Acclaim for V[illegible]

“VK Powell has given her fans a [illegible] read. The plot of *Fever* is filled with twists, turns, and ‘seat of your pants’ danger…*Fever* gives readers both great characters and erotic scenes along with insight into life in the African bush.”—*Just About Write*

“If you like cop novels, or even television cop shows with women as full partners with male officers…this is the book for you. It’s got drama, excitement, conflict, and even some fairly hot lesbian sex. The writer is a retired cop, so she really writes from a place of authenticity. As a result, you have a realistic quality to the writing that puts me in mind of early Joseph Wambaugh, before his writing became formulaic.”—*Lesbian News*

“*To Protect and Serve* drew me in from the very first page with characters that captivated in their complexity. Powell writes with authority using the lingo and capturing the thoughts of the law enforcers who make the ultimate sacrifice in the fight against crime. What’s more impressive is the command this debut author has of portraying a full gamut of emotion, from angst to elation, through dialogue and narrative. The images are vivid, the action is believable, and the police procedurals are authentic…VK Powell had me invested in the story of these women, heart, mind, body and soul. Along with danger and tension, Powell’s well-developed erotic scenes sizzle and sate.”—*Story Circle Book Reviews*

“This story takes some unusual twists and at one point, I was convinced that I knew ‘who did it’ only to find out that I was wrong. VK Powell knows crime drama, she kept me guessing until the end, and I was not disappointed at the outcome. And that’s not to slight VK Powell’s knack for romance.… Readers who appreciate mysteries with a touch of drama and intense erotic moments will enjoy *Justifiable Risk*.”—*Queer Magazine*

“From the first chapter of *Suspect Passions* Powell builds erotic scenes which sear the page. She definitely takes her readers for a walk on the wild side! Her characters, however, are also women we care about. They are bright, witty, and strong. The combination of great sex and great characters make *Suspect Passions* a must read.” —*Just About Write*

By the Author

Haunting Whispers

Justifiable Risk

Fever

Suspect Passions

To Protect and Serve

Haunting Whispers

by

VK Powell

2012

HAUNTING WHISPERS

ISBN 10: 1-60282-593-9
ISBN 13: 978-1-60282-593-2

This Trade Paperback Original Is Published By
Bold Strokes Books, Inc.
P.O. Box 249
Valley Falls, NY 12185

First Edition: February 2012

Credits
Editor: Shelley Thrasher
Production Design: Susan Ramundo
Cover Design By Sheri (graphicartist2020@hotmail.com)

Acknowledgments

To Len Barot, publisher extraordinaire, and all the wonderful folks at Bold Strokes Books—thank you for making this process so amazingly enjoyable and painless every time.

Brenda Allen—thank you for the expert advice and insight on issues beyond my mortal understanding.

My deepest gratitude to Dr. Shelley Thrasher for your guidance, suggestions, and kindness. You help me view my work through fresh eyes. Working with you is a learning experience and a pleasure.

For Sandy—thank you for your time and priceless feedback. This book is better for your efforts.

To all the readers who support and encourage my writing, thank you for buying my work, visiting my website (www.powellvk.com), sending e-mails, and showing up for signings. You make my "job" so much fun!

Dedication

TLP, for your assistance and support on this project, thank you!

Prologue

The militia group moved in just before dusk and blocked Arya's path to the extraction point. In less than an hour the team would leave without him, assuming he'd been captured or killed. They wouldn't look for him, couldn't even acknowledge he existed. Their orders had been clear, standard for clandestine ops in the shadow war against Iran: covert insertion, target elimination or recovery, and covert extraction. Anything else was unacceptable and created major repercussions for the US government. For the first time in his life, he had failed a mission—to move the wife of a high-ranking Iraqi official to safety—risk his life and his fellow operatives for a woman. *He wouldn't make it out this time.*

His body burned from the sand he'd burrowed under to conceal his location. The miniscule particles permeated his clothing like water and gnawed at already raw flesh. His lips ached and bled from three days' slow travel on foot through extreme temperatures. The little water that remained in his CamelBak was hot and couldn't quench his thirst. He sipped from the tube and let the liquid rest in his mouth, savoring the wetness and wishing it was ice cold and abundant. He'd need to ration what was left to fight off heat complications—in case he escaped. With the insurgents settling in around him, that seemed unlikely.

Some of the rebels prepared a campfire while others fanned out to plant mines and IEDs on the perimeter of their location. Arya held his breath as the men dug and carefully sowed their deadly seeds in the sand surrounding him. Then he waited for his partner, darkness, to arrive. The campsite eventually quieted, the fire died, and the night provided his only opportunity.

He'd tried to memorize the number of footsteps between explosive devices as the men prepared their traps, but without visual confirmation his estimates were merely guesses. Slowly he snaked his left hand through the sand and slid it easily until he met resistance. The metal had assumed the ambient temperature of the ground, but the consistency was unmistakable. He inched right and down before encountering another. His body was drenched with sweat, and the intensity of the process drained his energy. Hours passed before he located all the units in his immediate area. He was boxed into a six-foot space with barely enough room to maneuver.

Darkness had turned to the dull gray of morning before he'd inched far enough away from the devices to crawl on all fours. Arya rolled over the top of a dune and glanced back toward the camp. Dawn was breaking in their direction so he still had the advantage of darkness as he headed farther west toward the border. The pickup time had passed. His only chance was to make it across the Iraqi border and locate some friendlies.

He stretched his legs to relieve the cramps from hours of restricted movement and rose to a crouch. With one last look toward the militia camp, he ran. Perhaps panic finally registered or maybe he simply wanted relief from the sand, heat, and dehydration. He was trained to survive anything with practically nothing, but the days of exposure had wilted his resources and played games with his mind.

As the sky brightened with morning light, Arya pictured himself training with the other recruits. He was the gold standard against which everyone else was measured. His chest puffed with pride and discomfort as he pulled for breath in the dry desert air. How long had he been here? He'd stopped counting. And now he might die because of a woman.

He kept putting one foot in front of the other. Then a tremendous pain riddled his body, and he was flying through the air. He had no sensation below the waist other than the certainty that he was still running.

Arya jerked awake, the memories and pain from two years ago returning as violently as the explosion itself. His heart and lungs raced to see which would collapse first. As he stroked the injured and missing parts of his body, his rage returned anew. His original plan had been altered, but his determination to see it through never wavered. He'd waited so long to find his beloved, even following her to this dry-gulch town in the middle of nowhere North Carolina. The past would not deter him from having her once and for all.

Chapter One

"This might not have been the brightest idea I've ever had." Audrey Everhart mumbled under her breath as she circled the cinder-block Grantham Homes Community Center. The apartment buildings with boarded windows and graffiti-marred sides looked like one-eyed, tattooed pirates. Young men gathered on the street corners, making quick exchanges with passers-by while children played in close proximity. Clothes drying on an outside line flapped in the fall breeze like a warning.

She questioned her decision as disheveled men drinking from a bagged bottle gestured in her direction. Their unfocused stares followed her as she scouted the location for the mayor's press conference. Mayor Downing probably wouldn't approve of her coming here alone since the feds had endorsed his grant based on the amount of crime in this development. But Audrey didn't wait for others to take care of things. Her independence and resourcefulness had served her well so far. Besides, it was afternoon and she'd felt reasonably safe, until now.

A feeling of uneasiness settled like the gray clouds overhead, and she listened for anything odd or disturbing—white noise. She heard only the hollow echo of her own breathing, almost as if she was deaf to anything except the sounds of her body. Blood rushed through her arteries and veins, muscles contracted and extended as she walked, and her heart pounded more quickly as she understood the reason.

Danger. She'd felt this particular sensation only one other time in her life. In a matter of seconds her senses would shift into full alert and the stimuli of the outside world would rush in. Was it already too late? Hurried footsteps sounded behind her. Men, several of them, were coming for her. Why hadn't she noticed sooner? The white noise grew louder.

She ran from behind the back of the community center and headed toward the front parking lot. A few steps later she heard a crackling sound and a sharp pain shot up her back. The ground appeared solid, but the soft grass under her feet gave way. Her muscles twitched and convulsed. She had no control. The crackling noise again, more pain, and another surge pierced her body like lightning. She tried to catch herself as she fell, but her arms wouldn't cooperate.

❖

Audrey's skull still throbbed and the loud echoing voices nearby, one male and one female, weren't helping. She felt disoriented and unsafe. Her body ached, and she had no idea where she was, though the smell indicated a hospital. Why was she here? She recalled leaving the pavilion—no, an apartment complex. She kept her eyes closed, trying to block the voices and remember what happened.

"You know who this is, don't you?" The man's voice.

"Yeah, Audrey Everhart, the mayor's publicist. Though I have no idea why a town this size needs one. Why the hell was she at Grantham alone? I can't wait to get to the bottom of *this* one." The woman's voice, strong and professional, full of determination.

Only a cop would have such an immediate need for answers and justice. But cops also dug into people's lives, welcome or not, until they satisfied their curiosity. She had no interest in being a specimen for their dissection. Gathering a breath from deep in her aching chest, Audrey hissed through dry lips, "Shush."

The same female voice, too close and way too loud, responded, "Hey, can you hear me? Ms. Everhart?"

"Shush, don't yell."

"I'm whispering," the woman said. "You're at Kramer Hospital. Can you open your eyes?"

Audrey lifted her eyelids a fraction and pain streaked through her head like a sharp odor. She squeezed her eyes closed. "The light."

"Kill the overhead, Trevor. Try again when you're ready, ma'am. Don't rush."

The woman's concerned whisper made Audrey want to please her. She inched her lids open and stared into eyes as green as Irish shamrocks. Wavy auburn hair framed the woman's oval face and feathered toward full red lips. "You've got pretty eyes." She suddenly remembered those eyes and the woman behind them—Detective Rae Butler, Kramer Police Department.

"Must be the drugs," the man said.

Detective Butler squared her shoulders and stepped back from the bed. "I'm Rae Butler." She motioned to the short man with stark-white hair standing behind her. "And this is CSI Trevor Collins." The crime-scene investigator nosed the air in greeting. "Are you up for a few questions? I've just come from the scene."

The scene? That implied something bad had happened to her. Audrey blinked repeatedly to orient herself. She hated feeling confused and helpless. The sensation registered like a weighted block settling on an unstable foundation. "Where did you say I was again?"

"Kramer Hospital. You were brought in a couple of hours ago. Do you remember what happened?" Butler's comments shifted seamlessly from introduction to interview.

"My head feels fuzzy. I think I was in the Grantham Homes development. Then I woke up here with you staring down at me with those—" She stopped, certain that disorientation had hijacked her restraint.

Audrey had heard rumors about Rae Butler in her year with the mayor's office. It seemed odd that she could recall gossip more readily than the last few hours of her own life. Many of the Kramer cops aspired to emulate Rae as a detective or hook up with her romantically or both. Everybody seemed to like her. She was a good officer, friend to all, loyal to a fault—blah, blah, blah. Sometimes all the hype intimidated Audrey. It didn't help to be dazed in her presence.

They'd met when Audrey was going through rookie school, a requirement for non-sworn personnel in the police department and other key city employees. Rae had been an instructor in the training course and proved patient and knowledgeable. However, not only Rae Butler's professional skills had impressed Audrey. She was drawn to Rae as a person—as a woman—and that hadn't happened in years.

Rae's ability to discern the real from the bullshit had been so disturbingly accurate that Audrey avoided her whenever their paths crossed again. She couldn't afford the intimacy that friendships required or allow anyone to distract her from her goal. She needed access, and her position in the mayor's office provided it. She returned her attention to the attractive detective, determined to dispatch her as soon as possible.

When Audrey tried to sit up, Rae moved immediately to her side. She grabbed a pillow and started to position it behind her back. The gesture seemed like second nature, gallant and thoughtful in a way Audrey found endearing but a bit too presumptuous.

"No." Audrey shifted sideways and took the pillow. "I can manage, thank you." She couldn't let Rae Butler touch her. She needed physical distance, especially right now. She fought to control her senses at the best of times, but under duress she often failed.

Rae stood beside her bed, confusion clouding her eyes. How odd she must find Audrey—an injured woman frightened of the smallest kindness, the most benign touch. She continued as if Audrey's blatant refusal of her assistance occurred every day. Audrey thought that sad. "What were you doing in Grantham Homes?"

"Looking for a location to hold a press conference. Mayor Downing secured federal funding to revitalize the area and wanted to make the announcement on site."

"You went alone?"

"I didn't see the harm in the middle of the day." Trevor Collins pinned her with a look that shouted "idiot." She sensed his disbelief like a solid wall. Rae's expression remained neutral.

"Can you remember what happened?"

"Detective, my head aches. I hurt all over, and it's hard to focus." She ran her hand over her head and flinched as she struck tender spots on her scalp and matted knots of hair. "Jeez, I must look like death riding a crippled spider."

Rae flashed a grin that dimpled her cheeks, but quickly returned to business. "Anything at all about the assault would help."

Audrey's head pulsed as Butler's words registered. "I was assaulted?" She remembered walking around the community building, nothing more.

Trevor Collins grunted from behind Rae. "How else would you have gotten those bruises?" Collins either had little empathy or was socially challenged. She wanted him to leave but was afraid the request might sound like she had something to hide—which, of course, she did. No need to call attention to the fact so blatantly.

She looked at the purple splotches forming on her arms then back at Rae. The muscles in her abdomen contracted with the feeling that always accompanied her knowing. Inhaling deeply, she calmed the urge to throw up. She recalled pain and an eerie feeling of déjà vu. It's only a few bruises, she told herself. Why did it feel like more?

Rae glared at Collins and inclined her head toward the door. She either didn't like her sidekick's offhanded comments or she'd sensed Audrey's discomfort with his presence.

Audrey waited until he left. "I'm confused."

"Are you saying you didn't see who assaulted you?"

Rae Butler's tone indicated she found the possibility unacceptable. Most people who had never been victimized found it difficult to imagine the event itself or the ensuing aftermath. For some reason she thought cops would be different, or *should* be different. She wasn't about to test the theory.

"I didn't see anyone." That much was true. "I was walking around the Grantham Homes Community Center and then—nothing. For all I know, aliens could've abducted me. I'm not trying to be difficult. Really." How could she not know who assaulted her? She knew more than she wanted about most things, so how was it possible to be so clueless?

Detective Butler's brow furrowed as she regarded Audrey with suspicion. She clearly thought Audrey was being less than forthcoming. Audrey couldn't admit, *wouldn't* admit she'd been assaulted. Perhaps this once her feeling was wrong. Besides, the specifics of what happened were still blurred. The sparkle in Rae's eyes dimmed as she gathered her belongings and headed for the door. "Maybe you'll remember more when you've had time to recover. I'll be in touch."

Audrey wanted to cooperate to keep Rae Butler here a bit longer. While her questions were probing and uncomfortable, her presence soothed Audrey's unsafe feeling. Something more foreboding had or was about to happen. "I'm sorry I can't be more helpful."

"We'll get to the bottom of this. Rest now."

When she was alone, Audrey tuned the wall-mounted television to a music station and increased the volume as much as she could stand to block the noise inside her head. She focused on Rae Butler, regal in stature with a handsomely sculpted body, her movements fluid and efficient. She got what she wanted and didn't accept "no" easily. When Audrey failed to answer her questions, Butler was obviously disappointed, outwardly suspicious, and no amount of smiling could conceal her reaction. Upsetting Rae bothered Audrey more than it should.

She tried once again to reconstruct the afternoon's events. Perhaps she'd become too good at burying unpleasantness. No matter where she started in the scenario or how she tried to creep up on the memories, something stopped her when she rounded the corner of the Grantham community center. She felt the violence in her gut, not to mention the aches and pains that dotted her body like a well-placed beating. The nagging feeling that she was missing something obvious seemed like a premonition.

Audrey didn't believe in omens or fortune-telling. That was another world, another lifetime ago, and she was determined not to go back. She couldn't explain to Rae Butler—pragmatic, logical Detective Butler—that she had a *feeling* about the incident. If she ever shared those particular hunches with Rae, she would have proof, and she would find it on her own.

She shivered as a cold breeze swept through the almost-airless room. This day seemed to signal the beginning and the end of something that would change her life forever. She'd keep these thoughts to herself, along with the details of her past. Such information would only stymie her attempt at a new and different life.

❖

On the short drive from Kramer Hospital back to the crime scene, Rae thought about the first time she'd met Audrey Everhart over a year ago in the police basic introductory course. She'd initially been concerned that the petite, five-foot-five woman wouldn't make it in the intense, physically demanding classes. With her wispy blond hair and wide azure eyes, Audrey appeared like a fish in the desert—way out of her element.

In practical exercises, Audrey had shown tremendous insight, almost an uncanny ability to sense pending shifts in mood and potential danger. She wasn't as cocky as the male recruits or as reticent as the female ones. Audrey possessed a quiet intelligence that she wore like an old soul, a worldliness born of years of experience though she was only twenty-three. Rae wished on more than one occasion that she would reconsider a career in the mayor's office and join the police department.

However, Rae had also seen other traits that would not have served Audrey well on the job—fierce independence and emotional sensitivity. Audrey seemed determined to work through exercises on her own while simultaneously safeguarding the feelings of others by sharing her process. Her contradictory approach worked for her. She endeared herself to her classmates while keeping them at a distance.

Throughout the course, Audrey had been attentive, absorbing information like a gifted child. Sometimes she'd regarded Rae with the same admiring look rookies gave experienced officers, and maybe a little more. Audrey's gaze often lingered on her longer than necessary and seemed to hold unspoken questions.

Rae sensed the chemistry between them immediately, but convinced herself the mayor's publicist was only interested in learning as much as possible. Maybe Rae had just been particularly susceptible to the attentions of a young, attractive woman. She and Janet had started having problems, and her ego was more than a little bruised. Fortunately, she hadn't seen Audrey Everhart since the classes ended and didn't have to test her resolve.

When she'd found Audrey's hospital room earlier, Rae tapped and entered quietly. The ghostly pale woman lying in bed only vaguely resembled the Audrey she remembered. Her spiked blond hair appeared almost white against her colorless flesh. Nobody had mentioned an injury resulting in blood loss, though Audrey looked as though she'd been drained. Dark splotches were already forming on her arms. The thin sheet draped over Audrey outlined her delicate curves. What other injuries had someone inflicted on her?

Audrey's refusal of her assistance with her pillow could indicate deeper trauma, past or current, or simply a desire not to be touched. The sight of any victim altered by accident or intent always bothered Rae. The fact that it was Audrey gouged at a tender place inside her. She compartmentalized in order to do her job, but her compassion for the injured never waned.

As she parked in the Grantham Homes lot, Rae tried to recall any information about Everhart from the city's fertile grapevine. She seemed to work hard and keep to herself. If those were character flaws, Rae would count herself in that category since Janet left. Except for seeing a few friends semi-regularly, Rae had a social life right up there with Our Ladies of Perpetual Boredom.

She walked to the front of the community facility to join Trevor Collins, who stood with his hands perched on his hips. It was his what-the-hell-am-I-doing-here gesture. Rae had requested Trevor to the scene on a hunch. Another CSI had already processed the area, but she needed Trevor's years of experience. "I know they've worked it once. Try again. We missed something."

Recently her hunches amounted to little more than SWAGs—stupid wild-ass guesses. She'd virtually lost her intuition and instincts when her five-year relationship failed. If she couldn't spot a cheating spouse, how could she detect anything else? She trusted Trevor's eye for detail to augment her deficit.

"You think she's holding out, don't you?"

"Too soon to tell." Rae really didn't want to believe Audrey was purposely withholding information.

"Well, I do. How can she not remember being assaulted?"

"That's why you have all that white hair—too much deep thinking. Maybe you should wait until the evidence is in. Isn't that what you forensics types do?" Their banter had become almost routine. It offset some of the cruelty they encountered on the job.

"What, and leave all the wild speculation to you cops? Boring."

She followed Trevor patiently and waited for him to offer something significant.

He pointed toward the ground behind the community center as he talked. "Everhart walked from the front around this side. Her heels left very distinct impressions. She stopped here for some reason. The imprint is deeper in the soft ground. There's also a depressed area in the grass behind the shoe prints. Maybe a scuffle. Then drag marks."

"You're saying someone knocked her out and dragged her toward the back of the building?"

"I'm only telling you what I see. It's your job to draw conclusions. Look at these odd shoe prints."

Rae squatted beside him. "What do you mean?"

"They're consistent with a shoe size but not with any sole material I've encountered. It's almost like they were covered with fabric. See the wrinkles in the print? That doesn't happen with hard-soled shoes."

Disguising shoe prints indicated planning and intent, not a spontaneous or last-minute act. Was Audrey the intended victim or simply a convenient target? Still, it was a neighborhood known for frequent drug crimes and assaults. The shoe prints could be totally unrelated. She would talk with Audrey again tomorrow and maybe she could shed some light on the details. Perhaps she didn't remember everything yet, or was embarrassed.

Crime victims often used a variety of justifications to avoid facing the truth. Audrey Everhart didn't seem like that type. With a wave of nostalgia Rae realized she'd been wrong about a woman she thought she knew a lot better than Audrey. She turned her attention from a puzzle she hadn't deciphered in eight months and focused on a more solvable one—at least she hoped it would be.

"Thanks, Trev. Would you make a cast of the shoe print for me?"

While Trevor poured the casting agent into a bucket and mixed it to the ideal consistency, he kept glancing at her as if he had something to say.

She was too tired to play guessing games. "What? You're dying to tell me."

"Did you hear Ken Whitt is retiring?"

Rae wasn't in the mood for small talk, but Trevor was making a point. He didn't engage in idle gossip. "Yeah, he's in my unit."

"The captain of detectives is reassigning a serial of his—The Whisperer Case." Trevor lowered his voice at the end for effect. "You got any interest in taking that on?"

"Like I'd have a chance." She'd love the challenge of a serial case, and it would keep her mind off Janet. Even her worst days at work beat the hell out of pacing and dredging up the corpse of bliss passed. The Whisperer had stumped Whitt for the past year, so what made her think she was up to the task?

"The captain asked me to recommend somebody I can work with. I'm reviewing the forensics side. We do all right." He waggled his finger back and forth between them like they shared a special pact. "I could put in a word—if you're interested."

"Yeah, sure." Rae had no illusions that she'd get the assignment. She was junior in the squad and the case was too high profile. Her publicity hound of a sergeant would want his best detective on it. As she walked toward her car, she called back, "Keep me posted. I'm going home to get some rest. I've been up since yesterday."

Rae settled behind the steering wheel and rubbed her gritty eyes. She was too tired to think about victims or cases or even Audrey Everhart.

❖

Rae slammed the door of her condo and winced at the empty echo that welcomed her. The old chocolate-brown recliner, side table, and lamp faced off with her forty-six-inch flat-screen in the otherwise bare living room. Janet had taken most of the furnishings and accessories as compensation for their failed relationship. Rae had done little since to make this place a home, citing work demands as the culprit. Using the job as an excuse covered a multitude of sins.

She threw her backpack onto the small dining table that served as a desk and tried to shake her annoyance at her ex. It had been eight months, and Janet had obviously moved on with an associate provost at the university—someone more desirable, more educated, and up to her intellectual standards. The triple whammy, the three areas in which Janet found her constantly lacking. Maybe Janet had nagged to distract Rae from noticing her infidelity.

Whatever Janet's reasons, Rae hadn't really trusted anyone since. Today she'd let her uncertainty creep into an investigation. She'd doubted a victim's version of a crime, which was uncharacteristic. Irritable and jumpy, she needed to stay busy until she regained her self-confidence. She hoped it returned before the past destroyed her career and any hope of a satisfying future.

As if answering her thoughts, her personal cell vibrated against her hip. She wore it like an additional appendage, enjoying at least the perception that she was connected to others. Normally she became so engrossed in work she didn't notice the phone's silent demand for attention. She considered ignoring this summons, but curiosity prevailed and she plugged in her password. Three messages.

"Honey." Her best friend Deb's Southern voice strung the word out like it had a dozen syllables. "How are you?" She always paused as if she expected Rae to actually answer. "The other girls and I want to see you soon. We miss you. Call me." Rae smiled, made a mental note to do just that, and deleted the message before flipping to the next.

"Rae, this is Mrs. Cowan, your advisor at the university. I wanted to remind you that finals begin shortly, and you've missed a few classes. If you're interested in catching up, give me a call." Rae regretted being the cause of the concern in the woman's voice.

"I'm not sure what's going on with you. If you need to talk I hope you know I'm here."

Should she pursue her college education now? She'd enrolled to prove something to her family, but they'd disowned her when she came out. Then Janet became her reason to continue. Janet said it embarrassed her for her partner not to be a college graduate. She harassed Rae about her shortcoming and the amount of time it was taking to complete a simple four-year degree. Rae had been determined to finish in spite of her workload. When Janet left, Rae lost interest in almost everything. Maybe she wasn't worth the effort. Rae made a note to get in touch with Ms. Cowan, deleted the message, and skipped to the last one.

"Rae, stop avoiding me." Janet paused, and the air rushed out of Rae's lungs in a painful gush. "I know it's late, but I need to talk to you." Another pause during which Rae debated deleting the message. Some masochistic urge immobilized her. "You're probably out on a date or something. Rae, I miss you. I miss us. Can we talk? Call me, please."

The message ended and Rae steeled herself for the customary tears and pain. Looking around the nearly vacant condo, she waited for the outrage that accompanied betrayal. Feelings bottlenecked in her chest. Why couldn't she grieve any more? Perhaps that was the blessing.

She'd been a less than attentive partner, working all hours and expecting Janet to wait patiently until she had time for their relationship. Drained of emotion and disillusioned with the world, she'd come home unable to talk about their issues with the energy and consideration they deserved. The inhumanity Rae encountered at work had tainted even their enthusiastic but infrequent sex. But she couldn't just leave the job and pretend it all never happened.

In spite of the imperfections in their relationship, Rae missed the connection to another human being. It grounded her outside a profession full of harshness and brutality. Lately she felt terribly lonely and afraid that she deserved nothing more.

Chapter Two

"Ms. Everhart, wake up, honey. You're dreaming."

Audrey opened her eyes and sat up in bed. Her throat burned from yelling and her screams echoed in the unfamiliar room. The nurse rested her hands on Audrey's shoulders and Audrey felt the woman's emotions flood in.

"I'm fine. Please stop." She flinched at the woman's touch. "I'm sore."

Shying away from the unwelcome feelings, Audrey clutched the sheet to her chest. She edged out of the nurse's grasp, and the loose-fitting gown fell from Audrey's back.

"Look at those bruises. What the—?"

"I'm sure it's nothing. I'm fine." But it wasn't nothing, and she wasn't fine. Audrey simply couldn't bear to be touched. She didn't want to explain what came next or how she knew what the nurse was feeling. "Please."

"Honey, these look like stun-gun marks. I've seen them on folks the officers bring in. They'll want to take pictures. Did you tell the detective?"

At that moment the door opened and Rae Butler entered, filling the room with her vibrant energy. She was more handsome than Audrey remembered, dressed in black jeans, a burnt-orange turtleneck, and a black leather jacket that covered the weapon at her side. As Rae approached, the initial wave of exuberance settled into a comforting calm and Audrey felt almost safe. Cops and safety hadn't always gone together in her past. At this moment she was grateful to have Rae Butler beside her…as long as she didn't ask too many questions.

"Did she tell the detective what?" Rae's emerald eyes sparkled with anticipation and an I-thought-so glint. "Good afternoon, all."

Audrey gave the attendant a cautionary stare. The woman couldn't say anything about her medical condition without her permission. "That I'm going home. Right, Nurse?"

The unsuspecting woman nodded mutely and headed toward the door. "I'll get your paperwork together, Ms. Everhart."

"How are you feeling today?" Rae asked. Her gaze held Audrey's, the unasked questions almost like conversation bubbles above her head.

"Fine, thanks, ready to get out of here. I can't believe I've slept the day away."

"You didn't miss much. It was dreary. You're in luck now, though. I'm your personal escort slash taxi service."

Audrey couldn't imagine being confined in a vehicle with Rae for ten seconds, much less the ten minutes it would take to reach her apartment. In some cases, proximity was as risky as touch. Rae Butler would be such a case. How could she refuse the offer of a ride without getting into the idiosyncrasies that made her life so difficult? "That's not necessary. I can manage."

"I'm sure you can, but I don't have a choice. Mayor Downing's orders." Rae's smile let her know that she didn't consider the task unpleasant. Was Rae actually flirting with her?

"He shouldn't be throwing his weight around." Her boss's overprotectiveness bordered on imposition, but she accepted it as concern for her welfare. He couldn't possibly know what an inconvenience the police would be right now. Any minute Rae would launch into more questions, and Audrey needed time to prepare her answers. She wasn't ready to tell the truth until she understood what happened, but she didn't want to lie. Evasion would work only so long with someone as astute as Rae Butler. "Would you mind waiting outside while I dress?" Audrey found the pink flush of Rae's cheeks endearing. The stoic officer had a shy side.

An hour later Audrey stood in front of her apartment and waited for Rae to leave. She'd avoided probing questions by rattling nonstop about working in the mayor's office. She'd kept calm by almost hanging her head out the window, grateful for the winter chill in the air. Her brief respite was about to end.

Rae collected Audrey's mail from the box as casually as if she lived there. Pulling a note from the doorjamb, she added it to the collection, handed the stack over, and hesitated at the threshold. Audrey hadn't invited anyone into her apartment since she moved in last year. For the first time she actually considered it. She imagined Rae Butler sprawled across her old sofa, relaxed and tempting.

"Mind if I come in for a minute?" Rae asked.

Audrey shook her head to clear the image and reposition her defenses. "I'm not up for an interrogation, Detective."

"Rae. Would you please call me Rae? We have met before. I don't know if you remember. I was an instructor in your recruit class."

Could she ever forget the emotional pull she'd felt toward Rae Butler every day she entered the small classroom, stood beside her at a mock crime scene, or inhaled the light fragrance of her perfume? Those emotions had nipped at the edge of her consciousness for the past year, and each time they surfaced, she stuffed them back down. Now she distanced from Rae in order to focus on what she needed to do instead of what she felt. "I remember. You were very kind, not to mention knowledgeable and professional."

"Then talk to me, Audrey."

"About what, exactly?" Her headache returned like the sound of discordant drums. Evasion wasn't her forte, and the words sounded insincere.

"Tell me what happened and I'll stop bothering you."

"We can talk, but please, not today."

Rae started to leave then turned back. Her usually full lips pursed in a tight line and a frown formed between her eyes. "If you're afraid of someone, I'll protect you."

The wave of compassion from Rae was almost palpable. Audrey wanted to tell her everything but responded with the words self-preservation demanded. "I'm sorry. I'm just not sure what happened." Mostly true, but the accompanying guilt was relentless.

"Okay, but this case isn't going away. I'm already getting pressure from your boss and mine. If you do remember anything, give me a call. I'll check on you tomorrow." Before Audrey could insist that she didn't need to be checked on, Rae handed her a business card and left.

Audrey gingerly made her way into her apartment, closed the door, and looked around. Would Rae find the small one-bedroom flat quaint with its mismatched furniture and large secondhand stereo? Would she think it unusual that she didn't own a television like most people? The absence of pictures and decorations could be off-putting. An outsider would probably interpret her stark surroundings as the sign of a boring, uncreative person. To Audrey, it was necessary for a relatively peaceful existence.

She caressed the back of the blue-and-gray tweed sofa and thought of the day she and her mother, Nadja, bought it in a consignment shop. It had graced her mother's loft in Montreal and spent several years in a corner of Audrey's previous apartment before ending up here. Like a ruler on the doorframe, tiny pulls up the sides served as growth markers for their mixed-breed cat, Olga. She missed her mother and Olga, both passed on. She'd considered another pet but wasn't sure she could handle an emotional attachment to anything at this point. Her life seemed so colorless.

A faint beep distracted her and she followed the sound to her burgundy corduroy recliner. Reaching into the side cushion, she retrieved the cell phone she hadn't seen for two days. Audrey despised the invention, finding it more intrusive and disrespectful than public farting.

She flipped open the device and listened to the message. "Hey, girl, it's Yasi." The rhythmic sound of her best friend's Moroccan accent made her nostalgic. It had been six months since they'd seen each other. "Did you get my last message? We'll be in your area soon, and I'm trying to get an audience. Call me. Love you."

Audrey started to dial Yasi back but wasn't sure what to say. They'd been friends since adolescence, and she knew when Audrey wasn't being totally honest. Yasi wouldn't accept work as a suitable excuse for not seeing her. She'd overused that one the past year anyway. But she couldn't tell the truth.

Her old friends, especially Yasi, accepted people with all their imperfections—people from all cultures and ethnicities, rich and poor, stable and not so. They understood that life happens and nothing ever runs smoothly. They didn't judge. But they wouldn't understand her need to leave the past behind and start over. It would seem like the deepest level of betrayal. As guilt settled over her, Audrey couldn't disagree. She missed her friends yet she had to make some sacrifices. At least for the moment she had a good excuse for not returning Yasi's call.

She eased into the comfortable cushions of her worn sofa and clicked on the gas logs. As the chill lifted, she turned the stereo volume just loud enough to block the noise in her mind. Her body still ached with every movement. The headaches that had plagued her since the incident had slightly subsided. She intended to fill in the black holes in her memory before Rae Butler dug too deeply into her life. When she had the facts, she'd share them with Rae, maybe.

As she flipped through her stack of bills and junk mail, she stopped at the wrinkled note Rae had pulled from the door—a plain sheet of paper with no address, probably an ad or invitation to another community gathering. She opened it and read the typewritten message, *Sorry I missed you. Will try again.* Her neighbors were persistent; she'd give them that. She crumpled the note and threw it on the floor with the other sale papers and trash.

Finding nothing urgent in the remainder of her mail, Audrey stretched out and pulled the blanket off the back of the sofa over her. The headache was just bearable enough to allow rest, the music soothing enough to block distractions so she drifted to sleep.

Stop. Audrey dismissed the internal warning and stepped around the side of the building. It was so dark. She heard a crackling sound, then fear and a sweet smell overpowered her. She turned to check behind her but a stabbing pain stopped her. The street tilted. A bolt of lightning exploded through her body. She heard the crackling noise again, felt more pain, and fell backward.

She screamed. "No! Please!"

Drumming sounded in her ears as Audrey sat upright on the sofa, her sore body protesting the sudden movement. Her face burned and her skin was sticky with perspiration. She looked at the familiar surroundings of her apartment and relaxed only slightly. Before the snippets of the dream dissolved, she closed her eyes and reviewed each fragment.

The piecemeal images seemed like a disjointed recollection of the event at the community center. Chills covered her body as the warning voice and accompanying fear returned. Dreams could be random pictures of something real, something imagined, or a combination. One thing was becoming clearer; someone with a stun gun assaulted her. The marks the nurse had seen and her recollection of searing pain seemed to make sense. Who would do such a thing and why? The unsettled feeling she experienced when she woke up in the hospital returned, and she moaned in frustration.

Heavy pounding echoed through the apartment—the drumming again. She willed the noise to stop. Remnants of the dream swirled through her mind, mingling with the sound of someone calling her name from the direction of the front door. She shook her head and tried to stand. Steadying herself along the sofa, she edged slowly toward the entrance. "I'm coming," she whispered. The woodpecker hammering continued. She threw the door open, prepared to hurl verbal abuse at the intruder, and came face to face with Rae Butler.

"Are you okay?" The volume of Rae's voice galloped through Audrey's head like a stampede of wild horses. Rae scanned Audrey's body then swept the room behind her. "I heard screaming."

"I don't scream." Audrey motioned for her to lower her voice. "Not when my head still feels like scrambled eggs." Audrey was annoyed that Rae had come to her home without at least calling first.

And if she had called, Audrey would've put her off or insisted they meet somewhere else, anywhere else.

"Then you're not alone? Because I definitely heard someone screaming in this apartment. I was about to break in your door."

The haze in Audrey's head made it hard to concentrate. She looked behind her as if searching for another unannounced visitor. "I am alone, and I'd like to stay that way." She started to close the door, but Rae blocked it open.

"How are you feeling?"

The genuine concern in Rae's voice surprised her and she momentarily dropped her guard. "The headache's better. Now I have nightmares. That's what you heard." *God, why did I say that?* That's all Butler needed for an opening, even if her dreams had nothing to do with the assault. *Stop talking.*

"Do you mind if I come in?"

"As a matter of fact, I do. I'm not up to entertaining." She glanced down at the wrinkled dress pants and blouse she'd worn home the night before and groaned—obviously she looked as bad as she felt. She didn't want Rae Butler in her apartment. People made assumptions about your life based on your home, and Audrey wasn't ready for Detective Butler's judgment on the state of her world.

"If you're not careful, I could get a complex. That's twice you've refused to let me into your apartment." Rae's eyes flashed with mischief before turning serious again. "I was hoping we could talk about your case...and your nightmares if you want."

God, she was persistent. "If it can wait, I'd appreciate it, Detective."

"Rae, the name is Rae, and it's always best to get the facts as soon as possible. I promise not to take long." Without waiting for an answer, Rae walked past Audrey into the living area.

Audrey closed the door, followed Rae in, and turned off the stereo. This woman obviously didn't understand the word no. It probably made her both annoying and quite good at her job. Rae wore brown cords, a light-green striped shirt, Durango boots, and a leather jacket. She looked like she'd stepped off the pages of a top cop magazine—the outfit and the profession suited her perfectly.

She walked with a purposeful stride that made Audrey stare and stirred an unfamiliar feeling. She'd never seen a woman swagger so deliciously without looking totally butch. Did Rae's confidence extend to her personal life? Audrey dismissed her wandering thoughts as a side effect of head trauma and prepared for Rae's appraisal of her place. The feared evaluation arrived more quickly than she expected and not in the form she'd anticipated.

"What a nice place. It feels comfortable, just like a home should. My condo looks like it was burglarized."

In spite of herself, Audrey chuckled, then grabbed her head with regret. "Don't make me laugh."

"How long have you lived here?"

"A year. It's not much. I call it shabby without the chic." When Rae looked closer, she'd see the threadbare patches in the sofa cushions, ripped seams in the recliner, scratches on the coffee table, and blank walls. Audrey braced herself for the commentary to follow.

Rae Butler regarded her as if they'd bonded over the tag-team takedown of a perp. "Me, six years. Decorating isn't my thing. I feel like I live in a cold shoebox since…"

In spite of her joking, Rae's eyes looked sad. She would deliver no judgment. She seemed to accept that Audrey's life, like her own in some way, was in a state of flux. Did Rae realize she'd revealed something personal? A tenuous connection began to emerge between them like the silky thread of a spider's web. The formality she'd maintained slipped and she felt closer to Rae. She started to ask about the source of Rae's sadness, but her defensive mind once again overpowered her curious heart. Her own melancholy settled back into its hiding place as she watched Rae shift into cop mode.

Rae retrieved a notepad from her jacket pocket and referred to it before speaking. Unruly strands of auburn hair fell forward around her face and she blew at the shorter locks across her forehead. Silver slivers buried in the darker strands shone like tinsel on a Christmas tree, and Audrey childishly wanted to count each one. Rae shook her head and the tousled mop fell back in place, resting softly just above her collar. "Have you remembered anything else about yesterday?"

Rae seamlessly transitioned from developing rapport to conducting an interview. Some officers never developed the skill and many detectives never perfected it. "Nothing helpful, I'm afraid."

Audrey struggled with how to say nothing without revealing anything. She wasn't good at being purposely deceitful. It wasn't usually necessary. She easily steered superficial conversations of daily life away from herself.

"Well, humor me and go through what you do remember. Please." Rae's authoritative tone softened into a more conciliatory timbre. For a moment, Audrey lost herself in the ease with which Rae sensed her reluctance and reassured her. Then she saw it—the inevitable flash of pity.

Her body and her pride had already taken a beating, and having Rae look at her like a victim was too much. She wasn't anybody's sympathy case. She wouldn't tell Rae about the stun gun until she identified who assaulted her and why. Besides, what if this case led back to her past? She'd chosen to leave that life and couldn't chance the two worlds colliding until she was ready…if the time ever came. "I was walking around the building and then I wasn't."

Rae's eyes momentarily sparked with interest. Audrey imagined she'd inadvertently revealed something significant, until she realized the reason for Rae's expression. Her face was simply alight with the thrill of the hunt, the adrenaline high associated with risky situations. Rae thought she was going to tell her everything. She'd heard about cops who competed for dangerous calls and chased bad guys for that well-known drug. Maybe Rae was one of those adrenaline junkies.

Audrey cleared her throat to regain Rae's attention. If she knew how much her facial expressions showed, she'd try harder to conceal them. "So you're still convinced that I was assaulted?" Audrey asked.

"It's more likely than not."

The idea that Rae might find her lacking in self-protection or any other way irritated Audrey. She toyed with telling Rae about her *feeling* before the attack. But she would sound like a conclusion-jumping, highly emotional woman. She didn't want to appear flighty and unprofessional. Why Rae's opinion mattered so much, Audrey wasn't sure.

"We'll go with the assault hypothesis until a better one comes along." Rae clutched the small notepad in her left hand, stood, and offered Audrey her right, which she ignored. It simply would not do for them to touch. "If you think of anything else, let me know."

"Why don't you move on to more serious cases? I'm sure you have some." The statement sounded harsher than Audrey intended, but she had to scare or warn or plead Rae away from her assault. Audrey stood no chance of finding her assailant first if Rae Butler stayed on the case.

"All my cases are serious and I want to solve each one," Rae assured her.

Audrey held Rae's gaze and stood in front of her. The room seemed to recede as sensation from their locked stare surged through her. Overwhelming sadness and a sense of fear almost overcame her. She momentarily closed her eyes and tried to block the feelings. "I'm so, so sorry." The words, born of pure emotion, slipped out before Audrey could censor herself.

"Sorry for what?"

The flood of feelings ripped through her again. "Wasn't much help." She swayed and struggled to remain upright.

Rae reached for her but she stepped away, grabbing the edge of the sofa for support. "Audrey, are you all right?"

"Still a little light-headed, I guess." She *didn't* say that Rae's proximity, not the assault, precipitated this particular bout of dizziness. She *couldn't* say that contact between them would probably end any chance of even a friendship. She had no idea until this moment that mere physical closeness might have the same effect.

Chapter Three

Two days later Rae was summoned to Sergeant Sharp's office, where she surveyed his wall hangings and waited for him to end a personal phone call. He seemed to have a plaque or certificate for every Mickey Mouse class and seminar he'd ever attended—obvious overcompensation. Sharp, a twenty-year veteran, had probably collected on a favor to get the prestigious Special Victims' Unit assignment.

The troops referred to him as a pretty-boy leg humper who didn't know the meaning of real police work. Behind his back, they called him Sergeant Not So Sharp, or Not So for short. Fortunately, most of the detectives in the unit had experience and didn't require a lot of supervision. Coming from patrol, she was the exception, with only two years in SVU. If she needed help she asked a senior officer.

Sharp hung up the phone and waved her in. "Got a little present for you, Butler." He pushed a stack of overstuffed flex folders toward her. "The Whisperer case is yours now. Give it your best shot. I'm not assigning you a partner unless you turn up something. And if you do find anything, let me know. Got it?"

She got it perfectly. Not So didn't want her to bother him unless she turned up a lead resulting in clearance and/or subsequent publicity. He definitely wanted in on that. "Yes, sir."

In Rae's opinion, serial-assault cases should receive more hype and a higher priority, even if they were cold cases. The department didn't expend a lot of manpower on unsolved crimes unless they were homicides. This particular suspect had stopped short of killing. She picked up the files and turned to leave.

"One more thing. You don't have to worry about the Everhart case anymore."

"But—"

"Don't ask any dip-shit questions."

Screw that. Questions were her business, and she wanted to know why the sudden shift in priorities. She didn't believe in coincidences or the kindness of politically motivated supervisors. "Was a suspect arrested? Are you giving it to someone else?"

"I told you, it's no longer your concern, Butler."

"Three days ago the chief and the mayor were breathing down my neck for an arrest."

"And now they're not. You've got bigger fish to fry." He nodded toward the folders in her arms. "Count your blessings."

Not So was as intuitive as a hammer, but he was blessed with political acumen. He believed information was power, and he wasn't about to share any of his. She didn't like giving up cases before she cleared them, especially this one. It *was* only a simple assault, but she wanted to know what happened to Audrey. And her reasons weren't purely professional.

Then another thought occurred to her. Maybe Audrey had used her position in the mayor's office to call off the investigation. Not So would definitely jump at the chance to do the mayor a favor. Would the police department let that happen? Did Audrey have something to hide or was she simply concerned with the most productive use of departmental resources, as she'd stated? Dropping a case, no matter how insignificant, was sort of like cooking the crime stat books and generally frowned upon.

As she left Sharp's office, she considered maybe he was right to take her off the investigation. Rae couldn't even concentrate with Audrey staring at her. She lost track of physical tells and the facts while drowning in her blue eyes. Audrey could've spun an intricate tale of deceit while Rae focused on her sexy leg crossing. Rae was usually more attentive and much more certain of other people's reactions. If Audrey was hiding something, could Rae trust herself enough to ask the right questions? Audrey was simply distracting. But her delicate façade masked fierce independence and an almost-palpable depth of experience. Was what Rae saw in Audrey a reaction to some past hurt, a deeply buried scar, or the result of her recent assault?

Rae dropped the stack of folders on her desk and decided she had better things to do than chase a mystery no one wanted her to solve. The victims in these cases deserved her best effort. Her first serial case required that her skills be sharp and her instincts on target. It pained her to think she might not be up for the task, no matter how badly she wanted justice or how much she craved the challenge.

She tried to reason away her reservations. Sergeant Sharp wouldn't have given her the cases if he didn't trust her skills. Maybe he knew she'd fail and he could blame it on her inexperience. That didn't make sense. Failure would make him look bad. He must want her to succeed. She hated this—doubting herself and her abilities.

Rae quieted the uncertainty and pulled the first case file, dated almost a year ago, from the folder. Victim #1—she didn't allow herself to call the victims by name yet, except when conducting interviews. Some of her coworkers considered her method unsympathetic, but her approach served as an additional motivator and helped keep her emotions in check. When she made an arrest, she felt like she'd done her job and could then face the victims with pride and address them by name.

The no-frills verbiage of Whitt's follow-up report introduced Rae to the first victim and the severity of the offense:

White female, 21 years of age, blond hair, kidnapped from a high-traffic area and assaulted with a blade, possibly knife and/or scalpel. Victim on the way home from New Year's party, reports being subdued, possibly drugged. Woke up hours later near dumpster in deserted area with injuries. No information on suspect. Abrasions on victim's wrists from restraints. Toxicology report showed no signs of drugs in victim's system.

Erratic slicing-type cuts to upper abdominal area extending to lower abdominals above pubic region. Injuries appear random and frenzied. Victim reported suspect whispered "liar" to her repeatedly.

Rae slid the victim photos from the folder and stared in disbelief at the irregular cuts through the taut, young flesh. The weapon severed muscle tissue in some areas and barely dissected the skin layers in others. At first glance the injuries appeared to be a classic crime of passion, a hurried attack. The fact that the suspect referred to the victim as a liar could suggest a connection. Rae wouldn't assume that until she knew more about the victim's life. She pored over the other documents in the folder without finding anything significant. When Rae closed the first file with a combination of sadness and anger, her shift had ended. The case read like a blueprint of how to avoid capture for a felony assault, an investigator's nightmare of dead-end leads and inconclusive scientific results—the kind of case an investigator obsessed over.

Rae had already made an appointment with the primary detective on the cases, Ken Whitt, recently retired. She debated starting fresh without any input or opinions from him, but a cop's instincts were often the best weapon in solving cases. Whitt had been a detective for twenty of his thirty-year career. If he had any hunches or advice, she certainly wanted to hear it. She couldn't imagine retiring and leaving this suspect free to inflict more pain. And from what she'd read, he would strike again. Animals like him didn't stop. Their need drove them to torture and mutilate until they were caught and caged.

She stretched the kinks out of her back, gathered the file together, and headed toward the canteen. This case was too important to leave lying around open on a desk. It would be with her until she closed it by arrest. However, right now she needed a break. Too much violence at one time, even on paper, diluted her attention. Another jolt of caffeine and some fresh air would prepare her for the next round of reports and pictures.

She had to pass the crime-analysis unit on her way to the canteen located on the first floor above the police department. As she approached the door, one of the employees exited and she glanced inside. Audrey sat next to Loretta Granger, a red-haired, sultry records specialist who had attended the same recruit school as Audrey. Engrossed in something on the computer screen, they seemed very cozy, smiling and chatting as the printer tapped out copies. Rae stepped in before the door closed and slid into a cubicle behind Audrey.

She looked at the data displayed on the screen: a list of assaults for the past year. Several unsolved incidents were highlighted in yellow, including the Whisperer cases she'd inherited. Why was Audrey going through crime analysis instead of the chief's office for information about police cases? Perhaps the mayor was looking into something specific and needed to bypass the department, maybe an internal investigation of some sort. Rae tested her theory as she walked toward Audrey and gauged her reaction. "Ms. Everhart."

Audrey pushed away from the computer desk so quickly she almost toppled over. "Detective Butler, what are you doing here?"

"Funny, I was about to ask you the same question." Audrey's face flushed and she looked helplessly from the analyst to Rae. Even a rookie could call this one.

"Looking into a matter for the mayor. Research, you know, work," Audrey said.

Loretta rolled her chair closer to Audrey and immediately defended her. "I was helping her out, Rae. The crime-analysis folks were backed up." The smile Loretta gave Audrey said her services didn't have to end at statistics.

Rae found the visual leer inappropriate and almost said so, but Audrey's personal life wasn't her business. "Anything I can help you with?" If Audrey didn't want Rae to investigate her assault, she certainly wouldn't include her in a clandestine investigation. And Rae knew Audrey was doing exactly that. Research for the mayor, right.

"No, thanks. I have everything I need for the moment." Audrey grabbed a printout from the computer and started toward the door. "Thanks, Lo. Catch you later."

She should probably just walk away. If Audrey wanted to shut her out, fine. She didn't need the additional grief, especially not now. Instead, Rae followed her down the hallway and onto the elevator. When the doors closed and they were alone, she turned to Audrey. "If I asked your boss, would he know about this *investigation*?"

Audrey wouldn't face her. "Let it go, Detective. This doesn't concern you."

"You mean it doesn't concern me as in having a case taken away from me or as in it's not personal?" Rae heard the bite in her tone and didn't like it. She hated not knowing. If Audrey trusted Loretta Granger, why couldn't she trust her? Her rationale didn't make sense, but at the moment she didn't care. She couldn't handle one more secret and feeling that her instincts were faulty again.

"I simply suggested to Mayor Downing that the police department might have better things to do than investigate something that may or may not be an assault." She waved the printout. "And I was right. Quite a few unsolved cases could use some attention."

The air between them in the enclosed space shimmered with tension. Rae moved closer, and Audrey looked as though she was struggling to breathe. "Why are you trying so hard to convince yourself and me that you weren't assaulted when it's obvious you were? What are you hiding? Is someone threatening you?"

Audrey backed away from her as far as possible. The look on her face was almost fearful, exactly like two days ago at her apartment. What was she so afraid of? Maybe Rae had been too forceful. Maybe the attack was more traumatic than she realized and Audrey was having trouble coping. Rae cursed her errant instincts once again.

Audrey's expression shifted as the doors opened. "I can't tell you what happened. Why don't you focus on something more substantial? Besides, I'm so bored with these questions that my feet are falling asleep." With that final jibe, Audrey stepped off the elevator and flashed a smile as the doors closed behind her.

Rae punched the Open button repeatedly but the elevator was already moving. She couldn't understand Audrey's behavior. One minute she cowered fearfully in the corner and the next she made jokes. She didn't seem the type to jest about something as serious as assault. Rae remembered an earlier incident in the hospital and one at Audrey's home where she'd used humor to deflect her discomfort. Maybe it was a coping mechanism. If not, she'd seriously misjudged Audrey.

Rae returned to her desk. She needed a break from work and thoughts of Audrey Everhart. She shoved the files into her briefcase and made a quick phone call on the way to her car. "Deb, can you get the gang together tonight? My place will be fine. I need to vent, laugh, and celebrate. Not necessarily in that order."

❖

When the elevator doors closed, Audrey exhaled a lung-busting gush of air. Being in such close proximity to Rae had taken all her restraint. In addition to the uncustomary attraction, Audrey had also felt anxious and almost fearful, though Rae posed no threat. She had no idea what she'd babbled about during the ride. One thing was certain, Rae had been taken off her case and wasn't happy about it. Why didn't she tell Rae someone had assaulted her with a stun gun and she had no idea who it was? It sounded simple until she figured in all her secrets.

And gauging from Rae's scathing evaluation of Loretta, she would need to explain the records specialist soon. Could she justify forming a friendship with a woman solely to get information? When it became obvious Loretta wanted more, Audrey had utilized all her evasive maneuvers and jokes to keep Loretta close but not too close. Rae had seen something between them and drawn the wrong conclusion. Audrey would clarify everything, but not now.

She couldn't let her resolve waver, but feelings about Rae Butler kept surfacing: fear of what she might find out, apprehension about her opinions, concern about being judged and found lacking, and horror that these worries covered a deeper emotion. She had to focus on the facts, remain objective. Once she had some answers, maybe she could have a personal life.

As she walked back to her office, Audrey reviewed the dream she'd had and tried to make sense of it. Some of the pieces fit her recent attack and others were like bits of a nightmare. Maybe her mind was simply filling in blanks.

Her research about amnesia indicated that the memories of her earlier assault were probably still intact, blocked by her defense mechanisms. It also pointed toward partial or complete memory recovery. But it had been so long. Why could she *still* not remember? She could recite snippets of information provided by others but few of her own recollections. Perhaps she wasn't suffering from amnesia at all but blocking the dreadful memories. It seemed a cosmic joke. She was so extremely intuitive about other people and situations and so oblivious about herself.

Maybe the data she gathered from crime analysis would be a starting point. Solving her stun-gun attack might open other doors in her memory and her life. But how could she keep Rae Butler out of her business while she pursued leads? Audrey Everhart fought her own battles and she wasn't changing—no matter how attractive and compelling the rescuer.

After Janet moved out, Rae transformed the vacant sleeping quarters in her condo into a multi-functional space that served as an office, dart room, and alternate gathering space. Tonight she put Stephanie's favorite beer on ice, set Deb's Southern Comfort on a side table, and spread Ronni's preferred cheese and peanut snacks on a platter. Her friends weren't big drinkers, but they liked to sip and munch while they talked.

She'd met these three women through their public-service jobs with city-county government over the past five years. They'd become friends and weathered many personal and professional storms. When one of them needed a pep talk, a reality check, or a quick kick in the pants, the others rallied round.

Her oldest friend, Deb, arrived first, as usual. She liked a few minutes of private time with Rae before the others came. Without a good cover or diversion, Deb would see right through Rae's celebration ruse.

"God, I'm glad you called. I haven't had a day off in two weeks. The entire communications division is going to hell in a hand basket." Deb gave Rae a full body hug and waggled her pelvis against her in jest. She epitomized the Southern belle, voluptuous body and a drawl that made most men weak. Deb considered the effect a bonus in supervising the men in her unit and an annoyance otherwise, since she dated only women. "I love what you've done with the place. Nice spot for your dartboard. Stab anybody lately?"

"I'm considering it. How about a quick game before the others get here?" Deb looked at her with suspicion. She'd made a tactical error.

"Okay, what's going on?"

"What do you mean?"

"The last time you asked me to play darts was before you told me Janet was cheating on you. And if I recall, I broke two of your precious spinner thingies and destroyed the wall. You've got that woman-trouble look. Who is she?"

Rae needed at least one beer before she broached the subject of Audrey Everhart. Fortunately, the other two members of the quartet arrived before she was forced to answer Deb's question.

Stephanie, a robust butch with basic brown hair and brown eyes, worked as a firefighter. Her partner, Ronni, a gorgeously androgynous EMT, sported wavy black hair and dark-gray eyes. They were an unusual couple, but their relationship had lasted three years so far and showed no signs of trouble. They acted like teenagers in heat.

"What took you two so damn long? Stop for a quickie? I'm dying for a Southern Comfort." Deb gave each woman a hug and impatiently tonged ice into her glass.

"Nah, I took care of her while she drove," Steph answered. "Pass me a beer, Deb."

"Do we always have to start with sex?" Rae asked.

"Yes." They spoke in unison.

"I'm so horny you could snap me on the ass with a rubber band and I'd go off," Stephanie said.

Deb raised an eyebrow. "Well, let me see if I can rustle one up. That might be fun to watch."

"Might get noisy though," Stephanie warned. "Tell them, Ronni."

Ronni smiled her heart-stopping grin. She was the quiet one in the crowd. If she had something to say, she said it. If not, she didn't waste words or energy. She played it honest and true. "It's good to see you again, Rae. It's been a while."

Stephanie mumbled agreement then pinned Rae with a pleading stare. "*Please* tell me we're not here to unearth the bones of dearly despised Janet one more time. I'm not sure I can take it." Stephanie's profession suited her because she flew hot in seconds. Tact wasn't a skill she possessed nor one she tried to cultivate. Her emotions lurked close to the surface and she did nothing to temper them. Fortunately her peers wore fire-retardant clothing and had water hoses handy.

Deb moved to Rae's side. She had unofficially assumed the role of group peacekeeper and was surprisingly effective. "Now, Stephanie, darling, we have to be sensitive to each other's needs. We're here for support and encouragement…and the occasional wild gossip session."

"I promise I won't talk about Janet," Rae assured them.

They made idle chitchat while Deb played bartender and directed them to seats around the room. The small space could barely accommodate the settee and two dining chairs Rae had dragged in at the last minute. Stephanie and Ronni claimed the settee, leaning against each other in a picture pose of lesbian bliss.

"How are your classes going? Don't you graduate soon?" Deb asked.

Rae took more time than necessary retrieving her beer from the ice bucket, wiping it down, and sliding it into a koozie. "I'm not sure I will—graduate."

"What?"

"What?"

"What?"

She'd expected a passionate response and faced her stunned friends. "I've missed a few classes, after Janet—sorry. What's the point anyway?"

Her friends took turns encouraging her to pursue the degree she'd worked on so hard for the past five years. Their arguments made sense, and they were probably right. But she couldn't help but wonder what it would accomplish.

Ronni summed it up. "If you don't do this, Rae, you'll always regret it. A degree is good for you personally and professionally. Do it for yourself, not for anybody else." The others nodded agreement.

"Yeah," Stephanie added, "and start dating again."

Rae moaned. She hadn't thought about dating in eight months, until the past few days. "I don't know, guys. Love makes us either daredevils or cowards, and I don't want to be either."

"What's wrong with a little daring, as long as it's with the right person. You both have to be on the same page. Most women these days can't hold their sex. You sleep with them once and they think you're engaged." Stephanie looked at Ronni and grinned. "At least that's what I hear from our single friends."

Deb rolled her eyes. "I'd offer to loan you my address book to do some phone cruising, but my girls would be too butch. You go more for the femme types, like me."

"I don't have time to date. I've got other things on my mind." Talk about her sex life always made Rae uncomfortable, and thoughts of Audrey made it worse. She needed to change the subject. "I'd like to make a toast to the newest detective on the Whisperer case—me." Everybody clicked their glasses, took a drink, and waited for Rae to explain. She gave them a brief rundown, as if the case provided her ticket to investigative stardom.

"And this is good because?" Ronni asked.

Deb intervened. "Honey, this could move Rae up the promotion ladder, if she wants it."

Stephanie snorted. "It's career suicide. One detective has already retired because of it. Why do you think they gave it to a junior investigator, no offense intended?"

"If it's such a good thing, why aren't you more excited?" Deb passed around the guacamole dip and chips.

"I am excited." Rae took another swig of beer, and when she lowered the bottle her friends were all staring at her. They weren't buying it. "Mostly excited."

This group of women had been the only consistently stable thing in her life for the past five years. When she and Janet fought or when she changed positions in the department, they were there.

Each of them brought something different, something she needed. Stephanie's passion reminded her to grab life by the throat and squeeze for all its gusto. Ronni personified integrity. And Deb was the best best friend—fiercely loyal, brutally honest, nurturing, and kind. If emotions flowed, Deb wanted to share them. They were all good, reliable, trustworthy companions.

"If the most-decorated detective in the department couldn't solve this case, what makes me think I have a chance?" Rae couldn't admit the extent of her self-doubt even to them. Years of betrayal by her parents, associates, and lovers had taken a deeper toll than she realized. She didn't just distrust others now; she couldn't even trust herself.

"God, I hate her!" Stephanie jumped from the sofa and grabbed another beer. "That fucking Janet. She's made you question everything. Can I kill her?" Despite her rough exterior Stephanie didn't even hurt insects she found inside her house, so no one worried about an actual homicide.

Deb answered with a steely calm. "I'd prefer to handle it." She had everyone's attention. "I don't care that she's part Italian. The mafia's got nothing on a Southern redneck."

"Right," Rae said. "What can you do, twang her to death with your accent?"

The group cackled but Deb wouldn't be outdone. "I have deadly relatives. They could blind her with chewing tobacco juice at twenty paces or cold-cock her with a polecat before she knew what hit her." It took several minutes for the laughter to die down.

"It's a complicated case and I don't want to let these victims down."

"And that's why you won't," Ronni said. "Fresh eyes and that kind of compassion go a long way. You'll figure it out."

They sat in silence for a few seconds, as everyone seemed to let the truth of Ronni's statement sink in.

"Now, have you met anyone you're interested in yet?" Deb asked.

Anything except total honesty right now would undermine her cherished friendship with these three women. If she expected their allegiance, she had to give hers. "Maybe, I'm not sure…" The room suddenly went very quiet as they gathered closer for the scoop, but she didn't know exactly what to say about Audrey Everhart. "She's a victim in an assault, but not really. I think she's holding back information, but I'm not sure. She's different. I think she's attractive."

Deb responded first. "How did you meet her? How long have you known her? What's her name?"

"We met in her rookie school class over a year ago. I felt an attraction and that was all. You know, that immediate zing you get sometimes that usually doesn't mean anything. I hadn't seen her again until four days ago."

"And now she's a victim in a case?" Stephanie asked. "Well, you've got to nip that."

"You said, not really. What does that mean?" Ronni wanted to know.

Rae explained the situation with Audrey as best she could. The story didn't make any more sense out loud than it did rumbling around in her head. "Isn't this perfect? The first woman I like after Janet and she's obviously hiding something. I can't deal with any more deception."

The room was too quiet. Her friends didn't have any answers and they refused to give her false hope. Their silence confirmed what Rae already knew—run as fast as possible and don't look back.

However, Audrey had challenged her professional skills, piqued her personal curiosity, and aroused her sexual interest. It wouldn't be so easy to just walk away from her.

CHAPTER FOUR

Arya clenched his teeth against the pain coursing through him like electricity. Drugs were not an option. His plan required optimum performance. The medication dulled his senses and slowed his reflexes. What would've happened if he'd been medicated the other day when she needed him? His initial goal had been reconnaissance—surveillance and documentation of patterns and behaviors—the foundation of any successful mission. But the degenerates had forced his hand.

She walked toward the front of the community center, oblivious to her surroundings, as the three sloppy, untrained rogues approached from behind. He couldn't allow them to touch her, to spoil her in any way. Arya moved swiftly and immobilized the first one with a strike to the chest. The others ran like cowards. Then she was so close, the pull too strong. He wasn't ready. But she was waiting for him. His fever grew and the ache worsened—control fragile, desire overpowering.

He reached for his only non-lethal weapon and stepped closer. She would certainly turn at any moment and see him. After all, they were connected. Why didn't she turn? He placed the device against her back and pulled the trigger. Power surged through him into her. The craving swelled and burned between his legs. Rage exploded inside.

Her delicate body convulsed in grotesque shapes and she hit the ground. It wasn't supposed to be like this. It wasn't his way. He had a method, a foolproof plan. But circumstances demanded that he act to protect her. He had started to retrieve her body when the gangbangers returned with reinforcements. He had to choose between an altercation that would certainly result in their deaths and undue attention or leaving without her. He'd agonized over his choice since.

Afterward he waited outside her apartment for her return. His note hung loosely in the door. A car pulled up. He knew she was inside. Another woman opened her door, tried to touch her—someone he'd never seen—obviously a cop by the bulge under her leather jacket. The cop removed his message from the door. He'd almost shot her on the spot. It would've been so easy to eliminate this person who dared get between them. He intended his note for *her* only. Arya calmed himself and watched their interaction at the door. She hadn't allowed the cop inside her apartment. Good girl. She was still his special person and soon he would have to be closer.

❖

Audrey stared at the pages of assault cases spread across her kitchen counter, glad to have uninterrupted time to review them. Probably over a hundred cases, the printout hadn't seemed so daunting initially. Each entry consisted of a single-line account of a separate incident. Every item included time and date of offense, location, suspect MO and description, arrestee if any, weapon if used, and the identifying case number. If she expected to make any headway, she'd have to narrow the list.

She wasn't used to crime analysis or thinking like a cop. Her particular skills would come in handy later. At the moment she needed to concentrate on reducing the pool of possibilities. Perhaps the most identifying marker first. She highlighted the weapon category, then slid her ruler down the entries, counting as she went. When she finished, she noted only six incidents in which stun guns were used. After she read the other details, her spirits once again plummeted.

Five of the six cases involved women who used stun guns to ward off attackers, who in turn filed assault charges. What a crazy judicial system that turned the victim into the suspect for simply defending herself. The remaining entry sounded more promising. Jeremy Sutton assaulted Cris, could be male or female, utilizing a stun gun. She put an asterisk next to the case and looked around for her cell phone. Damn contraption. When she needed it, the irritating thing sprouted legs and crawled off.

A faint chiming noise alerted her to the direction of her phone and she followed it to the crumpled blanket on the sofa. She shook the cover and her cell skidded across the floor, its cry for attention louder. Ignoring the message tone, she dialed the number to the police records desk. If her calculations were right, Loretta would be on duty and could provide what she needed.

Her quick exit from crime analysis the last time Loretta helped her wouldn't win her any points. As she waited for an answer, Audrey regretted the two dinner invitations she'd accepted from Loretta to keep their link intact. She didn't like misleading people but seemed to be doing exactly that at every turn lately. Maybe it was time to do the decent thing and be honest with her about her lack of interest.

"Records Division, Loretta, can I help you?"

"Lo, it's Audrey."

"Hi. It's great to hear from you." Loretta's voice dropped an octave and lost its professional edge. "I've been hoping you'd call. You ran off in a hurry the other day."

"I know. We need to talk about that…and some other things too, but it can't be right now. Lo, I'm sorry. This is business. I need your help in a hurry."

"Okay, go ahead." Her disappointment came through the line like a chilly breeze.

She gave Loretta the case number and asked for the address of the arrestee, Jeremy Sutton. The short pause after Loretta conveyed the information told Audrey she was waiting for her quid pro quo. "I'll get back to you soon." The best she could do. She didn't wait for Loretta to acknowledge her obvious brush-off.

After a short drive, Audrey stood in front of Jeremy Sutton's house wondering for the second time in a week if this was a good idea. She scanned the area and got no unfriendly vibes. She hadn't sensed anything hostile at the community center until it was too late either. Audrey proceeded with caution. When she faced this man—and that's exactly how she would evaluate him—what would she say? Did Rae stand outside suspects' doors and wonder how to proceed in an investigation? She seriously doubted it. Audrey rehearsed a couple of possible scenarios in her head and knocked.

A handsome young man with wavy red hair opened the door. He smiled and Audrey felt at ease. "Yes?"

"Mr. Sutton?"

"That's right." His brown eyes showed no sign of recognition.

"I'm from the mayor's office. Could I ask you a couple of questions about your recent encounter with the Kramer Police Department?"

The man's friendly smile turned sour. "Is that what they're calling it now, an encounter?"

"I didn't want to be unkind or insulting. Would you mind a few questions?"

He assessed Audrey for a few seconds. "I've never heard of the mayor's office following up with wrongly accused people."

"Quality control. Please."

Sutton's demeanor softened as he stepped aside and waved her in. "Okay, but I won't be tricked or disrespected in my own home."

They sat across from each other in the immaculately decorated living room and neither spoke for several minutes. Audrey took in the hand-carved wooden sculptures in rich mahogany and soft pine finishes that accentuated floor-to-ceiling bookshelves. Accessories and live plants sprinkled the space with pops of vivid color. Audrey decided she'd made a mistake.

"Could I offer you a cup of coffee, some water?" Though his words sounded sincere, Audrey felt the offer came more from proper etiquette than genuine cordiality.

"Water would be great, thanks." When he returned, Audrey took a sip from the bottle of Pellegrino. She was again struck with the sense that Jeremy Sutton wasn't her attacker. But she'd come this far and a few questions would eliminate any doubt. "I'm sorry to bring up unpleasantness, but who was the victim in your assault case?"

"Cris Masterson."

"Male or female?"

"Male. He accosted me when I passed a bar on my way home. Apparently he thought I was gay. I defended myself with the only thing I had. If you'd read the report, you'd already know all that."

She felt like a complete incompetent. Rae would never have faced a suspect unprepared. She'd definitely made a mistake by not reading the initial investigation. She thought of the uncomfortable conversation with Loretta and realized she could've avoided that as well. The details of the case and the arrestee's address were documented in the full report if only she'd gotten a copy. Maybe amateur sleuthing was harder than it appeared. To cover the real reason for her visit, she asked a couple more questions. "And has your case come to trial yet?"

"He dropped the charges."

"How did the police officers treat you?"

"They were doing their jobs, misguided as they may have been." She sensed his obvious discomfort. Who could blame him? A stranger showed up at his door asking questions about an incident he'd prefer to forget. She would've felt exactly the same way.

"I see." Jeremy Sutton watched every move Audrey made, particularly her hands. "What kind of work do you do, Mr. Sutton?"

"I'm a woodworker. I love it." He indicated the sculptures behind him and his face lit up.

That accounted for his obvious interest in her hands. He was truly an artist. She admired creative people and doubted most of them were capable of violence. Maybe it had to do with their connection to the universe and that inspirational flow. "Well, thank you for your time, Mr. Sutton, and the Pellegrino."

"Sure." He smiled warmly and his eyes sparkled again with kindness. As he opened the door, he took her hand with such gentleness Audrey didn't attempt to move away. The extended handshake convinced her Jeremy Sutton would never intentionally harm anyone.

Audrey drove back to her apartment confused, dissatisfied, and full of self-recrimination. Usually firmly in control, confident of her actions, and determined enough to follow them through, today she'd acted like a complete novice. However, she had eliminated Jeremy Sutton as her attacker so she hadn't completely wasted the trip.

As she got back on the highway, her cell phone rang. The aggravating little thing wasn't helping her mood and she seriously contemplated throwing it out the window. She'd never gotten anything from it but bad news anyway.

"Yes, go ahead."

"Still hate your mobile, I see." Yasi chided her in her melodic voice.

"Oh…hi. I mean it's good to hear from you."

"Is that why you've been avoiding me?" Yasirah Mansour was the most compassionate person Audrey knew, so the hurt in her tone was almost too much to bear.

"I'm sorry, Yasi. Things have been a bit crazy around here."

"Are you okay? You sound strange, like you're out of balance."

"No, it's work."

"Whatever you say, but I'm not convinced. Are you home?"

"Almost."

Yasi hesitated, which was never good. She was a total extrovert and loved to talk more than almost anything. "I hope you won't be upset because I've done something."

The last time Yasi did "something" an equipment malfunction almost killed them. She hated to ask. *"What?"*

"You'll see."

"Come on, Yas, I'm not in the mood for games." She turned into her apartment complex and saw Yasi sitting on her vintage apple-red Corvette in front of her door. She looked like a graphic hood ornament with her womanly frame wrapped in a flowing multicolored kaftan. As Audrey parked beside Yasi's car, she felt a momentary pang of regret as her friend's dark hair whipped around her gorgeous face, dark eyes, and full lips. Why hadn't they ever been lovers? They felt the connection, even talked about it, just never took the next step. Audrey worried that it would destroy a perfect friendship. Now she loved Yasi like a sister. Even so, she wasn't ready to explain what was happening in her life—even if she'd been certain herself.

In spite of her reservations, she got out of the car and ran to her. She needed confirmation that someone cared. It had been too long since she'd felt loved in any form. "Oh, Yasi, I'm so glad to see you."

Yasi held her and rocked side to side, cooing reassurances. Her voice was like liquid love flowing from Audrey's ears directly to her aching heart. It hadn't been easy the past year only seeing Yasi randomly. She hadn't realized until now just how difficult and how lonely she'd felt.

"There, there. Now I'm certain something's wrong. You can tell me all about it, but first I have a present for you." She opened her car door, pulled out a shoebox full of holes, and with a grand flare presented it to Audrey. "*This* is what I've done. Please don't be mad."

Audrey didn't have to open the box. The distinctively disgruntled meowing and scratching from inside verified her suspicions. Yasi knew her so well and it *had* been almost two years since Olga passed. "How old? What color? When—"

"Why don't we go inside and find out?" She hugged Audrey to her as they walked into the apartment. They automatically headed for the sofa and stretched out like they'd done so many times as kids coming home from a movie. It was as if they'd seen each other yesterday, their intimacy intact.

Audrey placed the box between them and lifted the lid. A tabby kitten popped over the side and flung itself toward her, snuggling into the hollow of her neck. Audrey felt a connection immediately. "She can't be more than seven or eight weeks old. She's gorgeous."

"She's ten, weaned, has all her shots, and is litter-box trained—in other words, the perfect house pet. Don't you love her? And look at those darling little eyes."

Carefully dislodging the kitten from her neck, Audrey gazed into the most beautiful pair of mismatched eyes she'd ever seen, one deep green and one yellow. "Oh, my." She stroked the kitten's coat, amazed at its coarse, springy feel, unlike Olga's silken fur. The kitten's wiry hair was dense and formed little ringlets all over her tiny body.

"She's an American wirehair. I found her at the pound. They'd taken very good care of her. She's the friendliest kitten I've ever seen. Can you imagine anyone abandoning this little bundle of preciousness?"

"No." Audrey was immediately in love. "No, I can't. What's her name?"

Yasi smiled and produced an envelope from her purse. "I thought the three of us would take care of that together. Remember how Nadja used to name pets?"

Audrey smiled at the memory of her mother's naming ceremony. It was one of her favorite traditions and sparked a swell of warmth. "She let them choose their own names."

"Exactly." Yasi opened the envelope, shook, and little white squares of paper floated to the floor. "I thought it appropriate that the theme was famous circus acts. Turn her loose when you're ready."

Audrey kissed Yasi on the cheek, planted another on the kitten's forehead, and set her gingerly on the floor. The animal acted like she was on springs, bouncing from one area to the next, inspecting and scampering away again. When she eventually slowed, she walked carefully around the perimeter of the slips of paper as if stalking the entries, trying each name on for size. She stopped, sniffed, and stood completely upright with one piece of paper stuck to her mouth.

"That's it then," Yasi said as she retrieved the paper and read the results. "Meet Cannonball."

Audrey scooped the kitten up and held her in her palm. "Cannonball. Seems appropriate for the way you've been hurling yourself around. I might have to call you CB. Cannonball isn't very ladylike." Her new charge licked her wrist and Audrey could've sworn she smiled.

Yasi rolled off the sofa and started toward the door. "Well, my work here is done."

"Hey, wait a minute."

"Only kidding. I'll get the rest of CB's belongings from the car. I couldn't give you a kitten without the necessary accoutrements. That would be like having a computer without the Internet—basically no point. Be right back."

Cannonball sat perfectly still and stared at her as if trying to relay a message. "What is it, little one?" CB stretched out across Audrey's stomach and closed her eyes. "I'm glad you're here too."

Yasi returned with a pretty pink cat carrier lined with a heating pad and Hello Kitty blanket, a litter box and litter, and another bag full of food and toys. "Everything you need to make this little girl comfortable."

They spent a while deciding the best spot for CB's nest, locating her near the hub of activity to acclimate her to the new surroundings. Audrey put food and water in her dish, left it nearby, and turned the heating pad on low. When she opened the door of the crate, CB scooted inside and burrowed under the blanket, obviously tired from the naming exercise.

"Do you love her?" Yasi asked.

"Oh, yes." She hugged Yasi and pulled her back onto the sofa. "Thank you so much. I needed something to love." The statement was telling, but Yasi would've gotten it out of her eventually anyway.

"What's going on?"

Before she could censor herself, Audrey blurted out the entire story of her assault. She'd held it in for days and it felt good to finally tell somebody the truth. "I haven't told the police about the stun gun. I want to find the guy myself. What if it's all somehow connected to—you know, that summer."

Yasi's face turned ashen. "This is all too déjà vu. That's why you left without an explanation. When you finally contacted me again, I couldn't believe it. Everybody thought you were busy with the new job. I was sure it was all connected. You hadn't ever disappeared so completely, not even while you were away at school."

Audrey's college experience had been like four years of high school on steroids. Cliques and game playing trumped real friendship, and she couldn't master either. The daily teasing aggravated like a persistent outbreak of zits. She was the mark of rich and poor, bright and dim-witted, freshman and seniors—an equal-opportunity target. The constant judgment and rejection contrasted starkly to the love and inclusiveness of her childhood and formative years. How could two segments of the same society be so diametrically opposed? After a while she retreated, coming out of her room only for meals and classes. She led a solitary existence—punishment for her unwillingness to face the truth?

"Sweetie, have you remembered anything else about last summer?" Yasi's soft voice was tentative. She knew how much it hurt Audrey to talk or even think about that time.

Audrey shook her head. This was the part that made her seem loopy. She was chasing ghosts without knowing the dearly departed—no idea where to start or what to look for.

"You have to let it go, Aud. You're not equipped to deal with things like this. Let the police handle it."

"The police? Really? I can't believe you're giving me *that* advice. What would I tell them? I either don't remember or I'm blocking everything. *I* have to do this. It's changed my entire life. Besides, I can't tell them what I am."

"Don't you mean *who* you are?" Yasi pulled her close and slid a hand up and down her arm in a soothing motion. Yasi knew Audrey's fears, even when she denied them. "Did it ever occur to you that your gift might actually help this one time?"

Audrey pulled away from Yasi, annoyed with the topic and at how quickly it made her defensive. "My *gift?* You mean this unholy *curse* I've been saddled with all my life? This *thing* that possesses and drives me like a mind-altering disease? If there was any good in it, why didn't I sense the attack? How could I miss *that*?"

"Oh, sweetie, don't be so hard on yourself. Give it a chance."

"I can't, Yas. I've left all that behind. It's not part of my life anymore. It can't be."

"Aud, I know it's—"

"I love you, Yasi, but you *don't* know. You have no idea what it's like. The logical, thinking part of me questions everything while the intuitive part of me trusts only what I feel. And when I need it most, the damn thing misfires. It's like being schizophrenic, but fully aware that you are. How can I possibly share that with someone, with *anyone*? It was bearable when I was young, with all of you. Not now. Most people can't understand and wouldn't accept it. Trust me, I have to do this by the rules of the real world—not woo-woo psychic universal law."

Her pride wasn't at stake as much as her decisions, her loyalty, and her past. She'd left everyone she loved a year ago because of a stranger and regretted it ever since. Initially fear kept her away. As time passed it became easier to stay away, more difficult to admit her mistake, and impossible to face failure. Her new path wouldn't mesh easily with the one she'd left behind. Now she was afraid some diabolical force was drawing the two together.

Audrey rested her head on Yasi's shoulder. "I'm so tired of running, Yas. So tired of fighting this battle alone. I know I chose it but I can't seem to stop."

"You were always so damn independent. We can't do everything ourselves. At some point we all need help. Don't you know anyone you can trust?"

After everything else she'd shared with Yasi, what was one more revelation? "There is one possibility. A detective named Rae Butler. She already thinks I'm withholding information. Perhaps I should trust her. She's very…" How could she describe Rae and the feelings she tried to ignore?

"Wait a minute. Wasn't she that instructor during your class—the one you liked but wouldn't admit it?"

"Yes." God, she hadn't meant for that to come out. Audrey had forgotten she'd told Yasi about meeting Rae. Then it had been general conversation about someone she'd probably never have contact with again. "I mean, what the hell. Yes, and I still like her. She's competent, reliable, trustworthy, and—"

"Sounds like you're vetting her for a job. You're attracted to her, aren't you?" Leave it to Yasi to nail the situation with the fewest words. "Never thought I'd see the day."

Neither did she. And simply telling herself *not* to feel anything for Rae was like waving the proverbial red flag in front of an angry bull. Rae remained in her mind, consuming more space as they spent more time together. The feelings came whether she wanted them to or not.

Every time she encountered Rae it was more difficult to misdirect or to simply withhold, harder to keep the distance her life demanded. She *wanted* to tell Rae the truth, to enlist her professional assistance. What if she was like other cops Audrey had come across—intolerant, heartless, and callous? The picture didn't fit Rae Butler.

Yasi went into the kitchen and put on a kettle for tea, leaving Audrey alone with her thoughts. She always knew exactly the right thing to do for her. It was like being of one mind with someone who truly knew you and loved you in spite of your faults. Would she ever experience that with a lover? A seductive picture of Rae sweaty and flushed, brushing unruly curls from her forehead, flashed through her mind. The image ignited a shiver of arousal.

"Here." Yasi handed her a cup of chamomile tea. "Drink, then we'll sleep and talk again in the morning. You look exhausted."

"You mean you're spending the night?"

"Try to get rid of me. I'll need a T-shirt to sleep in."

"Got you covered."

Yasi laughed but Audrey was too distracted to get the joke. She was just glad to have the subject of Rae Butler at least temporarily tabled. As they drank their tea and prepared for bed, Yasi made small talk about their friends and work. They moved to the only bed in the apartment with no questions or awkwardness. She and Yasi had slept together many times without discomfort, and tonight would be no different.

She shivered as cold wind brushed across her face. Just a temperature response, but she looked around anyway—nothing except her excitement.

Turning toward the bar, she thought how strange that the sky had suddenly gone dark. Remnants of a shattered streetlight littered the path. That sweet smell. A stabbing pain pierced her. Liquid fire oozed down her spinal column and branched out into her body. Her muscles seized and she dropped to the ground like a stone.

"No more," she begged. "No more."

CHAPTER FIVE

Rae woke at dawn and shuffled into her dart room/office by way of the coffee pot. Her eyes burned from lack of sleep and her marathon Whisperer case review. She examined the timeline and victim photos thumbtacked to the massive display board again as she twirled one of her favorite darts between her fingers.

She'd taken up the sport as a teenager to avoid her family's constant nagging about her first girlfriend. Janet hated darts so Rae kept the set packed away to avoid an argument. She enjoyed having some personal space back, though she was occasionally lonely. As she perused the crime board, the sleek, perfectly balanced dart teetered on the tip of her finger, reminding her of the precariousness of life.

Four attractive women assaulted in similar fashion. She absently rolled the streamlined Viper dart shaft and sipped her coffee. Her extensive background checks indicated the four women had nothing in common. Though they were striking in appearance, she couldn't find enough similarities between them to establish a victim type for the offender.

What was she missing? Rae positioned her right foot and angled about seventy-five degrees to the dartboard. She visually lined up the target, stroked the dart flight between her fingers for luck, and accelerated through the throw in one fluid motion. Only her arm moved, shoulder and body still and grounded for the perfect shot. The follow-through ended with her hand aiming at the center of the target.

The dart spiraled beautifully toward the bristle board, struck a spider that separated the segments, and bounced to the floor. She often bargained with herself before release that if she made the shot she'd uncover one clue in her current case. Her delivery proved much more reliable than the crime-solving gods. Frustrated with her game and the lack of significant leads, Rae headed for the shower.

She was dressed and on her way out the door when her cell phone rang. "Butler."

"How soon can you get here?"

"Sarge?"

"Of course it's me. I need to see you ASAP. And yes, I know it's Sunday."

As Rae drove to the station, she wondered what kettle of fish had boiled over and ruined Sergeant Sharp's suit. Not So didn't ruffle unless he sensed danger to his perfectly coiffed career. A few minutes later she found out the reason.

Sharp paced behind his desk in a pair of khaki slacks and golf shirt. Was his sour expression because his game had been interrupted or because of the news he was about to deliver? Either way she wouldn't be a winner. "It's that Everhart woman."

"Excuse me? You took me off that case two days ago."

Not So waved a computer printout in the air then shoved it toward her on the desk. "See that?" He pointed to the pages, crumpled around the edges from his vigorous fanning. The data was the same information Audrey had gotten from crime analysis, with one entry circled.

She waited for the point. It wasn't her case any more and the sergeant seemed more agitated than a simple assault would warrant. "Am I missing something?"

"The suspect in this case," he stabbed the paper with his index finger, "Jeremy Sutton, was murdered yesterday. Homicide is on it. And guess who paid the guy a visit?"

"Aud—Ms. Everhart?" Not So nodded. "How do we know she went to see him?"

"Homicide dicks scanned the computer database for the last person who ran a check on this guy—Loretta Granger in records.

She flipped like a cheap whore and gave up your girl. You're wasting time, Butler."

"Just because she ran a check on him doesn't mean she went to his house or killed him."

Sharp looked at her like she was as thick as a layer of bricks. "What do you want, an engraved confession? They found her fingerprints on a bottle of Pellegrino—get a move on. We're not here to try the case."

"And I get this honor because—"

"You already have *rapport* with her." Sharp emphasized the word as though it held some unpleasant meaning, not like a concept he utilized every day in his ladder-climbing career.

Rae laughed. If what she and Audrey Everhart had was rapport this would be a very unproductive trip. "Any idea of the connection between the two of them?" Rae had a feeling she already knew, but wondered how much Sharp had pieced together.

"That's what I want you to find out before the homicide boys rain a shit storm down on her. Mayor Downing called me personally and asked that I intercede."

Did Not So seriously think they could "intercede" in a murder investigation? If Audrey had visited this suspect alone, she was more independent than Rae thought...and more unpredictable. Was there a connection between Sutton and her attack? *Audrey, what are you hiding and why won't you let me help?* Rae could only pray this was a huge misunderstanding.

"Talk to the woman, find out her side of the story, and get back to me ASAP. The mayor wants to be ahead of the game if there's bad publicity."

That made sense. The mayor certainly looked out for his political ass. If Audrey was implicated in a homicide investigation, he could fire her for some flimsy reason and ask questions later. Political fallout was like a foul odor, permeating and contaminating everything it touched. She didn't want to see Audrey dragged to the cleaners...if she wasn't involved.

"Right, I'm on it." On the way out of the building, she tried to call Audrey but got no answer on her cell. She played out the worst-case scenario and tried to imagine Audrey killing someone. The picture wouldn't materialize. Violence didn't fit her image of Audrey.

Rae pulled into the parking lot and approached the apartment. She'd straighten this out quickly and get back to her active case. As she listened at the door, she was pleased to have a legitimate reason to see Audrey Everhart again. She stepped to the side and knocked.

After several attempts, Audrey answered. "What are you doing here? It's Sunday." Her blond hair stood out from her head in wispy sprigs and the lids over her cerulean eyes were at half-mast. She looked like a sleepy kid on the first morning of school. "Don't you believe in calling?"

"I tried. Sorry to wake you. I need to talk to you rather urgently." When Audrey turned and walked back inside, Rae followed. Every step Audrey took rewarded Rae with a glimpse of her perfectly curved bottom under the tail of her short T-shirt.

Rae was so distracted she almost bulldozed a bright-pink kitten carrier in the middle of the floor. "Oh, this is new." Rae knelt and offered her curled fingers to the little bundle of tabby inside the crate. The kitten licked and chewed her knuckles.

"Her name is CB." Audrey gave the kitten a few strokes, promised food would be coming shortly, and turned to Rae. "Coffee?"

"That would be nice, thanks." Rae sat at the counter and watched Audrey retrieve cups from the cabinet. She inhaled Audrey's lingering perfume combined with a trace of her distinctive aroma. Arousal reared its elusive head, and its force surprised Rae. The form and scent of a woman had always incited Rae's baser instincts, but she'd never been this excited without touching. Rae indulged in the sight and fragrance of Audrey Everhart a few seconds more, wishing her reason for being here was different. She'd suspected early on that friendship with Audrey wouldn't be enough. As she sat in her kitchen, stimulated by her mundane activities, she was certain of it.

Now she was in the untenable position of evaluating and assessing Audrey on a professional level. The conflict between attraction and work could throw her instincts off, but add to it the shredded state of her psyche, and the fact that Audrey might be withholding something, and Rae couldn't trust any of her feelings. She'd better stick with the facts.

"Aud—" A fair-skinned beauty exited Audrey's bedroom wearing little more than Audrey and holding a terry-cloth robe. "I'm sorry, sweetie. Didn't know we had company." She flashed Rae a stunning smile. "Thought you might need this." The woman held the robe open for Audrey and tied the sash as gently as a lover. After a hug, she turned to Rae.

"Good morning, I'm Yasirah Mansour."

She offered her hand and Rae shook it with all the professionalism she could muster. Rae struggled not to immediately interrogate her about her relationship with Audrey. Under normal circumstances, she would've tactfully persisted, unearthing everything about the beautiful Ms. Mansour. However, now wasn't the time for a personal digression. Sergeant Sharp's urgent task demanded she stay on track.

"I'm Detective Rae Butler. Sorry to disturb your morning. I need to talk with Audrey, privately if possible."

Yasi placed her arm protectively around Audrey's back. Rae caught a momentary flash of something as it crossed Audrey's face—concern, pain? "Audrey can speak for herself. However, I'd prefer to stay."

Audrey and Yasi stared at each other several seconds, assessing and deciding. The look relayed so much emotion Rae felt like a voyeur. Then, without speaking, Yasi poured herself a cup of coffee and disappeared into the bedroom.

Rae couldn't stop the unedited words that rushed out with too much emotion. "That was impressive. I don't think I've ever seen two people communicate so clearly without saying a word. You're obviously very close."

Audrey placed a steaming mug in front of Rae without responding to the comment. "What exactly do you need to discuss with me? It is Sunday, after all."

"Why does everybody feel the need to remind me of that fact? I'm aware it's the weekend. Unfortunately crime doesn't take a break, so neither do I." Her words were sharp and unfriendly. Audrey's failure to clarify the relationship with Yasirah Mansour bothered Rae more than she realized. It shouldn't, but everything about Audrey affected her in some way. She sipped her coffee for a few seconds to regain her composure. "Sorry. I'll get to the point. Did you visit a man named Jeremy Sutton yesterday?"

Shock registered clearly on Audrey's face as she turned to stir sugar and cream into her cup. Rae tried not to read too much into the obvious stall tactic. When Audrey faced her again, she looked defeated. Rae placed her hand on her back to reassure her that she could trust and confide in her. Audrey's response was not what she expected.

"Don't do that. It hurts." Audrey flinched as powerful emotions and pain coursed through her. It was the first time Rae had touched her, and she wasn't prepared for her reaction.

"What did I do?"

Every nerve ending in Audrey's body seemed to coalesce at the point of contact and beg for more. The feeling almost paralyzed her. Rae's touch had the depth of a mother's affection but was profoundly more sexual. She searched for an explanation. The sensations in her body overruled reason. She'd never experienced anything like this—and she couldn't allow it now.

Audrey focused her awareness on the physical pain radiating from the injuries on her back. The discomfort was preferable to the unexplained feelings Rae's touch conjured up. She backed away from Rae and immediately regretted her action.

"You're so flushed. What hurts?" Rae stood next to her looking like she'd tipped the ashes out of Aunt Tilley's urn.

"Where you touched me." Audrey felt silly and light-headed. She had no viable excuse for nearly passing out from a touch. The truth poked at her insides, demanding release. "It's my back. An injury from the assault."

From the look on Rae's face, Audrey knew she'd said the wrong thing. "Mind if I see for myself?"

At least Rae had focused on something tangible and not Audrey's fragile emotional state. "You certainly may not." The last thing she wanted was Rae Butler's hand on her naked flesh, yet it was the only thing she wanted. "I'm sure it's nothing."

"What if it isn't? Please, Audrey. This could be important." Rae crossed her heart with her fingers. "I promise this isn't a ploy to see your naked back, though I'm sure it's quite spectacular."

Audrey's pulse doubled at the thought of Rae Butler looking at any part of her exposed flesh. However, if she resisted further, she would only increase her anxiety and extend the unannounced visit. "Okay, just a glance, no touching."

Rae waited as she lowered the robe to her waist, tied it off, and raised her skimpy T-shirt. "Jesus H. Christ. What the hell?"

When she looked over her shoulder at Rae, her eyes had gone dark and cold. Her jaws worked in time to the kneading of her hands at her sides. She looked like she wanted to hit something. "Rae, you're scaring me. What *is* it?"

"You were hit by a stun gun."

Rae's fingers traced a light path across her back and sent chills up Audrey's spine. Then she pressed against a tender spot below her shoulders and the pleasurable sensation turned into a pulsing ache. Audrey almost came off the floor. "You're touching."

"The marks are pretty obvious on your lower back." She gently touched the area again.

Audrey struggled for a response that didn't reveal how long she'd withheld this piece of information. Any comment at this point should clarify the truth, not cloud it further. Before she could respond, Rae stared at her, brows furrowed, lips tightened into a thin line.

"You already knew." The look in Rae's eyes signaled more pain than accusation, as if Audrey had attacked her personally, in some way offended her sense of integrity. When she spoke again she clearly sought understanding instead of information. "What have I done to make you distrust me?"

Audrey was unsure how to answer such a simple question. She hadn't done anything wrong, hadn't violated any law or hurt anyone, until now. She wanted only to find answers—her way. It should be so easy to tell the truth. She couldn't. Instead she watched with disbelief and apprehension as Rae reached for her cell phone.

"I need to call the lab to get some pictures of this."

"Wait a minute." Audrey pulled her shirt back down and squared off with Rae. "Hold everything."

Rae stopped as her finger hit the Send key.

Audrey didn't like this part of herself, but she had to draw the line. "Put down the phone, Rae."

"Let me get Trevor on the way. We need to document these injuries."

"Put down the phone."

"What's going on here?" Yasi exited the bedroom, her deep-brown eyes almost glowing with anger. It took a lot to rile her, but seeing Audrey scared and obviously rattled was enough. She stepped between Audrey and Rae, the sight almost comical. Rae towered over Yasi by at least four inches, but she didn't back down. "Get away from her. Right now."

Rae closed her cell and stared at Audrey—probably trying to figure out whom to address first—Audrey for her reluctance to pursue her attacker or Yasi for her threatening stance. "Why are you fighting me on this, Audrey?"

How could she convince Rae to let this go? Did she really want her to back off or did she want and need her help? No, she couldn't pull Rae into her quagmire of a life. It might lead to other revelations she couldn't and wouldn't share. Audrey struggled for a compromise that would allow them both to get what they wanted. "If I let you take these pictures, you have to promise they'll never leave your possession."

"They'll be evidence in your case when I catch this guy. I'll have to turn them in."

"Rae, you're off the case. I don't want to pursue it any further. There's no need for photos. If you insist on taking them, you'll have to meet my terms." Audrey didn't think Rae would agree. Without a case, photos were unnecessary. Rae would have to concede the wastefulness of utilizing city funds for useless "evidence."

Yasi nodded and her stare dared Rae to question Audrey's logic.

"Okay, you win." Rae raised her fingers in the Scouts' honor sign and started to reach for her cell phone, but a knock at the front door stopped her.

Audrey couldn't believe Rae actually agreed to her conditions. She'd played a bluff, and Rae had called her on it. Now what?

"Why don't I answer that?" Yasi said, shaking her head at Audrey and Rae's stare-down. She opened the door for a Kramer Police CSI with a digital camera and evidence bag. "Looks like we have another cop-type visitor," she called over her shoulder.

Trevor answered Rae's question before she could ask it. "When you punch a number into your cell phone, hit the Send button, and the other person picks up, they can hear you. I asked the dispatcher for your location and voilà. Besides, I was in the area on another case."

Rae waited until she and Trevor stood in front of Audrey before giving him his instructions. "Look, this is pretty sensitive. I don't want anybody else to see the pictures you're about to take, and I do mean *anybody*. When you finish, put the camera card in an evidence envelope and give it to me. Understand?" She obviously wanted to make sure Audrey was as comfortable as possible and that she kept her word.

"No, but since when does that matter? I do as I'm told," Trevor said.

Audrey sat on the sofa and wrapped the robe as tightly around her as possible. Her insides quivered as if cold had settled deep inside her. Feeling lost and very much alone she took a deep breath and mentally distanced for the invasive touching about to take place. She seldom allowed anyone to touch her, especially not strangers. The only person in this room who had any idea of her agony was Yasi.

Without being asked, Yasi settled beside her on the sofa. "Here, sweetie, let me hold up your shirt."

While Audrey clung to the robe covering her chest, Yasi eased her T-shirt up and Trevor snapped several pictures of the injuries to her back. It was taking too long and Audrey grew irritated with Trevor's dawdling. The skin over her abdomen stung with cellular recall at the touch of fabric. She flinched, wanting desperately to remain covered but feeling the terry cloth like a weapon against her flesh. It was difficult to determine which was more painful and insidious, the stranger who touched her back now or the memory of another who'd defiled her before. Trevor dropped his hand to Audrey's waistline and rubbed.

"What the hell are you doing?" Rae asked as Audrey lurched forward out of reach.

"Sorry, I was making sure there weren't any injuries farther down. This one is pretty close to the waistline." He pointed to the lower mark. "You okay, Audrey?"

"I'd appreciate a little warning next time."

"All finished." Trevor clicked a last shot and stepped away from the sofa. He removed the camera card, dropped it into an envelope, and handed it to Rae. "Anything else?"

"No, thanks, Trev." When the door closed behind him, Rae knelt in front of her. Audrey could tell she wanted to touch her, to reassure her but kept her distance. "I'm sorry about that."

"Are we done then?" Audrey gathered a pile of papers from the floor beside the sofa, shuffled into the kitchen, and threw them into the trashcan. The waves of emotion that she'd held back hit her full force. A strange man's hands on her body, an appealing woman kneeling in front of her—the combination of revulsion and desire rolled through her like a blast of heat. She opened the refrigerator door and stood in the cool air praying it would ground her in the moment. Clinging to the sides of the refrigerator, she mentally wiped her mind of the images.

"Are you all right, sweetie?" Yasi asked, hovering nearby.

"I'll be fine." She stood in the cool air a few minutes longer before turning again to Rae Butler. "Now what?"

"If you're up for it, I have a few more questions."

"And if I'm not, will you go away?" The words sounded harsh and accusatory, but Audrey didn't have the emotional energy to be tactful.

"If that's what you want." Once again her careless words had wounded Rae. Audrey felt the underlying turmoil as Rae seemed to struggle before she spoke. "There's a good chance I'm wrong about this, Audrey. Maybe you've already told me everything that happened at the community center and I'm way off base. My instincts haven't been great lately." She coughed, a throat-clearing noise almost stifled by emotion. "I *really* need to know…if I'm wrong again."

Rae's confidence clearly had evaporated and doubt seeped in like water through a sieve. Audrey's heart ached for her, so raw and exposed. What had happened in the past to make her question something so basic? She'd revealed a vulnerability that obviously caused her pain. Rae Butler didn't trust easily. If Audrey diminished the significance of this moment, she might never experience it again.

As she stared at Rae her anger disappeared, replaced by compassion. No one had ever spoken to her that honestly about her insecurity. Rae touched her deeply even as Audrey tried to be her most resistant. "We might as well talk. You won't rest until you have all the answers."

She motioned for Rae to join her on the sofa and waited for the barrage of questions that she dreaded. Rae's green eyes had turned springtime again, warm and open. Audrey wanted to surrender, to fall into that openness and let someone else help. Could she?

"If you knew your attacker used a stun gun, why didn't you tell me sooner?"

Maybe she could tell Rae the truth, to a point. "I wanted to take care of it myself. You have no idea how demeaning and disempowering it is for people to consider you a *victim*. They look at you differently, like you're at fault, like you asked for it."

Rae didn't speak for several minutes and her gaze scanned the room before settling on Audrey again. "I actually do know what that's like. I was assaulted off duty once. And trust me, it's worse when fellow cops look at you like you deserved it because you couldn't protect yourself. I want to help every victim reclaim what was taken from them in some way."

It wasn't the callous response she'd expected from a cop or the meaningless platitudes of the near-strangers in her life. She relaxed, pleased and surprised that someone understood—that Rae understood. Maybe she'd misjudged her and maybe other people would be supportive as well. She hadn't allowed herself to even consider the possibility, much less try to find out.

"Would you mind going through what happened step by step, please?" Rae asked.

Audrey recounted the assault, remembering everything and seeing nothing. The energy around her had shifted and become very dark during the incident. She'd tried to focus on her assailant's feelings but had seemingly stepped into a storm cloud of static cacophony. It was frustrating. She'd agonized for days, warring with herself about telling Rae, and now that she remembered, her recollection wasn't helpful.

"Do you know anyone who would want to harm you?"

"No." She answered too quickly, without conviction. Calm down, Audrey told herself. Rae is only trying to help. She doesn't know anything that can hurt you and won't find out unless you tell her.

"Are you sure, Audrey? Think carefully. There has to be something."

"I moved to Kramer a year ago for my job, and the people at work are the only ones I know. I've barely had time to get acclimated, much less make enemies." Exactly what Audrey had wanted to avoid—Rae or anyone else delving into her past. Audrey read the apology on Rae's face. She looked like she'd unintentionally wronged a friend and didn't know how to fix it. At least she had the decency to realize she was being intrusive.

Rae reached for Audrey's hands but stopped. It felt like the right thing to do, to comfort and reassure her for prying into her life. Audrey hadn't been receptive to her touch before, and Trevor's misplaced contact earlier had seemed to genuinely disturb her. How could she reassure Audrey and encourage her to cooperate? Rae sensed Audrey wasn't telling her everything—maybe not about her assault, but about something.

The stun-gun marks provided the first real clue that someone had actually assaulted Audrey, aside from a shoe print of questionable value and a few nondescript bruises. Why the reluctance? Suddenly another possibility occurred to her. What if Audrey knew her attacker and was protecting him or her?

It made sense. Maybe the entire I-can't-remember thing had been a ruse to give Audrey more time to fabricate a plausible cover story. She wouldn't be the first person to risk her integrity for someone she cared about. However, this seemed a bit out of character for her. Audrey could've been seriously injured and didn't seem like the kind of person to accept abuse and cover it up.

The look in Audrey's eyes was not that of a lying woman afraid to be found out. It was the frightened stare of a cornered woman unsure where to turn. Rae breathed a little easier. She didn't want to believe Audrey was capable of lying, but reminded herself that anyone was capable of deceit when it served their purpose.

She doodled in her notebook as a list of possible suspects spun through her mind: an angry ex-lover, a jealous current one, disgruntled coworker, someone with a grudge against the mayor or city government in general. Maybe someone from her past. "So what about where you lived before? Surely you had time to make a few acquaintances, maybe even a few enemies."

"There's no one."

"Are you sure? Nobody lives their life without pissing off someone unless they live in a bubble or don't stay put for long."

Audrey rubbed her temples and repeated, "No one."

"Why don't you give me your last address anyway and I'll snoop around a little. If it's somebody from your past, I'll find him." Crime victims often needed additional assurance that they'd be protected during the process. Maybe Audrey's reluctance was about personal safety.

"What part of *there is no one* don't you understand, Detective?"

Rae looked up from her pad. "But—"

"But what? You can't resist the opportunity to nose around in my life? Isn't it enough that this investigation can blow apart my present without dredging up history? Trust me, the mayor won't be happy to have one of his staff involved in this unseemly business."

Dumbfounded, Rae had no idea where Audrey's anger or defensiveness came from, only that it was aimed at her. "Audrey, believe me, I don't enjoy poking around in people's private lives.

Sometimes it's the only way to get answers. If you're hiding something, you could have been assaulted because of it."

Audrey vigorously massaged her temples as the blood drained from her face. "I need for you to leave now. I'm not feeling well."

"I'm sorry. What can I do?"

"You can go—and you can stay out of my past. It has nothing to do with this."

Rae stared into eyes so vividly blue and full of emotion that they seemed to churn like ocean swells in a storm. She didn't respond to the statement. She'd heard it too many times in other cases and it was often proven wrong.

She couldn't bear the anguish on Audrey's face or her resulting Pavlovian response to come to her rescue. Audrey looked like a child who'd come home and found her family moved without her. Rae felt capable only of doing her job, but that wouldn't address the other desires that Audrey Everhart conjured up in her.

Rae felt the attraction between them, the edge of interest every time they were near. But the look in Audrey's eyes each time she avoided Rae's touch had been one of shock and maybe a bit of fear. Still, the current that sparked between them was real, desire so thick it was almost edible. If Rae couldn't maintain a professional distance, perhaps she was as inadequate a cop as she was a partner.

Audrey Everhart sparked suspicion in her like a match in dry timber. Audrey's soft voice made Rae irrationally want to believe anything she said. But Rae's twelve-year career had taught her that people *always* had a motive for their behavior.

As Rae approached the door to leave, she remembered her reason for the visit. She'd forgotten all about Jeremy Sutton and hated to bring him up now. She couldn't return to Sergeant Sharp without answers.

"Audrey, I'm sorry. I have to ask about Jeremy Sutton. Did you go to his place?"

The pained expression returned to Audrey's face. Her shoulders slumped and she appeared exhausted. "Yes."

"Why?"

"I told you, I wanted to handle it myself. I thought he might be connected to my assault. Obviously I was mistaken. We chatted a few minutes and I left. Why?"

"He was murdered yesterday." Rae had delivered death notices many times and could read the range of emotions from barely fazed to totally debilitated. Audrey Everhart seemed completely shocked. She paled and grabbed the door for support. She clearly had no idea and absolutely nothing to do with Sutton's death.

"How…what…why?"

"His throat was slashed. No idea why. The homicide squad is investigating. Someone will come by to question you later, I'm sure. They found your prints at the scene."

"Was this my fault? Because I went to his house?"

What a strange question. Why would Audrey's visit endanger Jeremy Sutton? Did she also know more about his death than she was saying? An uncomfortable gnawing sensation settled in Rae's gut again. She expected suspicion when dealing with suspects, but not with victims. It always surprised her when it happened.

❖

Arya hadn't planned to kill anyone. He was supposed to watch over her, protect her, and eventually claim her. He followed her to a stranger's house and stared in disbelief as she went inside. She didn't know this man. During his weeks of surveillance, she had never visited the location before. Why did she constantly place herself in danger, first at the community center and now this? She needed him more than he'd realized. When she walked into the house, Arya resisted the temptation to break down the door and rescue her. Instead he'd crept to a side window and watched their interaction, ready at any moment to defend her.

They talked about *him*. She was trying to find *him* but didn't know it. He smiled, happy that she sought him even without knowing who he was. She sensed him, just as he'd imagined the first time they'd met. Their lives were intertwined, of that he was certain. Soon she would understand why they had to wait, why he couldn't go to her as they both wanted. In the meantime, he kept constant vigil, keeping her safe and unspoiled.

Then it happened. As she walked out the door, the man stopped her. He captured her small, delicate hand and clung like a predator. The familiarity of the image seared into Arya's brain like a brand. His blood pounded fast and hot. No one could touch her except him. This man dared to violate the sanctity of his agreement with her. He would be held accountable.

Arya escorted her home and made sure she was safely inside before returning to the man's house. When darkness came, he knocked on the door. As it opened, Arya struck, one quick slash across the throat at the precise spot. He spun sideways, avoiding the scarlet spray, and watched as his prey staggered backward and slumped to the floor.

"You should *not* have grabbed her. She is *mine*." Arya whispered loud enough for him to hear. The dying man's eyes grew wide, lost their shimmer, then clouded over. He debated severing the man's hands for touching her, but the longer he stayed the greater the chance of being seen or leaving evidence. Arya waited until death was his only companion in the room then slipped out.

Chapter Six

The next morning Rae sat in the university coffee shop, Ken Whitt's choice, not hers, waiting for him to arrive. People darted through the small café securing their early fixes of caffeine, sugar, and news before heading to work or school. Faculty members stuck out from students, each in their personalized version of the academic uniform, each making her uncomfortable in a different way.

She'd spent her youth working instead of getting an education. Her decision often made her feel out of step with her more educated peers. The professors evoked deeper, more personal responses—inadequacy and failure. Janet had left their relationship for one of her own kind. Rae evaluated each person and imagined what he or she possessed that she didn't, besides a degree.

Such thinking only confused her and kept her rooted in the past. She sipped her bitter, almost-cold espresso and read the class notes her advisor, Mrs. Cowan, had forwarded. Her professors had agreed to let her take finals if she made up the work she'd missed. Exams began in a few days, and she was nowhere near ready.

"Heard you missed a few classes. Is everything okay?"

This is why she hadn't wanted to meet Ken Whitt here. She'd reasoned that it was Janet's day off so the likelihood of running into her was minute. So much for reason. Janet's voice contained a hint of concern, which elicited conflicting emotions. Rae took a few seconds, calmed her breathing, and finally looked up.

Janet looked as beautiful as ever. Her tailored business suit clung to her curves, and an open-necked blouse flashed a tasteful exposure of flesh. Her jet-black hair was closely trimmed and accented high cheekbones. The brown of her eyes shimmered with flecks of gold that Rae associated with excitement. In spite of her mental protests, Rae's body responded as it usually did to Janet, with arousal. And, damn, Janet knew it.

Without asking, she sat down next to Rae, laid her hand over Rae's forearm, and squeezed. "I miss you." She'd always admired Janet's ability to get to the point, but now she hated it. She didn't want or need to hear that, true or not. "I'm serious, Rae."

"Yeah, I've noticed my phone ringing constantly since you left." Rae regretted the angry sarcasm in her voice, a dead giveaway that Janet's betrayal still hurt.

"I know you're upset and I don't blame you. I handled the situation badly. Will you give me a chance to explain? Can we talk sometime? Not here." She looked around as if someone might overhear. If this campus mirrored other microcosms of society, everybody already knew they'd broken up and why. The gossip probably made the grapevine for a day or two before the academic community became bored.

"We don't have anything to talk about, Janet. You made it clear I'm not what you want."

Janet raised Rae's hand to her lips and lightly kissed the backside. "That is so not true. I've always loved you. You were never there for me."

"My job is unpredictable and so are my hours."

"It wasn't all about the job, Rae. Even when you were there, you weren't. It's almost like you stopped feeling, stopped caring. I don't know if it was your work or me."

Why couldn't she tell Janet the truth? She'd felt left out of a relationship that used to sustain her. The nagging about college felt more like criticism than encouragement—more a validation of Janet's stature than Rae's self-improvement. Maybe she'd used that as an excuse as her feelings waned. As much as she wanted a scapegoat, it wasn't fair to blame Janet entirely for the failure of their relationship.

"It was both, the work and us." It surprised Rae how easily she'd given up, yet the anger and disappointment over Janet's betrayal remained. Janet cheated for months, and Rae hadn't seen it. Maybe her anger was self-directed.

"Can we talk about this? Please, Rae." Her grip on Rae's arm tightened.

"Excuse me. I'm obviously interrupting." Ken Whitt stood behind Janet, eyeing her hold on Rae's forearm.

Rae didn't bother explaining. She'd been open with her squad and her sexual preference had never been an issue. The guys had just become less guarded in their discussions about women. Ken Whitt, though, was always a gentleman—watching, appreciating, but seldom commenting. "It's okay, Ken, we're finished here." Rae stood and shook his hand before turning back to Janet. "I'm sorry, this is business."

She could tell by Janet's expression that she wanted to fling a sarcastic comment. Instead she said, "I'll call you…about that talk."

Rae didn't respond.

As Janet walked off, Ken gave her an appraising once-over and nodded at Rae as if to say nice choice. They engaged in small talk about mutual acquaintances and sized each other up for several minutes. The ritual resembled a gut polygraph—establishing a baseline to determine normal responses before moving on to challenging topics. While they knew each other, they'd never worked closely together on a case. The feeling-out process was a must.

Whitt looked like an average man by conventional standards. He'd be unremarkable in a lineup, as likely to be identified based on his similarities to everyone else than by any differences. The two things most often associated with Ken Whitt were his newsboy-style cap and his devotion. Behind his back the guys affectionately referred to him as Mother Ken. He worried about everything: cases, victims, fellow officers, and his family and friends. He would fret about all his unsolved cases after retirement, especially the serious ones.

"How did you get so unlucky to draw the Whisperer cases?" The question seemed innocent enough. Was Whitt implying she wasn't qualified, or was her insecurity showing again?

"Maybe Not So wants somebody to blame when it all goes sideways."

"Not even that self-serving douche bag would be so stupid. You're a good detective and he at least knows that much." Rae relaxed a little. Ken Whitt was investigative royalty, and his comment was as close to a compliment as she'd ever get. "Now, what can I do for you? All my notes are in the case file."

"But we don't always put *everything* in our heads in the file, do we?"

Whitt pushed back his cap and scratched the top of his balding head. "See, like I said, smart. Where do you want to start?"

"What did your instincts tell you about this guy, things you couldn't prove?" Rae had read the file several times and wasn't interested in the facts now. She wanted the intangibles that floated around the edges of a case, the bits that stuck in a cop's mind and often led to arrests. These details were never written down, could never be used in a court of law, and would be completely useless in the hands of a rookie; yet they were investigative gold.

"The obvious thing, he's a flaming psychopath."

Rae smiled at his choice of words. In the two years she'd worked with Whitt before he retired, she'd never heard him say one curse word. That alone made him an anomaly in law enforcement, and she admired him for it.

"He's got to have some type of ploy to get close to these women. They don't walk up to him and offer to be kidnapped and mutilated. It takes a sick person to do what he does to them. But I never understood why he didn't kill them. He came close enough."

The same question had occurred to Rae. Rage or passion seemed to fuel the injuries, but those types of suspects were often impulsive and disorganized. It was as if an apparition had committed the crimes, the scenes entirely scrubbed of evidence. That took planning and a tremendous amount of control.

Rae nodded her agreement. "He might kill soon. He's getting more violent."

"I always thought this guy was military. I never had any concrete proof, just a gut thing."

Rae's skin dimpled with expectation. She relished this part of the job, the speculation and hypothetical scenarios. They provided the foundation on which every case was built. Once she established a workable premise, she proceeded until the evidence disproved that theory and she needed another. Locating the culprit's slimy trail and following it—that was the challenge. Whitt apparently worked the same way. "Why did you think military?"

"First, we got nothing. If it walks like a ghost and acts like a ghost, it's probably a freaking ghost. What organization trains people to get in and out of places without leaving a trace—the government? Aside from the medical profession, what other career instructs in torture without killing—the military? What beats the humanity out of young men and women until they act like zombies—war training? *And* who provides reacclimation and coping skills for these folks when they return? You guessed it, not a flipping soul."

The resentment and emotion in Whitt's voice told Rae that he'd been a recipient of the military's proficiency and incompetence. How had the experience colored his premise? On the other hand, everything he said had theoretical merit. The Whisperer wouldn't be the first serviceman returned from the war damaged beyond repair. "Did you find *anything* to support your idea?"

Whitt hung his head like a scolded dog. "Not So wasn't fond of my hypothesis. I tried to work the angle in my off time. Do you have any idea how many vets have returned from combat in this area over the past couple of years? I needed something to narrow the field and never found it."

Rae's earlier excitement evaporated. "Everything else is in your notes."

"Yeah. I checked out everybody in each victim's circle and came up empty. I couldn't even find a connection between the victims."

"Maybe there is no connection. Maybe they were victims of convenience, wrong time and place, whenever the urge struck," Rae said.

"He seems too organized for that."

"Or else he's in a constant state of readiness, which lends credibility to your military theory."

"Could be, Rae, but I think something else is going on with him, and I'd bet my badge that it stems from his combat service." Whitt seemed to be deciding whether to verbalize his thoughts.

"Whatever you're thinking, say it. Can't hurt."

"This whispering thing—always bothered me. Usually if a perp disguises his voice, it means the victim knows him. And the things he was saying sure sounded personal to me."

Rae flipped through her notes and reviewed the whispered phrases: *liar*, *unclean*, *destroyer*, *poison*. "I wondered about that too. The language is a bit stilted but definitely personal. And you got nothing from friends and known associates?"

"Nothing, and I grilled every guy even remotely connected to these women. No one was the least bit hinky."

Rae's thoughts bounced around like pinballs. One of Whitt's comments would elicit a checklist of possibilities, and the next one would dash them. The path to a criminal arrest was never straightforward. "How do you think he subdues them? Some kind of drug?"

"Would have to be, and that would require at least some pharmacological knowledge. The amateurish slicing sure doesn't seem like anyone with medical experience. So where does that leave us?"

"Wondering what type of drug can be administered without leaving a trace, can knock a person out temporarily, and can't be detected in the bloodstream."

"Apparently he wants them unconscious long enough to restrain them but not long enough to miss the cutting. He wants them fully aware of what's happening. He gets off on the control and the fear. Filthy freak."

"W*hy* does he do it?" Rae wondered aloud.

"You know that's usually the last thing we find out, if we ever do. Maybe somebody stole his teddy bear when he was a child. Maybe he was mentally or physically abused. Maybe his mother didn't breast-feed him. Or maybe he's just a warped individual."

Rae cringed at this part of her job—getting inside a criminal's head. She couldn't imagine what motivated such depraved actions.

If she allowed herself to dwell on it, poking around in the mind of such an individual could depress her.

Across the table from her, Ken Whitt clenched his big fists until the knuckles turned white. "Sorry I can't be more help. This one eats at me every day."

"I can see why." When he rose to leave, Rae shook his hand and offered a final promise. "I'll find this bastard, and thanks for the help." Officers were often cut out of the information loop when they retired. The omission seemed cruel—trusted and included one day and excluded the next. Whitt had given his life to public service, and she respected and honored him for it. She hoped someone would do the same for her one day.

"Thanks, I appreciate that." As he walked away, Rae felt compassion for Ken Whitt and a deeper need to solve this case. Neither of them would get much sleep until she did.

❖

On her way to work Audrey thought about Yasi's visit and wished she could have stayed longer. Two nights was barely enough time to settle a baby kitten in her new surroundings, much less catch up with a lifelong friend. Yasi had a way of putting things in perspective. She even pointed out Rae's protectiveness when Trevor had touched Audrey's back unnecessarily. Audrey had been too distracted to notice. This time, Yasi's usually sage advice wasn't so easy to follow—leave the investigating to the cops.

Maybe she was finished with amateur detecting. After Jeremy Sutton's death, she couldn't shake the nagging feeling of responsibility. She wasn't cut out for the uncertainty and guilt of a cop's world. Letting Rae help her was another issue entirely.

When Audrey entered the mayor's complex, a couple of shorthaired cops rose to meet her. Nerves knotted in the pit of her stomach. She couldn't deal with another interrogation. It was a big day for the mayor, and she needed to be at her best. Their expressions made it clear she wouldn't have a choice.

"Ms. Everhart?" A tall black officer with a rumbling voice approached her and held out his hand. "I'm Detective Brown and this is Detective Greene." He nodded toward his partner, a short, skinny, almost sickly looking specimen.

Audrey almost laughed aloud. *Brown* and *Greene*, seriously? They sounded like code names for some clandestine alphabet agency.

Brown offered a half smile. "I know. The guys call us the Colors." Then the pleasantries ended. "Is there somewhere we can talk, privately?"

"This isn't a good time. The mayor has a press conference shortly, and I have to make sure everything is in order."

"It's important. I didn't want to do this at our office, but—"

"I see." Translation, if you don't talk to us here and now, we'll haul you downtown with the utmost humiliation and detain you as long as possible. She motioned toward her office. "Would you wait for me in here, please?" She closed the door behind them and turned to the mayor's elderly secretary, who had been straining to catch every word.

"Mrs. Honeycutt, would you tell the mayor I'll be in shortly?"

"What was that all about, dear? Anything wrong? I couldn't quite hear."

"It's all right, Mrs. Honeycutt. This won't take a minute."

The secretary gave her a disappointed sigh and laboriously nodded her consent. Audrey steadied herself and entered her office. She took a seat at her small conference table, and the detectives joined her.

"Do you know why we're here, Ms. Everhart?" Greene asked.

"I assume it's about Jeremy Sutton."

"And why would you assume that?"

Was it a cop strategy to ask stupid questions or were they being purposely annoying to put her off guard? "I went to see Jeremy Sutton and now he's dead. It makes sense you'd want to talk with me. You don't have to be a police officer to figure that out."

Brown asked the next question. "Why did you visit Mr. Sutton?"

Audrey recounted her assault and unsuccessful attempts to find her attacker. A police report had been filed, and Rae was following up. She was certain they already knew the answers to their questions. Her best and most expeditious course of action was complete honesty. A little contrition wouldn't hurt either. "I realize now these things are best left to the professionals."

Greene nodded in agreement. "Did you touch anything while you were there?"

"A bottle of Pellegrino. I was there only a few minutes. Mr. Sutton was very kind and understanding of my questions. It was a shock to learn that he'd been…murdered…and so soon after I left."

For the next several minutes Brown and Greene batted questions back and forth, going over points she'd already covered, obviously searching for discrepancies in her story. When it felt she couldn't answer one more redundant question, Mrs. Honeycutt announced over the intercom that the mayor was ready to see her. The detectives closed their notebooks and stood.

"I think we've got everything we need, Ms. Everhart. Thank you for your cooperation." Detective Brown shook her hand. Greene merely nodded.

"Is that all? Am I, how do you say, cleared now?" Audrey felt tense and quite unnerved, even though she was totally innocent. She needed to hear that she was no longer a suspect.

"We have to cover all the bases." Greene answered from the doorway, his retort swift and unresponsive. She was content to have that particular chore off her list so she gathered her folder and headed to the mayor's office. She had more than enough drama in her life at the moment without adding a murder investigation to the mix.

Audrey stepped into Mayor Downing's plush brown-leather-and-oak office and glanced over his event schedule again while she waited. The press conference at the community center started in an hour, and he hadn't read his speech yet. Charles Downing's charisma had kept him afloat in the political-hotbed town of Kramer for the past six years. Their bedroom community, which skirted the state capital, was home to most of the county's wealthiest residents. They made many political demands.

Mayor Downing handled each challenge with tact and flair. He was tall and handsome, though not intimidating, well educated, and as honest as any politician. To his employees he was kind and generous, to his opponents ruthless but fair, and to his constituents loyal and obliging. When he spoke, people listened and wanted to believe his message.

Today he would unveil a plan to renovate the Grantham Homes public-housing development on the outskirts of town. He had secured a federal grant for the work, which pleased the Kramer taxpayers and garnered resounding support. The more public funds Downing saved on government projects, the more private money he received for his own extravagances like an armored car, an elite security force, and an unnecessary publicist.

Audrey didn't know why Mayor Downing needed her or any of the other excessive perks of his position. In the past year she hadn't seen any indication of corruption or malfeasance, so she accepted her good fortune. She glanced at her watch and gave him the windup signal to end his call. He needed to be shaking hands and kissing babies on site in fifteen minutes. When he hung up, Audrey followed him out. They would do the final briefing in the car.

The crowd of nearly fifty was impressive for a workday political gathering with no promise of food or beverages. She disliked this part of her job most—the throngs of people pushing and touching. At times she felt emotionally overwhelmed and often positioned herself along the sidelines, humming to block the external noise and remain internally focused.

Audrey left the mayor with his security team, effectively avoiding the handshaking, and checked the makeshift stage for last-minute changes. The city banner and state flag flanked the podium, attached to the platform of a flatbed pickup. Magnetic campaign stickers decorated the sides of the truck, confirming in bold print that it was an election year.

The small stage would barely provide enough room for the mayor, his security detail, a few well-placed benefactors, and her. Since last year when the spring breeze whipped his speech off the stand, Downing had insisted that Audrey accompany him onstage with an extra copy at the ready. She tried to delegate the task to one of his guards, but he wouldn't relent. Audrey didn't want the exposure that came with the local news coverage.

When the mayor and his entourage walked to the stage, she stepped between the broad-chested security officers and blended into the background. Downing began his speech and Audrey visualized herself by a quiet river humming the Lakmé Flower Duet. The cacophony around her slowly dulled.

Audrey relaxed with the steady rhythm in her head, but swept her gaze over the area surrounding the stage. Her assault here a week ago felt fresher, more recent. What if her attacker was in the crowd waiting for another chance? She dismissed the thought as paranoia. She'd been a victim of circumstance, nothing more. No one was brazen enough to risk an assault in front of so many people—no one but *him*.

The thought chilled her. He *was* here, at this moment, watching her. She felt his presence like a sickness, intrusive and malevolent. Why hadn't she picked up on it before? As distasteful as it was, she followed his energy to the source. She concentrated, opening her mind, willing him to allow her entry.

Their connection was powerful and turbulently contradictory. He personified darkness and evil; she held the light. She struggled to see him, to spot the person who hid behind indistinguishable images and blank spaces. One whispered word floated to the surface over and over like a mantra, *unspoiled, unspoiled*. Her intense concentration made her dizzy, but she wouldn't stop until she identified him. Her body weakened, and she swayed side to side.

One of the mayor's security officers, John or Marc, grabbed her elbow and steadied her. She released the mental link with her attacker and regained her composure. The guard remained close until she indicated with a subtle nod that she was okay. She searched the crowd for him but locked eyes with Rae Butler instead. The concerned look on Rae's face said she was wondering the same thing as Audrey—*what the hell just happened to her?*

CHAPTER SEVEN

Audrey glanced across the table and tried not to grimace at Loretta Granger's blatantly seductive stare. Even with her limited experience, she could see the intent in Loretta's eyes. Perhaps lunch at the Thai Palace only three blocks from the municipal building wasn't far enough away. She hoped the muted lighting didn't scream *date* because that certainly wasn't her objective. After she'd put Loretta in such a bad position with the homicide detectives, she had to clear the air.

"Lo, sorry it's taken so long to get together. Thanks for meeting me."

"You've been busy. I saw the mayor's press conference a couple of days ago. There's bound to have been calls, good and bad, with the announcement."

"You have no idea." Audrey appreciated Loretta's understanding and was grateful her job once again provided a plausible explanation for her lack of communication.

"This is about that Sutton thing, isn't it?"

"Not entirely. Can we have lunch first? I'd like to enjoy some time with a friend before we get into other stuff." Audrey was being selfish. It wasn't fair to let Loretta think she had a chance romantically, no matter how badly Audrey needed her help. Once the real purpose for this meeting came out, she doubted Loretta would consider them amiable acquaintances, much less share another meal with her. Still she hoped to salvage a casual friendship.

"Sure, whatever you want." Loretta seemed happy to postpone the serious discussions while they exchanged city rumor-mill gossip and ate.

Halfway through the meal, Audrey saw Rae Butler enter the restaurant with an attractive, smartly dressed brunette. As they followed the hostess toward their table, Rae scanned the room and her eyes settled on Audrey. She almost smiled until she noticed Loretta. They exchanged a brief nod of recognition, and Rae headed in her direction. Audrey wanted to run.

"Nice to see you again, Loretta." Rae's greeting sounded formal. When she turned her attention to Audrey, her tone softened noticeably. "Are you okay?"

Audrey looked up at Rae's statuesque figure looming over the table. Her auburn waves cascaded over the collar of a crisp pale-blue shirt and reminded Audrey of a sunrise over desert sky. Casual slacks supported by a wide leather belt rested low on Rae's hips, and Audrey had an irrational urge to grab the restraint and yank it off her. She swallowed a sizable lump the image conjured in her throat. "Of course, why wouldn't I be?"

"You seemed a little rattled at the press conference the other day."

Audrey didn't want this conversation with Rae, especially in front of Loretta. "The heat probably got to me." Audrey realized immediately she'd chosen the wrong excuse.

"It was forty degrees that day."

She wanted the topic closed. "I'm fine. Now, if you don't mind, I'm trying to have lunch with a *friend.*" She purposely emphasized the last word to dismiss Rae as quickly as possible. It worked.

"I'm sorry to have bothered you." She nodded to Loretta and returned to her table.

"What was *that* about?" Loretta asked. "I could cut the tension between you with this dull butter knife." She raised the utensil and slashed the air in a dramatic demonstration.

"Nothing."

"It certainly seemed like something. I think Rae has a crush on you. She obviously wasn't pleased to see us together." Loretta nailed the situation.

"Don't be ridiculous."

"I know women, and I know that look. You can tell me."

"There's nothing to tell because nothing's going on." Audrey regretted acting like such a brat to Rae, but she refused to discuss private matters with a woman she was attracted to in front of a woman she wasn't. Why was life so complicated?

Her concentration fluctuated during the rest of the meal as she gazed too often at Rae and her friend. For the first time, she tried to imagine the type of woman Rae would be attracted to. This one seemed to fit: slightly shorter, curvy, longish hair, open and attentive, definitely sexy. From the way Rae stretched across the table toward her, she agreed with Audrey's assessment.

If that was Rae's type, she didn't stand a chance, hypothetically speaking. Audrey didn't consider herself particularly attractive, maybe even a bit too short and not curvy enough, not at all sexy or appealing, and certainly not open and communicative. Based on the flashes of insight she'd picked up from Rae, she would not only need but also demand an honest relationship. Audrey couldn't offer that openness, at least not right now. The limitation bothered her so she returned her attention to her own lunch companion.

She finished her meal and pushed her plate to the side. "Loretta, I wanted to thank you for your assistance since we got out of recruit class. I know some of my requests have put you in the middle. It means a lot that you'd help me."

"You're welcome. And I'm sorry for ratting on you about the Sutton info. The detectives were grilling me, and I had to tell the truth. I didn't know it would get you in trouble. Somebody *killed* that guy." She shook her head in disbelief.

Guilt and regret radiated from Loretta, and underneath another emotion struggled for expression. Audrey hated knowing other people's feelings. She was the worst kind of voyeur: one who went beyond physical leering into the secret places intended to remain protected and secure. Her mother had taught her that unlimited knowledge came with great responsibility.

Silence was no longer an option. She'd let it go too long. Saying nothing would be another violation. "Lo…about us."

Loretta's face brightened as she scooted forward in her chair. "I've been waiting for this. I would've preferred a quieter place, perhaps a glass of wine."

"Loretta, I like you—"

"Good, because I like you, a lot."

Audrey started to take Loretta's hand but the sensations would've prevented her from saying what she needed to. One of the great injustices of her knowing was the inability to freely touch. "Please listen. This is difficult." Loretta's expression changed as her words registered. "I *like* you, as a friend. We can't have anything more."

Loretta exhaled a deep breath and her fair skin paled as she sat back in her chair. She studied Audrey for several minutes, looking back and forth between her and Rae. "Is there someone else?"

Her inevitable assumption that there was another person didn't surprise Audrey. Perhaps it was easier than not feeling good enough or blaming yourself. A concrete reason was a better scapegoat than some abstract concept. "No, there's no one else."

"It's Rae Butler, isn't it? I knew something was going on. I could see it."

"There isn't anyone, especially not Rae Butler." But was she being totally honest? Did wanting count? How about fantasizing? At what point was she lying by claiming disinterest?

"Then why not give us a chance? You might be surprised."

Audrey searched for an easier way to tell Loretta she simply wasn't attracted to her. Nobody wanted to hear those words, and few people could be so brutally honest. "I have a lot going on in my life right now and can't get involved with anyone." That much was definitely true. "Please try to understand. I'd like to be friends, if you're willing."

Loretta seemed to consider Audrey's offer. "Was it an act from the beginning? Were you using me to get information without going through the police department?"

The incisive question caught Audrey off guard. If she valued her friendship with Loretta, she deserved the truth. "Initially I was probably after information and access, but then I got to know you. I like you, and I'm sorry. I never wanted to hurt you."

Loretta's posture sagged a bit as some of the tension seemed to drain from her body. "I believe you, and yes, I'd like to be friends. I'm glad you were honest with me before it went any further."

As they rose to leave Loretta placed her arm around Audrey's waist, and they walked companionably toward the door. Now the energy between them was clean and clear, and Audrey felt no reservations about hugging her good-bye.

Rae squeezed the spring roll she held as Audrey and Loretta exited the restaurant. The sight of Loretta's arm around Audrey's waist reminded Rae that Audrey had specifically avoided her attempts at contact.

"I guess you know those two?" her lunch companion asked.

Dana Thompson had been Rae's therapist for the better part of an hour after Janet left. When the session ended, she decided the process wasn't for her. They had become friends, meeting periodically to unofficially check in. "Barely know them."

"Your poor spring roll would suggest otherwise." She nodded toward the mangled appetizer in Rae's hand. "Want to talk about it?"

She didn't, and the reason bothered her. How could she explain her feelings for Audrey when she didn't understand them herself? The attraction was real but wasn't logical. They hadn't spent enough time together to even develop a friendship. And if her instincts were accurate—which was still questionable—she couldn't trust Audrey. That was a deal breaker. "I'd rather talk about this guy who's attacking women."

"Poor deflection, but it's your angst. Tell me about him." Rae provided the few details she'd pieced together and prayed Dana could fill in some of the blanks. "You won't like what I have to say."

"Try me." Rae needed a lead, a direction for her investigation. At this point, she'd take speculation over nothing.

"Broad strokes, he's probably an aggressive, narcissistic personality, a pathological liar with no guilt, remorse, or empathy. He lacks genuine emotion and doesn't accept responsibility for his actions. I just have generalities and conjecture. You know the drill, white male, 25-40 years of age, no real long-term goals, early behavioral problems, sexually promiscuous."

As Rae listened, her hope faded. What Dana said didn't ring true for this particular suspect. She couldn't put her finger on why, just another feeling.

"I'm sorry to disappoint you. I know you wanted something more concrete. We're not miracle workers. What does your gut tell you, Rae?"

Rae understood why Dana was one of the top therapists in the state. She'd probably mentioned her lack of confidence when they initially met, but Dana never pushed. Now she tactfully broached the issue at exactly the right time. Rae's insecurity, this case, and Audrey Everhart were like Alpine peaks in her mind. If she couldn't overcome the first obstacle, she had no chance of tackling the others.

Dana's question hung in the air between them. "It feels wrong, but I can't—"

"Trust yourself?" Rae nodded. "Baby steps, my friend. Play with your instincts on small things first. Test the outcome. Soon you'll believe again." Dana touched Rae's hand and flashed one of her most encouraging smiles. "Any contact with Janet lately?"

"Have you been stalking me or what? She wants to talk."

"How do you feel about that?" The question was probably one of the most overused and dreaded ones a therapist could ask, but Dana's concerned delivery made it feel genuine.

"I don't see the point. We were falling apart before she cheated. I realized that today, so what else do we have to talk about? It's over…so why do I still miss her?" She expected Dana to comment but she remained silent, as if allowing Rae to hear and reconsider her words. After a few minutes, she asked the inevitable question that Rae couldn't answer.

"Do you miss *her* or the idea of her?"

❖

Audrey returned home that afternoon exhausted from the emotions of the day. She plucked Cannonball from her crate, gave her a wet smooch on the nose, and buried them both in a blanket on the sofa. The kitten's rhythmic purring relaxed and comforted Audrey as she imagined the advantages of being a cuddly pet with no problems. Kittens didn't have to worry about challenging conversations like the one she'd had with Loretta or the draining exchange with Rae Butler.

Rae's obvious enjoyment of another woman's company had bothered Audrey. She had no claim on Rae, her time or attention, but still it rankled. Her attraction to Rae surpassed her most infatuated phase with Yasi or her first quasi-lover. Normally she was too preoccupied with other people's feelings to entertain her own, but she couldn't dismiss these. She recalled the only time Rae had touched her and shivered with desire.

Why *this* woman? She constantly challenged everything Audrey was avoiding in her life. And Rae's reference to the press conference brought up another set of issues Audrey purposely hadn't addressed.

That afternoon had taxed her more than she wanted to admit. She hadn't expected a flashback or a round of psychological intercourse with her attacker. It was unusual for her to mentally connect with someone, to be allowed initial entry then denied full access. The disparity felt like a scrambling device emitting white noise. The vacuum sucked and consumed her emotionally until she almost fainted. She'd barely had enough energy to disconnect. True to form, Audrey had sidestepped when she asked about her struggle today.

She stroked CB's back. "Promise you won't become one of those females who asks prying questions and breaks my heart, and

I promise to feed and love you forever." CB licked the side of her neck as if agreeing to the terms. Audrey tuned in to the contented purring, blanked her mind, and drifted to sleep.

Throngs of people pushed in around her, cheerful and celebratory. Even the close contact of strangers couldn't dampen her spirits. Tonight they would gather to toast their success before moving on. Her steps quickened as she hurried to meet her friends.

Something was wrong. As she looked down at her feet, the shoes she'd worn changed into gold sling-back heels and her slacks into a red, form-fitting dress. A sickly sweet odor burned her eyes and made her nauseous. Light reflected off metal in thin streaks. Her stomach ached. She couldn't scream. A voice whispered unintelligible words. Then she ran down the dark street—naked, alone, and terrified.

Audrey jerked awake so quickly Cannonball went flying across the room. The kitten landed on her feet and stared at her with a shocked expression. "Sorry, darling," Audrey mumbled as she tried to clear her head. Parts of the dream memory made sense but not entirely.

Her previous nightmares had centered on the assault at the community facility. This one was different. The emotion of it felt like that summer, the pain too real, but the other images were still murky and the clothing totally unfamiliar.

She drew her legs underneath her and curled into a ball on the sofa. The air around her thickened with unpleasantness. She turned on the stereo and adjusted the volume to block outside stimuli, but the discomfort remained. The room felt almost foreign, even her furnishings emitting an odd energy. Cannonball stood in the middle of the floor, and the wiry hair on her back bristled. Time to go. She couldn't be here alone right now.

Audrey picked up her purse and wrapped Cannonball in a bath towel on the way out. As she settled in her car and turned the ignition key, she realized she had no idea where to go. In the past she would've gone directly to Yasi, but that wasn't an option. She was out of state at the moment, and Audrey wasn't sure when she would be available again. Perhaps she could call Loretta—definitely not. That would give entirely the wrong impression.

Digging into her purse, Audrey prayed her cell phone was where she'd left it for once. She felt the cool, slim device at the bottom and pulled it out, then fished around for Rae's business card. As she stared at it, she wondered if she was making a mistake. Was she overreacting?

Audrey looked back toward her apartment and decided she most certainly was not. Her instincts were seldom wrong, especially in matters of bad news or danger. She placed the call and simply asked if she could come over. The answer was an equally simple yes. As she drove, Audrey realized she was headed to the one place she'd feel relatively safe but had absolutely no right to be.

CHAPTER EIGHT

When Rae disconnected, she wondered what had precipitated Audrey's call. They weren't close friends who occasionally dropped by to chat. Audrey had consistently maintained her distance and privacy. Maybe something else had happened or she'd remembered more about her assault. She'd sounded a bit shaken. Whatever the circumstances, Rae would be patient and let Audrey come to her. That was the only way to establish trust.

It was almost seven in the evening. Should she offer her something to eat? Did she have anything to offer? Her best meals consisted of ready-made purchases nicely arranged on paper plates. She wasn't exactly a cook, but this wasn't exactly a social call, was it? It certainly wasn't a date so she didn't have to feed or entertain her guest. The sound of a car outside her door ended the internal debate.

Rae opened the door and watched as Audrey approached with a bundle in her arms. She still wore her work clothes, though slightly wrinkled. The habitually unruly strands of hair poked out at odd angles as if she'd just woken up. Her forehead was furrowed in distress and the usual spark in her eyes was absent.

Audrey stopped at the threshold. "Don't you hate people who drop in unexpectedly, especially bearing unwanted gifts? Do you mind cats?"

Rae stepped aside. "Of course not. Come in." Audrey was definitely upset. Her attempt at humor failed in enthusiasm and delivery.

"I couldn't leave her there alone."

"Has something happened? Are you all right?" Their exchange felt stilted, but Rae forced herself not to push.

"I'm fine. Maybe a bit vulnerable after all that's happened. You're very kind to let me come over."

"You're welcome any time. I'm glad you're okay." This was an unusual though welcome glimpse of Audrey's softer side. Rae had seen it occasionally in recruit school, hardly at all since. Recently Audrey had been too concerned with protecting her privacy and asserting her independence to let her emotions show.

Rae's compassion for Audrey swelled, and her protective side strengthened. She'd have to take it slowly for both their sakes. Rae wasn't ready for even a casual relationship, and Audrey always seemed primed to bolt. Why hadn't Audrey gone to Loretta? They'd seemed very chummy at lunch today. Rae dismissed the unpleasant thought, glad that she'd come to her.

Audrey looked around the small condo and smiled. "Now I know what you meant when you said your place looked like it had been burglarized."

Rae felt her cheeks flush with embarrassment.

"I'm sorry. That was insensitive. It doesn't suit the picture I had of your home."

"And what was that?" Rae was curious about Audrey's preconceived ideas about her and thrilled that she'd thought enough of her to form them.

"A warm, comfortable place full of soft furniture, fall colors, and lots of greenery. I guess I imagined your home as your refuge from the type of work you do."

Her assessment was exactly what Rae wanted her home to be. At least Audrey understood the need for a safe haven. Janet had never seemed to. Rae motioned Audrey toward the space with the most furniture, her dart room/study. "It used to be." She noted the hint of melancholy in her voice and quickly changed the subject.

"I was about to order a pizza. Interested?" Totally not true, but she had to eat. Besides, the idea of feeding and entertaining Audrey had become more enjoyable since her arrival.

"If you're sure I won't be a bother."

This was a completely different Audrey Everhart than Rae was used to. She was too agreeable. Something had definitely shaken her confidence and maybe even scared her. Rae put her thoughts aside, remembering Dana's suggestion about testing her instincts on small things. If she was right, Audrey would tell her soon enough.

"Have a look around while I find the delivery menus."

Audrey walked into the small room, placed a swaddled CB on a side chair, and took in Rae's belongings. She felt oddly comfortable among her things, though sparse and utilitarian. She sensed a variety of activities in this room, some light and carefree, some serious. This was the part of Rae Butler she'd wondered about for over a year, the person behind the officer.

She scanned the space and mentally catalogued each item. On one side of the room, a dartboard sprouted several darts in the bull's eye, and a case of the shiny projectiles rested on an ottoman nearby. A settee, another side chair, and a small table that served as a desk occupied the other side of the room. Audrey pictured Rae and her friends here talking, laughing, and sharing their lives. The setting had a playful vibe that Audrey absorbed and breathed in like fresh air. The room felt like Rae, grounded and substantial, and a feeling of peace swept over her. She had come to the right place.

She'd expected Rae to question her about the sudden call and showing up on her doorstep, but she hadn't. Rae's concern had been with her well-being, and Audrey sensed her sincerity. The more she learned about Rae, the more she liked her and the harder it was to be around her without revealing herself.

"What's your pleasure?" Rae fanned an assortment of delivery menus for Audrey to choose from.

"I'm partial to thin-crust with everything."

"My kind of woman." Rae pulled her cell out and placed the order. "Thirty minutes, perfect." She hung up and waved her arms around the room. "Not much, but it's mine."

Rae was obviously embarrassed by her meager furnishings, and Audrey wanted to dispel her discomfort. "It's a lovely place. This feels like you. Is that your work area?" On second glance around the room, Audrey noticed a corkboard mounted above the desk area covered with notes and crime-scene pictures. The images leapt out and bombarded her with sensations, the data overwhelming her. Audrey quickly looked away and hummed to herself to stop the flow.

As if Rae realized Audrey's discomfort, she lowered the cover over the exposed layers of information. "Are you all right?" Audrey could only nod. "I'm sorry. That's not exactly entertaining for guests. I throw darts while I think. It helps."

Rae had provided the perfect distraction. "Tell me about your interest in darts." She focused on the sound of Rae's voice and slowed her breathing.

Rae's face lit up like an excited child and she started talking. It was as if Audrey had flipped a switch and allowed the current to reach Rae at last. She practically hummed with unrestricted exuberance. "I started playing when I was a teenager. I enjoy something about the feel of the grooved barrel in my fingers, and stroking the flight before release is like blowing on the dice for luck before a craps roll. It's a physical experience that requires concentration."

Rae's explanation sounded almost sexual. Audrey could feel the cool metal in her hands and the fan-shaped tail as if her own fingers stroked the instrument. Darts wouldn't have been the kind of extracurricular activity she pictured for Rae. It wasn't physical enough, not engaging enough for someone so athletic. Yet the precision required to release a true shot into the center of the board demanded practice and consistency, which she certainly associated with Rae Butler.

"Though dart throwing requires concentration it's also distracting. That probably sounds bizarre, but it helps me focus."

"Not at all. I completely understand the need to be distracted in order to focus. It happens to me all the time." Audrey had so empathized with Rae that the words were out before she thought about their implication. They told much more than she intended.

Rae gave her a curious smile. “What do you need distracting from?”

Everything. If you only knew. “Just life.” Audrey wasn’t fooling Rae. The evasive maneuvers didn’t escape her sharp intellect. To her credit, Rae didn’t press. Maybe her propensity for probing questions was only a professional tool. Perhaps she allowed personal relationships to develop organically. At least she was opening up a bit, and Audrey was more than willing to listen and learn as much as possible. “And what about you?

“My parents weren’t very fond of my lifestyle, so I needed an outlet growing up. That’s all it was initially. I tell everybody darts got me through school, my first breakup, and finally leaving home. I’ve kept the sport up pretty consistently. I play on an amateur team occasionally.”

“Why would you ever stop? You obviously enjoy it so much.”

The light in Rae’s eyes dimmed. “Janet, my ex, didn’t like it. She said it was one more thing to keep us apart.”

“Was she right?” Audrey was surprised how easily Rae slipped into sharing personal information. She had briefly experienced Rae’s caring, open side during recruit school. Then during the investigation of her assault, Rae had seemed suspicious and more reserved. Something had obviously changed Rae in the past several months, affected the way she interacted with others, and it wasn’t for the better.

“I don’t think so. It helped me de-stress. She didn’t enjoy it, so I stopped.”

“I’m sorry.”

Rae picked up a dart and twirled it in her fingers. “No, I’m sorry. I seem to have slipped into the dregs of my past. Want to try your hand?”

The intimacy of the moment passed, and Audrey could almost hear the door slam shut around Rae’s emotions. The void left Audrey and the room decidedly cooler. “Sure.”

Rae stepped closer to the dartboard and pointed to a strip of tape on the floor. “This is the throwing line. With time and experience, each player develops their own stance. I find it easier to angle my body a bit so the shoulder, elbow, and wrist have a direct line to the target." Rae displayed a smooth throwing motion, but didn't release the dart.

As Rae positioned her body toward the dartboard and demonstrated the action, Audrey watched her thighs flex beneath her worn jeans. Her squared shoulders brought Rae's posture into perfect alignment and maximally enhanced her slight breasts and perfect backside. Audrey's appreciation of the instructor almost eclipsed the procedural display.

"Hold the dart in a comfortable combination of the thumb, forefinger, and middle finger, firmly but not too tight. Visualize the dart leaving your hand in a straight line and hitting the bull's eye." Rae released the dart and it flew directly to the red center point. "Voilà."

When Rae turned toward her, Audrey was still staring at her backside. "Impressive." Rae flushed pink, and Audrey knew she'd been caught. God, what was she doing here? Playing with fire was such a cliché, but in this case it fit. She'd already experienced the overwhelming sensations that being around Rae Butler elicited. Something was different now, but she couldn't put her finger on the cause. The energy between them was as charged as before; however, it didn't make her anxious or afraid. She wanted to understand what had changed. In order to do that, she'd have to reach out, to touch Rae. She wanted the connection but couldn't risk what she might discover.

"Are you going to try it?"

"Try it?" Audrey shook her head to clear the image the question aroused. "Darts…of course." She took the instrument in her hand, glad for the tangible feel of something solid. Trying to mimic Rae's position, she turned sideways to the dartboard, fingered the dart, and let it loose. The brightly colored flight wobbled side to side as the projectile flew through the air and landed on the desktop, stuck in a pile of papers. "Oh, my, I'm so sorry. Metal has never been a good conduit for me."

Rae gave her a puzzled look. "A *conduit*? I've heard darts called many things, but never a conduit. You're an interesting woman, Audrey Everhart."

"Is that a good thing?"

"Definitely." Rae picked up another dart and stepped closer to her. "Let me walk you through it. Position your feet, relax your legs, take it in your fingers, and I'll help you with the release."

Audrey's heart pounded faster the closer Rae stood. Her words sounded like erotic instruction, and Audrey struggled to pay attention. It had been years since her mind and body jumped so immediately to sexual innuendo and responded so readily. She'd practiced keeping such feelings contained. Now this woman seemed capable of crashing her barriers with the tiniest effort.

Rae moved behind Audrey, lightly gripped her wrist, and raised her arm shoulder-high. Audrey braced for the flood of thoughts and feelings that usually accompanied another's touch, but it didn't come. She felt only the distinctive warmth of Rae's skin and a sense of comfort and peace. How odd. It was both a welcome and disturbing revelation. She tried to tune into Rae but failed. Instead of the mental and emotional influx she'd expected, her body absorbed every ounce of physical stimulation like a dry sponge.

Audrey let go and allowed Rae to guide her. Rae's hand covered hers, and she enjoyed the slight friction as their arms rose in unison and thrilled with the jolt that brought their bodies together at the moment of release. Heat seared as they pressed closer, Rae still at her back.

"How was that?"

Rae's voice was soft and close to her ear, her breath hot on Audrey's neck. "Great." Their arms were outstretched toward the dartboard and Rae still held her hand. With what seemed an effortless motion, Rae brought Audrey's hand to her lips and kissed it.

She should object but couldn't grasp a coherent reason to do so. Liquid fire seemed to infuse her insides. She'd never experienced anything so tender yet so poignant. "Just great," she repeated. Then the image of Rae and the brunette from lunch flashed through her mind. If they were a couple, Audrey wouldn't interfere. If they weren't, she wouldn't be one of many. When she chose to give herself, it would be completely and exclusively. "What would your girlfriend think about you kissing another woman's hand?"

"Don't have a girlfriend. You?" Rae's voice was still soft but more teasing, and her breath was dangerously close to Audrey's ear.

"Don't have one either. What about your lunch companion?" Audrey hated herself for asking. Her question sounded so juvenile. Damn it, she wanted to know.

"A friend…and Loretta?"

"Friend who wants more."

"Yasi?"

"Childhood friend." With the simple exchange, they'd cleared the playing field. Rae made it hard not to open up when they were so close. Audrey often imagined, but had never experienced such a reaction to anyone before. If she wasn't careful, Rae Butler would know all her secrets before they ever kissed.

As if reading her thoughts, Rae turned Audrey to face her. She didn't need any special skills to read the desire so clearly broadcast on Rae's face. "Audrey, I'd like to—"

Audrey saw what was coming. She wanted it desperately, and she had to prevent it. Audrey had too many secrets to resolve before allowing herself pleasure. She placed a finger over Rae's luscious lips. "Thank you for letting me come over."

Rae stepped back, clearly surprised by the sudden change. Audrey imagined the disappointment mirrored on her own face. For an instant she considered hugging Rae again and accepting the kiss. But the gesture would be paramount to offering goods under false pretense. Rae had no idea who she was or what she was capable of. For the moment, Audrey would have to be content with sharing bits and pieces of the truth that served her purpose.

"I had a dream, and when I woke up I was terrified to be in my apartment alone. That's never happened before. I'm usually very comfortable in my little space. I'm in your debt."

"You're welcome, anytime." Cold air enveloped Audrey as Rae moved to the desk and retrieved the errant dart.

"And I've stabbed your paperwork. I hope it wasn't anything important."

"Only the most difficult case I've ever had. I inherited it after another detective retired. It's a serial-assault case, pretty horrendous.

This guy attacks attractive women and—Sorry, that's not good social conversation, especially after what you've been through."

"One of your victims wasn't wearing a short red dress and gold sling-back heels, was she?" Audrey laughed, remembering her dream and trying to deflect the focus from herself. When Rae didn't join in, she stopped. "Did I say something wrong?"

Rae didn't have to answer. As Audrey moved toward the desk, all the anxiety and fear she'd experienced in the elevator with Rae that day returned. She'd been holding the same folder. The uncomfortable feeling she'd experienced then and now originated from this file, not from Rae.

Now her reaction was more focused and specific. The feeling morphed into a series of terrible sounds and visions—all unpleasant, scary, and painful. Something in her dream was connected to Rae's case. She was certain of it.

"As a matter of fact, one of my victims was wearing exactly that. How did you know?" Audrey suddenly had Rae's full attention again, and not in a good way. The sparks of passion had turned to suspicion, and the softness in her eyes hardened.

She struggled for a plausible explanation and decided on partial truth. "I didn't. I dreamed about a woman wearing the same thing. I imagine red dresses and gold heels are pretty common."

Audrey could almost see the wheels turning as Rae tried to put together the disparate pieces that made no sense. Audrey's flippant remark hadn't distracted her. "I guess you're right." Audrey had always been able to count on the logical mind to discount or disregard what it couldn't explain. Rae wasn't buying it.

"I can see this case has you worried. Anything I can do to help?"

"Not unless you're a psychic." Rae's grin suggested the idea was totally absurd.

"Have you tried it?" Audrey was fishing, testing Rae's view of the extrasensory.

"Yeah, right. It's one of our most dependable and widely utilized investigative methods." Rae must've seen the change in Audrey's face. "Are you serious?"

"Is it such a ridiculous idea?"

"Of course it is. Those people are parasites who prey on victims desperate for answers. They're only interested in blowing their own horns and making money."

Audrey's insides roiled with conflicting feelings, and she struggled not to run out the door. Rae's words felt like darts piercing Audrey's heart, cold and true. Negative energy threatened to overwhelm her. She retrieved a stretching CB from the side chair and cuddled her into the hollow of her neck. The contented purring helped ease the discomfort brewing in Audrey's chest. "So you've worked with a psychic or clairvoyant before?"

"Not personally. One of our detectives consulted one a few years ago. It was a total waste of time."

"Maybe he didn't speak to the right one. I'm sure it's like everything else, some are good and some bad at what they do." Audrey couldn't believe how adamant Rae seemed on the topic or that she was actually broaching it with her. Their exchange reaffirmed her belief that her previous life and her new one could never blend seamlessly. These were the types of preconceived and prejudicial attitudes that kept them apart.

"It sounds like you've had a more positive experience."

"Let's say I've had more exposure and have kept an open mind. You might try it sometime." She hadn't meant to snap. Rae's surprised expression told her the statement had hit its mark. After several seconds of silence, Audrey stated the obvious. "I should be going. Thank you for taking me in."

"What about the pizza?"

"I hear it's good for breakfast. Night."

Rae shook her head in disbelief. At least she'd been right about Audrey's reason for coming to her—she was frightened. Her instincts passed the mini-test and Rae felt good about that. Maybe she was recovering her intuitive skills. But God, Audrey was frustrating. The evening had started so well. She felt as if someone had changed the channel in mid-scene. One minute they were about to kiss and the next Audrey was gone.

Audrey's body drew her like gravity. The softness of her curves fused with the firmness of Rae's and made her weak with possibility.

It had felt so natural to take Audrey's hand, to kiss it, and to want more. And they *had* almost kissed. The warmth of Audrey's breath was so close Rae could taste the sweetness of her mouth. Then Audrey had pulled away with a question about girlfriends and a conflicted expression.

Rae had never formulated a personal opinion about the supernatural, but Audrey obviously had strong opinions about it—one more interesting thing about her.

Chapter Nine

Arya was finally in the perfect place to keep watch over her. He'd taken longer than usual to position himself and move equipment in and out so no one would notice. The arrangements complete, she would now always be safe. From his vantage point, he observed her comings and goings and could intervene whenever necessary. While he waited, he would finalize his plan. One more obstacle stood between them. He was not yet worthy. She had proved to be the perfect choice, but she would have to pass a final challenge as well.

Recently she had taken too many chances, branched out too far from the safety of her apartment. Last evening she'd visited that police officer's home unescorted after dark. Arya was unable to establish observation into the residence, and the short time she'd remained inside had been agony for him. What was the purpose of her visit? What had she told the police? Had she turned against him? He was anxious and edgy, on the verge of forcing entry and extracting her when she emerged.

Demons awakened in him. The cop had become a nuisance. She stood between them and that was not allowed. He thought of the red-haired man who had touched her and his fate. Perhaps this cop would end up the same way. An attack on a police officer would cause unwanted attention, though. And he wasn't sure if the cop had actually touched her. Arya was honorable in meting out justice and needed to be certain before he acted. He could deal with her later. His first responsibility had been to see his beloved safely home.

This morning he watched her lock her apartment and begin her daily walk to work. He shadowed her, mingling with the crowd, stepping into doorways when she looked back and paralleling her route on side streets. When she arrived at her destination, he blended into the masses of people around city hall and assumed his place in the world. He'd done it hundreds of times in the past year, and she never knew.

Sometimes he wondered why she couldn't sense his presence, why she didn't see through his ruse and recognize him. In those moments of worry, he reasoned that she was aware of him and simply chose to let him set the timing of their joining. She knew her place and deferred to his superior intellect.

When Rae reached her cramped office, she had a feeling she'd forgotten something important. She hadn't thought about anything except Audrey since last night. She'd attempted to study for finals, but even the tough course material didn't distract her. The result was poor concentration and little sleep. It wasn't normal for her to lose track of her investigations because of a woman.

"Forget something, Butler?" Not So asked from her doorway. His expensive suit seemed to shine in the morning light, and not a single strand of his carefully combed hair was out of place. Real police officers got dirty, looked tired, worried about people and their cases, and even appeared disheveled sometimes—not Sergeant Sharp. His perfect appearance made her wonder what he actually did all day and it made her not want to see him, especially first thing in the morning.

"Sarge."

"I'm glad you didn't say good morning because it's not. A woman has been waiting for you in the conference room for fifteen minutes."

"Jeez." Rae fingered her hair in frustration. That's what she'd forgotten. She was interviewing the Whisperer assault victims today, and fifteen minutes of her allotted two-hour slot with number one was already gone. "I'm sorry, Sarge. Guess I got sidetracked."

"Don't apologize to me. Get your ass in there and grovel to that poor woman."

Rae grabbed her files, slid past the sergeant, and hurried to the conference room. On the way she looked up the woman's name. In a face-to-face interview, they deserved to be identified and respected as individuals. "I'm so sorry I'm late, Ms. Flynn. I'm Detective Rae Butler."

Carol Flynn sat at the rectangular table with her hands clasped in front of her, staring down. She didn't look up when Rae entered but nodded in response to her apology. Her brown hair was pulled back in a French twist exposing a pleasant face. The report indicated she was an accountant. She had a strikingly understated elegance, but someone had stolen her confidence. "Would you like a cup of coffee or tea before we start?"

"No, thank you." She finally looked up, gave Rae a visual assessment, and asked, "Why am I here? My attack occurred a year ago. Where is Detective Whitt? Have you located a suspect?" The hope in her eyes was almost painful for Rae to see. She hated to be the one to extinguish it.

"Detective Whitt retired, and I've taken your case. I'm afraid we don't have a suspect yet." The woman's shoulders sagged as if in defeat. "I'm going over everything once more. Sometimes a fresh pair of eyes helps. I know this is difficult, Ms. Flynn, and I apologize for putting you through it. Would you tell me the events of that night again, please?"

Carol Flynn clutched her purse to her chest as though for protection. She sighed with such depth that Rae knew the retelling of events would be like opening an old wound. No matter how quickly she told the story, it wouldn't lessen the pain. "I was walking home from the New Year's Day celebration downtown. It was late, almost two in the morning. I'd passed the new condo construction at the corner of Smith and Elm Streets when someone jumped out of the shadows and grabbed me from behind."

Ms. Flynn's recitation had the precision of repetition. She'd probably been over it again and again in her mind, searching for new details, putting everything in exact chronological order, and trying to make sense of the unconscionable.

"I never got a look at him. He put something over my mouth and nose, and I must've passed out. When I woke up, I was restrained in a small space, blindfolded and gagged." She reached into her purse, retrieved a water bottle, and took a couple of long sips.

"Why do you say it was a small space?"

"It felt closed in, like a container of some sort. When he talked, I mean whispered, I heard a faint echo. It was definitely an empty space, nothing to absorb sound."

This was new. None of the other victims had described the space they were held so clearly in their original statements. She would ask each one about it specifically today. "Go on, please."

"The pain was…excruciating. He whispered one word over and over—*liar*, *liar*—and the more he said it, the more agitated he became. It was as if he wanted something from me that I couldn't give. I expected him to rape me or kill me. He just…sliced my abdomen every time he called me a liar. I—" Her voice cracked and her eyes welled with tears.

"It's all right. Take your time, Carol." No matter how many victims' statements Rae heard, she never got used to the brutality. Every incident stripped another layer of joy from life. "Do you have any idea what type of weapon he used?"

She shook her head. "It was cold and extremely sharp. That's all I know. After what seemed like an eternity, he put this cloth over my mouth again and I passed out. When I woke up this time, I was beside the dumpster at the construction site almost exactly where he'd taken me from, completely naked and in tremendous pain. And before you ask, I can't describe his voice. He only whispered and said the one word. Any other sounds were just noises."

Rae became immediately more attentive. "What kind of noises?"

Carol Flynn appeared to struggle for exactly the right words. "Rustling…and frustrated noises, like grunts and heavy breaths."

"And he didn't assault or touch you sexually? You're certain."

"Yes, I'm positive. That's the one thing I'm grateful for."

"The rustling sound, what was that like? Describe it for me."

Carol searched for the right description. "Plastic, I think. It sounded like rustling plastic. And it felt like I was lying on very thin plastic. It stuck to my skin."

Rae had never conducted an interview a year after an incident that produced so many fresh details: the size of the confinement space, noises made by the suspect, and the plastic. They might never prove useful, but they added to the overall picture. "Anything else you can remember?"

"No. I go over this every day of my life. I can't think of anything new."

"You've done very well." Rae made a few final notes and closed the file. Two hours had passed as they slowly worked their way through the incident. Carol looked exhausted. "How about that cup of coffee now?"

"Make it a Coke and you're on." Carol seemed a bit more assured than when they started. Maybe the feeling that she'd actually helped was comforting. Rae vowed that soon she'd be able to tell Carol Flynn her assistance led to the suspect.

"Follow me. I'll get you the coldest Coke in the canteen vending machine." Rae tried to lighten the mood, and Carol seemed grateful.

As they approached the entrance to the canteen, Audrey was coming out. She glanced at Rae and half smiled before her gaze swung to Carol Flynn and froze. Her face paled and her bottom lip trembled slightly. She placed a hand over her stomach as if she felt sick.

Carol automatically reached to comfort Audrey, her hand resting on Audrey's shoulder. The touch seemed to weaken Audrey. Her knees buckled and she gasped for breath.

"You—you've—I see—" Audrey stumbled back as if stricken by something in Carol Flynn's face.

Rae grasped Audrey's elbow to steady her and guided her to a seat. "Are you all right?" Audrey's gaze moved from Carol to Rae. "What's wrong?"

"I'm fine. I felt light-headed for a moment." She turned her attention to Carol but didn't make eye contact. "I'm so sorry."

"No need to apologize," Carol said. "Detective, I'll take a rain check on the soda. Thank you for your help, and please do keep me posted."

When Carol left, Rae turned to Audrey. Her instincts told her something other than a dizzy spell had just occurred. "Let me get you something cold to drink. Water?"

Audrey nodded.

Rae placed a bottle in front of her and studied her face as she sipped. The scared look in her eyes slowly faded as her breathing returned to normal. What could have provoked such an intense response, and what, if anything, did it have to do with Carol Flynn? She'd learned to pursue a scared suspect but back off a frightened victim. Right now, Audrey seemed very much like a victim.

"Thank you for this." Audrey raised the water bottle. "Guess I was dehydrated. I don't usually have dizzy spells, believe it or not."

"No, you don't seem like the dizzy type at all. Very resilient, I'd say."

"You're always coming to my rescue, Detective."

"Wait until you're really in trouble. I can be rather handy."

Audrey paused as if deciding whether to continue. She looked like what she was about to say was either hard for her to imagine or would be so for Rae. "That was one of your assault victims, wasn't it?"

"What makes you think that?" Rae's answer was nonresponsive, but she didn't identify crime victims. It seemed the least she could do to help them maintain some sort of dignity.

"Something in her eyes. She was cut, probably with a very specific type of knife." Audrey stood so abruptly she caught Rae by surprise.

"How—" Before she could finish the question, Audrey was gone. Specialized forensic pathologists and criminalists had studied the victims' cuts and been unable to definitively determine if the weapon used was a scalpel or knife. The wounds were so smooth and the skin so elastic they had preliminarily thought it to be a scalpel. Why did Audrey think it was a knife?

The nerves in the pit of Rae's stomach tightened, the gut feeling she got when things went very wrong. Her experience taught her that only suspects or those with intimate knowledge of the crime possessed these kinds of details. If that was true, why would Audrey implicate herself by divulging this information? Rae couldn't wrap her mind around the possibility.

No matter how many ways she considered the facts, none of them produced Audrey as a reasonable suspect. The person she knew and was attracted to could not do such a horrible thing. Besides, the victims were all certain the assailant was a man. That didn't mean Audrey couldn't have been an accomplice, an accessory after the fact, or be acquainted with the suspect. Rae simply didn't want to believe it. Audrey couldn't drop information like that and not expect questions. But at the moment another victim was waiting to be interviewed.

❖

Audrey fled the canteen so fast she nearly plowed over a man exiting the elevator. When she'd gazed into the decimated eyes of the woman with Rae, she'd felt her pain and despair. It was as if they were connected somehow. Then the flashes began: the bits of information she didn't want, blurry images, stomach-turning smells, and haunting sounds. The only clear pictures were of a very sharp, menacing knife and the clothing she'd dreamed about. And without thinking, she'd blurted the information about the knife to Rae, only to regret it seconds later.

Now Rae probably thought she was either a mental case or a criminal. Either way, Audrey couldn't face her again because she couldn't explain what she'd seen without lying or telling the truth. Once again she was trapped between her past and the present with no clear escape. Could she ever tell Rae the truth about being a psychic?

How could she explain to a woman who lived and breathed facts and logic that she saw, felt, and knew things other people didn't? It wasn't like she'd developed a marketable skill or aptitude through the years. She'd been born with this ability and had tried to ignore and deny it since she was a child. Ironically, denial became increasingly harder. The more things she saw or predicted, the more pronounced her gift became. She still hoped it would eventually disappear like neon clothing or mood rings.

Today she'd abandoned caution in the face of overwhelming grief and injustice. She found it impossible to remain silent when another human being had been so violated. This recurring theme had always haunted her.

Her mother often said that Audrey's gift came with great responsibility. What she did next would mark the course of her life forward. Her conscience pulled her one way, her sense of self-preservation another.

The remainder of the day Audrey shuffled the mayor's schedule, wrote mundane speeches, and grappled with her choices. If she hoped to have even a friendship with Rae, she'd have to tell her who and what she was. She couldn't base their relationship on anything except honesty. Tonight she'd tell Rae the truth, or at least part of it, and face the consequences.

When a light tap sounded at her office door, Audrey was startled to see Rae framed in her doorway wearing an unusually wide smile. She looked delectable in faded jeans and a snug green cashmere V-neck sweater. "What are you doing here?" The question sounded more accusatory than Audrey intended.

"I was wondering if you'd like to go for a drink…and maybe talk afterward."

It wasn't exactly what Audrey had planned, but perhaps a little socialization and a bit of lubrication before the heavy conversation would make what she had to say go down easier. "That's a good idea."

On their short walk to the corner bar, they chatted about the routine details of their days without saying anything important. Audrey wished for something substantial that would reveal more about Rae. At the same time, she dreaded the connection that would establish. Maybe she wasn't ready for the inevitable exchange of histories, trust building, and intimacy an actual relationship required.

Rae held the door for her, and as they entered, the place exploded in a chorus of greetings. When her eyes adjusted to the dim lighting, Audrey located the source of their welcome. Three women at a table in the back waved their arms and shouted, "Over here, Officer."

"Great," Rae mumbled. "I'm sorry about this, but I have to say hello. Those are my best friends. I'd like to introduce you to them, if you're okay with that."

Audrey considered the backhanded invitation. Maybe they would give her some insight into how to approach their conversation later. "I'd like that…if it won't put you in a spot."

"They'll just rag me forever about you, that's all."

Rae introduced Audrey to Deb, Stephanie, and Ronni. She felt only slightly uncomfortable as they greeted her warmly and offered her a seat. Meeting Rae's best friends all at once was daunting. Audrey held her breath for their version of the Inquisition. If she introduced a woman to Yasi, the questions would go on for hours. But these women were gentle. They ordered drinks and checked out the other women in the club, all while throwing in an occasional question to include Audrey in the chatter.

Pretty soon she was relaxed and engaged with the cordial banter, watching Rae transform from police officer to a cheerful and much-kidded friend. Her genuine belly laughs filled their corner of the room, one of the most beautiful sounds Audrey had ever heard. Her gaze caught and held Rae's, her emerald eyes danced and sparked. Neither of them seemed willing to look away. Any doubt about being attracted to Rae evaporated in that instant.

"Excuse me. Who are *you*?"

Audrey almost jerked at the shrill and unfriendly tone coming from a woman standing over her. "I—"

"She's our friend," Deb answered, pulling Audrey closer to her side.

"*Whose* friend?"

"Don't do this, Janet." Rae stood and tried to steer the obviously unhappy woman away from their table.

"I'm not doing anything except asking a simple question. Is she mute?"

Audrey didn't know Janet but already didn't like her. She stood to face her inquisitor. "No, I'm not mute. I'm quite capable of speaking for myself when addressed civilly." The snickers from the women behind her indicated she'd scored points with Rae's friends.

Rae intervened. "Janet, let's talk somewhere else. Don't make a scene."

"We can talk while we dance." Janet took Rae's arm and pulled her to the dance floor.

Audrey watched in amazement as Rae allowed herself to be womanhandled. "The ex, I presume?"

Stephanie said, "What was your first clue, the razor-sharp fangs or the green skin tone?"

"What's she like when she's not foaming at the mouth?" Audrey asked.

Deb got to the point. "You mean what were she and Rae like as a couple, don't you?"

She nodded because that was exactly what she wanted to know. She could care less about Janet the ex, but she was very interested in what Rae Butler was like in a relationship—her kind of woman, what she liked, disliked, how she felt, everything.

"Great chemistry, not much in common. They tried to make it work for five years until Rae caught her cheating."

Audrey was beginning to understand Rae's distrust and insistence on honesty. Her family's rejection of her lifestyle at an early age and a cheating spouse had left scars. "Are they still in love?"

"No." Ronni's answer was emphatic. It was the first time the dark-haired woman had spoken since Janet crashed their table. "Janet was never in love, and Rae can't forgive her deception."

But Rae could still be in love with her, Audrey thought, as the two women danced. They made a striking couple with Rae's auburn hair and fair complexion and Janet's Italian features. Rae's lean body fit nicely against the voluptuous curves of Janet's breasts and thighs. They danced awfully close for two people who didn't care any more. Audrey felt an uncomfortable prickle of emotion as Janet maneuvered her leg between Rae's. Her uneasiness increased when Rae didn't move away.

"I should be getting home." Audrey stood to leave. "It was nice meeting all of you. I hope to see you again."

The women tried to convince Audrey to stay, but she'd seen enough. As she walked home, the thoughts of telling Rae the truth about herself seemed less clear. If Audrey allowed Rae's ex-girlfriend to stop her from helping people in need, what did that say about her? Rae's personal situation shouldn't influence her decision to do the right thing. Her logic sounded good but felt awful.

Chapter Ten

The image of Rae in the clutches of her ex annoyed Audrey on her walk home, but she wasn't sure why. Maybe because the day before, Rae had held her, only a breath away from a kiss. She wanted to be in Rae's arms again, to finish what had almost happened…and couldn't believe she wanted it. She pushed the idea aside, along with all its disturbing feelings.

As Audrey neared her apartment, it sounded like a party was going on in the parking lot. The upbeat music filled her with a déjà vu feeling of familiarity and warmth. She danced the last block, ready to join the revelry as she opened the gate to her complex and stopped.

"Surprise!" Her seven closest friends smiled and ran toward her like Cheshire cats gone mad. She mentally identified each one as she'd first seen them years ago: the Romanians Melvin and Tony; the Chinese girls Grace, Hope, and Charity; the Kenyan Sam; and the Moroccan Yasi.

"What are you doing here?" The question didn't relay the surprising sense of joy and gratitude she felt. "I mean…it's great to see you. Why are you here?"

"I told you we were coming this way. I didn't realize we'd be so close," Yasi said. "When I told everybody you lived in Kramer, they had to come. And we brought our own refreshments." They held up bags and bottles as peace offerings for showing up unannounced and in the hopes of an old-fashioned party.

Audrey greeted the friends she hadn't seen for too long. Each one held a special place in her memory and in her heart. They had helped her adjust to a life she didn't understand and didn't want at the time. Melvin and Tony, with bodies like Greek gods, had taught her that strength and flexibility aren't mutually exclusive. Grace, Hope, and Charity epitomized inner peace and instructed her in meditation. Sam, her dark-skinned sidekick for years, demonstrated how to play and not take herself too seriously. And Yasi had always been her foundation, her stability. When Audrey bounced around emotionally like a windswept balloon, Yasi calmed her and helped her work through the madness. It seemed that since she'd lost contact with her friends, she'd forgotten all she'd learned. Seeing them now, she realized how much she'd missed everyone.

"I'm so glad you're here. I have something to tell you."

Audrey ushered them inside and introduced them to Cannonball. The little ball of fur seemed disturbed by all the excitement and refused to come out of her protective crate. Her friends gushed over the addition to her family, made themselves at home with snacks and drinks, and settled in for an update on her life. No one spoke as they waited for her to begin what would be one of the most difficult discussions of her life.

"I guess you're wondering why I left so suddenly."

Yasi was the first to answer. Though she'd known months after the incident, she'd never shared Audrey's ordeal with anyone. "Sweetie, you don't have to do this." Everyone else nodded in agreement.

"Yes, I do. All of you were…and still are…my family, and I couldn't share what happened to me that night when we were supposed to meet. I still can't because I don't remember. You do know I was hurt, and that's about all I know. I didn't leave because I couldn't trust you. I was afraid…of everything and needed a fresh start.

"This year I've tried to put it behind me, to keep the past and the present separated. It isn't working. Things are starting to come back in bits and pieces. I miss all of you terribly." What Audrey didn't say was that the time had come to remember and to deal with the events of last summer. Her friends couldn't help with that. She'd have to tackle that task alone—or with Rae's assistance, if they were still speaking after tonight.

"We miss you," Sam said. "We worried when you didn't show that night. All of us, we looked, but didn't know where you'd gone. It was strange. We always handled things together."

Audrey placed her hand on Sam's broad shoulder. "I know."

"How can we help now?" Hope asked. "Anything, we will do."

"Your being here is exactly what I need." It wasn't what they wanted to hear. They *had* always worked through each other's problems together. Being left out would feel like another slight. "I'm sorry for leaving so suddenly and not getting in touch. Can you ever forgive me?"

Melvin and Tony rose from their seats on the sofa and flanked her, placing muscular arms around her waist. "Nothing to forgive. We all do what is necessary. When the time is right, you'll call and we'll be there," Tony said.

Sam raised his glass. "One for all, we are one." His bright smile always reminded Audrey of happy times. "Do you remember the Yasi and Sanjana dance routine?"

"Oh, no, Sam, not that story," Yasi said. "Must we always rehash that one?"

"Your *friend*," he inclined his head toward Yasi, "convinced you to join her in a dance routine."

"And almost got us killed. She kept saying, 'I have a surprise for you.' It's made me a bit anxious about her gifts ever since." Audrey flashed Yasi a loving smile to let her know she was only joking.

Yasi tried to defend herself. "How was I to know the sash was threadbare? Nobody told me that box of stuff was for the garbage dump."

"Lucky for you that I was close by." Melvin smiled and flexed his biceps.

Audrey felt as if she'd stepped back in time and they'd never lost touch. Laughter filled the room and joy settled in her heart again. It was nearly midnight before they decided it was time to leave and said their good-byes.

When Audrey opened the door, Rae Butler stood on the other side poised to knock. "What—I thought you were—" Nothing coherent would come out of her mouth.

Rae stood silently surveying the group of people standing behind her in the doorway.

"They were just leaving," she said as her guests filed out.

As her friends passed Rae, they introduced themselves and bid her a good night. Audrey thought how surreal. Her past and present seemed determined to collide. It was probably best, as she'd already decided to tell Rae the truth. But she hadn't planned to tell her about being psychic *and* a circus brat all at once. One of those things would probably send Rae running in the opposite direction, but combined she was certain to lose her. Audrey waved Rae in. "Is your *party* over so soon?" She hated the bite in her words yet couldn't seem to help herself. She didn't control jealousy well.

"That's why I came by, to explain about Janet."

"You don't owe me an explanation." Audrey tried to show disinterest, though she longed to know the real story. She assumed a casual expression before turning to face Rae. "That's none of my business."

"I'd like to clear something up. Janet and I aren't together anymore. She cheated, and I can't forget it. If I lose trust in the person I love, it's over for me."

Audrey relaxed and a stressful ache across her shoulders dissolved as she listened to Rae's words. She wanted to believe Rae, but she'd let Janet handle her like a lover, in public, in front of her friends...and Audrey. "You sound pretty certain."

"I am, now more than ever, and I wanted to tell you...so you wouldn't misunderstand what you saw tonight."

"It was quite a display, and you seemed to enjoy it."

Rae blushed an endearing color of pink that was such a contrast to the self-assured cop she was used to. "Not really. She knows the buttons to push...and we always had a healthy—" She stopped as her color deepened. "Sorry."

Audrey didn't enjoy the visual that popped into her head—Rae and Janet hot and sticky from each other's sweat and other bodily secretions. She forced the image from her mind. "She obviously doesn't want it to be finished."

"She doesn't have a choice. It's over." Rae shrugged like she had nothing more to say on the subject, and Audrey tingled in relief. Her words rang true.

"Sorry if I interrupted your evening. It looked like you were hosting an international conference, or were they friends?"

Audrey took a deep breath and steeled herself for Rae's reaction. "Actually, they're more like family."

Rae's expression didn't change. "They seem very nice. How did you meet such a diverse group of people?"

"Why don't you sit down? Would you like something to drink?" Audrey stalled for time. She needed a few more seconds to mentally map her strategy.

"No, thanks." Rae took a seat at one end of the sofa with Audrey at the other.

"I met those people when I was young, in the International Cirque."

Rae's gaze never left hers, her eyes full of attention and interest. An involuntary twitch in her brow was the only indication that the comment registered as unusual.

"My mother, Nadja, was a dancer with IC originally, exquisitely creative and coordinated. When she retired, they kept her on as a dance recruiter and instructor until she died." The memory of her mother and her amazing career brought a wave of pride and sadness. She fought to control the swell of emotions. "From my earliest recollections, we moved every couple of weeks from one venue to another. The small cirque family became my family. We were close-knit and lived together in the beginning. Wherever we went we had a few rooms and everybody shared space and resources. Everyone had a job—fixing meals, educating the children, planning events, transportation, or housing. It was like a busy little ant hill."

Audrey looked to Rae for an indication to continue. Her face was softer than she'd ever seen. The small worry lines that usually creased her forehead had disappeared and her eyes shone with kindness and curiosity. So far so good, but this was the easier of the two bombs to drop.

"Please go on."

"When I was old enough to work, I chose to become a clown. The more experienced performers took me under their wings and gave me on-the-job training. Melvin and Tony are trapeze artists. Hope, Faith, and Charity are tumblers/gymnasts. Yasi is an exquisite dancer. Sam and I developed a clown routine—Sam and Sanjana."

Rae looked confused. "Sanjana?"

"In Sanskrit it means soft, gentle, untouchable. I chose it for the act. Sam was the Charlie Brown to my Lucy. I was a Queen of Hearts jester with a hood hat, comedy and tragedy masks, curly toed shoes, and oversized gloves. I never handled anything directly. I carried huge tongs in my back pocket. I'd start to touch something or shake Sam's hand and change my mind at the last minute. Silly, I know, but the crowds loved us."

Rae smiled. "I'm trying to envision you dressed in that costume acting onstage in front of thousands of people. You're so private now. I bet you had a great childhood, full of fun and adventures."

So far Rae's reaction hadn't been what Audrey expected. Her background had no more adverse effect than any other person's recollection of their childhood. Rae seemed interested and asked questions, showing no signs of judgment or disapproval. "It was a happy time until I went away to college."

"Did you stop performing?"

"I returned at summer breaks and did a few shows, because I loved it so much and it kept me in touch with friends. My last one was a year ago." Audrey remembered the night of her final performance. The arena had been packed and they'd done shows back-to-back. Afterward she'd changed clothes and was walking to join the others at a nearby bar to celebrate. Her memory always faded at this point. She hadn't figured out if the blockage resulted from the incident or her refusal to remember it.

"You look sad. Did something happen?" Rae asked.

Audrey barely contained her feeling of helplessness. She couldn't tell Rae this part of the story until she remembered everything. To unearth the past, she had to stop running in the present. "I'm getting ahead of the story. I wanted to tell you about myself because I find it difficult to make new friends without being honest."

Rae's bright eyes sparkled and her face seemed to glow. The corners of her very kissable mouth curved into a smile. It was as if Audrey had given her a gift. "You can tell me anything, Audrey. If you want it kept confidential, just say so." Rae reached for Audrey's hands but seemed to reconsider. "May I?"

It took every ounce of Audrey's resolve to refuse Rae's touch. "I'd prefer you didn't. I need to stay focused. This part is the shocker." Audrey wanted Rae to hold her and tell her everything would be all right, no matter what she revealed. She wanted to be loved and accepted exactly as she was, but that hadn't been her predominant experience.

"Say it, Audrey. What could be so bad anyway?"

"I'm psychic."

Rae's head tilted to the side sharply as though she hadn't heard properly. "What?"

"Psychic, clairsentient, seer, clairvoyant, whatever you want to call it. If you tell anybody else, I'll have you put to sleep." Audrey joked in the hopes of dislodging the stunned look from Rae's face. It didn't work. Rae's eyes opened wider and her gaze bounced around the room before settling on Audrey.

"The conversation we had the other day, was that a trick of some sort?"

"If I recall, you brought up the subject. I tested the waters."

"And I failed miserably."

"Please don't start with the jokes. I've heard them all. What's a blond psychic's greatest achievement? An in-body experience. Why do psychics have to ask your name? Where do fortunetellers go to dance? The crystal ball. They're all pretty lame."

The jokes weren't helping. Audrey could feel the confusion rolling off Rae. She had no idea what to say. Her attitude toward psychics had been clear, and her opinion of Audrey had probably gone off the scale on the negative side.

Rae stood and paced in front of the sofa, her mind spinning with Audrey's revelations and her new willingness to be so exposed. While the conversation felt genuine, almost intimate, the news disturbed her. "How do you know you're…psychic?" Even the word didn't flow easily off her tongue. She wasn't sure how she'd reconcile Audrey with her idea of a clairvoyant.

"I apparently come from a long line of similar relatives, gypsies, actually. I know, I'm blond and blue. We're not all dark-haired, brown-eyed vagrants, basket makers or chimney sweeps—a common misconception. My mother was the first to break the mold and refuse to use her gift to make money fortunetelling. At first I denied I had any intuitive ability, then I ignored it, and finally I refused to use it."

The conflict on Audrey's face made Rae wince. It was obviously painful for her to reveal something so personal and controversial. No wonder she'd been so secretive about her past. This wasn't the kind of thing you told folks in casual conversation. It actually wasn't the kind of thing you told at all. Her response to Audrey's news would be crucial.

"I'm not sure what to say." Honesty was her only hope of getting through. "Can you tell me how you realized you could do this? I confess total ignorance on the subject."

Audrey seemed to relax as she released a deep sigh. "I used to watch my mother make predictions for friends, help find lost children, or send clues to the police, but I never understood how she did it.

"When I was ten, a lady in the cirque came to ask about her daughter, who had been missing for months. My mother didn't see anything, but I did. It was a horrible flash of a body inside a car in a junkyard. I blurted out, 'She's dead.' It made no sense how I knew that, yet I was certain it was true. Mom hurried me from the room, scolding me for being insensitive and giving me the *rules* for delivering bad news to people."

"Did it scare you, the first time it happened?"

"I thought I was a terrible child and was being punished. If I saw bad things, it had to mean I was bad. I couldn't tell anyone about it. At that age all you want is to fit in, to be normal, and I definitely wasn't. I felt so alone. Mother tried to convince me I had a great gift that I would grow to appreciate and utilize to help people. To me, it felt like a curse."

"Your mother and your friends…?"

"Accepted me the way I was and helped me cope. The people who come to circus life are a little different anyway. I find them more tolerant than most. I fit in there."

"And when you went away to college?" Rae asked.

The pained expression returned to Audrey's face. "I got a bitter dose of reality when I realized that the world isn't made up of open-minded circus people. Teenagers can be so cruel, especially if you don't conform. I tried to intellectualize everything and ignore my feelings. My entire system felt constipated, emotionally and spiritually blocked. Does that make any sense?"

Rae imagined Audrey denying her feelings, obstructing that vital part of herself. She thought about her recent crisis of confidence and decided Audrey's experience must have been many times worse. "Maybe a little. It's like losing your internal guidance system."

"Exactly." Rae's answer seemed to please Audrey.

"What's it like to have this…ability?"

"You mean physically?" Rae nodded. "It can manifest in several ways. I sometimes get a tingling sensation on my face or hands or feel pressure in my head. It could be a chill, a scent, or a hazy vision or image. I might zone out for a few seconds. Sometimes I feel like my body is wrapped in fiberglass. My physical reaction often depends on what I'm picking up. And occasionally the energy around me is so disturbing I have to completely shut down. That's the dark side of this gift."

Rae's heart ached for the huge burden Audrey had always carried. She believed some people had extrasensory perception and were gifted with occasional insights unavailable to the masses. But she couldn't imagine being privy to other people's feelings or constantly receiving unwanted images and information. She couldn't fathom wading around in the sick minds of some of the deviants she'd encountered. Rae found it hard to accept that this could be a way of life for some. And if it was, the emotional consequence and responsibility were bound to be tremendous.

A strange sensation crept over her. Was Audrey reading her, knowing she had trouble absorbing all this? Rae based her knowledge of the world mostly on facts and tangibles. "Can you read everybody's mind?"

Audrey smiled and shook her head. "That's another common misconception. I'm not a mind reader. I sense things from people's energy, an object, or even a picture. It's usually necessary that the person opens the door or invites me to read them fully. Otherwise, I read their surface energy—are they a nice person, is it safe to be with them, generic things."

"So you don't know what I'm thinking right now?"

"You seem to be one of the few people I can't read very well. I'm not sure why."

"Maybe because you like me too much." Rae was fishing but couldn't help wishing.

"My mother used to say that reading close friends and family was psychic cheating. Who knows, maybe it's nature's way of leveling the playing field. I don't need to be psychic to see your apprehension and disbelief, maybe even confusion. That's normal. I'm asking you to stretch your perception of reality."

"I'll say. How do you turn it off, or can you? I imagine it gets pretty exhausting."

"It would be if I engaged everybody I passed on the street or met each day. I listen to music, hum, or cuddle my kitten. It soothes and distracts me from the bombardment of stimuli. I don't own a television. The news is always negative and drains me. I don't only see things, I also hear, smell, feel, and taste spiritually."

Rae caught herself right before she shook her head in disbelief. When she didn't understand something, she investigated and questioned until it came together in a coherent picture. However, the more Audrey talked the more conflicted she became. She'd handled cases where people were institutionalized for espousing such things as Audrey had. Rae desperately wanted to believe in her, because it had taken tremendous courage to expose herself so completely. Rae simply couldn't embrace this notion of psychic ability. She was too realistic, too by the book—*too closed-minded*?

Audrey patted the sofa beside her. "Please sit down. You're wearing a hole in my carpet. Don't be so hard on yourself. Most people would find this difficult to grasp. It violates their preconceived notions of God versus the Devil, religion versus the occult, good versus evil. You're having trouble too, aren't you?"

"Forgive me, I'm thinking like a cop. It could take a while to wrap my head around it."

"Ask your questions. It's best to get them out."

"That comment about the red dress and gold heels—was that one of your—I don't even know what to call it. Did you really dream that?"

"Yes, I dreamed it, and I had no idea it was connected to your victim until later."

Rae raked her hands through her hair in frustration. "See, that's what I have trouble with, the whole it's-connected-to-my-victim thing. What about the knife? Where did that little tidbit come from, another dream?"

"I had a momentary image when your victim touched me. I felt her pain, saw her dressed in those clothes, and flashed on the knife slicing through her flesh."

"My mind tells me that's not possible unless you were involved in the case. And I don't want to believe you were."

Audrey was obviously struggling to explain the reality of her situation. "Consider for a moment that I might be authentically psychic. Would you turn down my help if it led to a suspect in these cases?"

"I'd have no choice but to turn it down. They'd laugh me out of the office, not to mention the courtroom. Anything you told me as a result of your ability would be inadmissible and unquestionably discredited—and my reputation along with it. We deal in facts of law, Audrey, not psychic perceptions."

"And the law isn't about perceptions?"

"You know what I mean," Rae said.

"Actually, I don't. If I'm not mistaken, your job depends greatly on a cop's intuition and ability to read people. Just because you can't see it doesn't mean you dismiss it."

Rae thought about her conversation with Ken Whitt and acknowledged the heavy credence she'd given his insights into the case. None of them were based on facts. She'd specifically asked him to speculate, to give his opinion and gut instincts. "It's not the same thing at all. We operate on valid hunches, not dreams and visions." Rae regretted the comment the minute she said it. Audrey's cobalt eyes darkened and her lips closed in a tight, decidedly unpleasant grimace.

"The sad part is you believe that. I obviously made a mistake by sharing this with you."

The statement landed like a blow. Rae had done the one thing she wanted to avoid—lost Audrey's confidence and trust. Why hadn't she taken more time to think everything through before automatically reverting to the rational? "Don't say that."

"What else can I say? I expected the usual logical, information-gathering questions and that you'd have to process and formulate an opinion. Then, I even expected you to dive into the professional queries. But I prayed you'd be different, that you could see beyond the hypothetical arm's length. Maybe I misjudged your capacity for compassion and understanding. Perhaps the woman I wanted to see isn't the woman who actually exists." Audrey rose from the sofa and headed toward the door. "I think you should go now."

Rae hadn't thought she could feel any worse. She'd disappointed Audrey on a profound level, and the result hurt her more than she could've imagined. It never occurred to her that she could betray someone instead of vice versa. The dish was bitter from either side. She didn't believe Audrey and basically rejected her for admitting who she was. And the wound would have been even deeper if they'd been closer. Rae had essentially destroyed that possibility. "I'm sorry." As the door shut behind her, Rae thought she heard a soft cry from the other side.

Audrey slumped to the floor as her hope that Rae would understand and accept her disappeared. For a moment she was back in college with her peers pointing and laughing at her, the rejection sharp and damaging. She tried to muffle the sorrow that rose in her throat but failed. The cry sounded like a tortured animal as it escaped her lips. When would she learn not to trust people? What made her think Rae Butler was different, special?

It was common to have philosophical and ideological differences, but they could also be grounds for disagreement and serious conflict. Now Rae probably thought Audrey was a crazy circus freak who should take her act back to the big top. Audrey would've had more luck revealing herself to the mayor. At least he didn't cling to some antiquated idea of truth as only black and white or right and wrong. She had challenged the very foundation of Rae's just-the-facts mentality and been rebuffed. What had she been thinking? She'd trusted a *cop*.

If Rae didn't believe her, she wasn't the person to help uncover the remaining mystery in her life. Once again she was on her own, struggling to understand something she didn't even remember. Her instincts had brought her to Kramer for a reason, and it had to be connected to her forgotten past. Nothing else made sense. She would eventually unravel the convoluted threads and come up with the answer with or without help.

Audrey drew her knees to her chest, feeling alone and strangely uncomfortable. Looking around her little apartment, she wondered why it suddenly felt vast and unwelcoming. Cannonball nudged her legs, and when Audrey stretched out, the kitten nestled in her lap. The tiny creature licked her hands and seemed to be trying to console her. If only people were as nonjudgmental and accepting as animals, life would be much easier. She gently stroked the wiry hair on her kitten's back. Had she seen the last of Rae Butler?

❖

Arya bit the inside of his lip until he tasted blood. Strangers surrounded her all night. Those strange people from her past, touching her, talking, laughing—always touching. The annoying woman who delivered a pesky animal had again brought disruption.

It burrowed into his soul and made him crave retribution. He wanted to punish them for their violations. Instead he was forced to watch without taking action. His rage always flared when he felt helpless. She needed him and he could do nothing.

And then the cop returned. She was becoming more of a problem with each visit. This time she'd tried to touch his beloved, but she had thwarted the advance. Good girl. If only he could've heard them, but the voices were muted.

The cop had upset or hurt her in some way. She sat crumpled on the floor like a wounded thing, and he couldn't comfort her. At least maybe now she understood that she could trust only him. The list of those who deserved punishment grew longer. Soon his passion would demand that he seek revenge to quench his thirst or finally take possession of her…or both.

CHAPTER ELEVEN

Rae stared at the blank page and tried to formulate a response to the final-exam essay question. Everyone else in the packed classroom hunched over their papers and worked furiously. For her the stark institutional gray walls closed in and blotted the information right out of her head. She looked at the clock, ten more minutes. The question wasn't hard. She simply couldn't put the answer together. Her mind wandered to her conversation with Audrey three days ago, the psychic connection, as she now referred to it. They'd had no contact since.

Rae felt like a narrow-minded bigot, unwilling to look beyond the veil of her own reality. She theoretically accepted life beyond our universe. To think otherwise was not only unenlightened but also egotistical. So why was she having trouble acknowledging Audrey's abilities? Maybe she could only deal with the mystical in theory but not in her well-ordered life.

Cops and psychics didn't mesh. Their approaches to solving crime, and to life in general, were too different. Police officers, skeptical by nature, questioned anything they couldn't see or touch. Those who collaborated with seers were ridiculed and their careers suffered. She'd seen the disastrous results. No one ever took them seriously again, regardless of the case's outcome.

Psychic ability was simply mumbo-jumbo, guesswork, and everybody guessed right occasionally. The last psychic who *assisted* on a case shotgunned such a massive amount of vague information that some of it hit the mark. The victims wanted details so desperately they only remembered the correct bits, and the media sensationalized the results. The leads he provided were anecdotal at best, never anything concrete. Rae wanted to believe Audrey was different and was willing to suspend her disbelief long enough to investigate further. If she didn't, she'd never forgive herself. Audrey made her feel things she hadn't thought possible, and she couldn't walk away.

"Five minutes," the instructor announced.

Rae returned her attention to the exam and scribbled a quick answer to the question. She wouldn't say she'd done her best, but she'd done all she could. She either passed or she didn't. Rae had a more difficult test now, understanding and accepting Audrey—warts and all.

On her way home, she called and left Audrey a message asking if she'd stop by on her way home from work. She at least owed her a face-to-face apology for her earlier behavior. Rae spent the afternoon researching psychics and clairsentients on the Internet. She might be mildly intolerant but she didn't have to be completely uninformed. Most of the sites were advertisements or testimonials geared to solicit money—another unpleasant connection Rae associated with psychics—money grabbers who preyed on the weak. The searches didn't help.

While Rae waited to hear from Audrey, she threw darts and reviewed the Whisperer details she'd pinned to her case board. She studied the pictures of each victim's wounds and wondered if a forensics weapons expert could narrow down the type used to inflict the injuries. Rae added the task to her to-do list with a shiver of excitement. What if Audrey was right and the weapon had been a very specific knife? If they could identify the style of weapon, it could be her first solid lead.

How would she explain where the information came from? That's where merging police work and the supernatural got murky. Maybe she didn't have to say anything about Audrey's vision. Rae always explored every detail in her cases, and narrowing down weapon type was certainly on the list. If she considered Audrey's information like any other lead and verified it, the source wouldn't be a problem. It wasn't like this would be a recurring issue. Audrey wouldn't be involved in the investigation any further.

Rae breathed a little easier. At least she knew a bit more of Audrey now. A circus upbringing wasn't anything to be ashamed of, so why had she kept quiet? In Rae's opinion a unique background made her more interesting. Perhaps she was concerned that others wouldn't understand. People judged one another on money, power, and position or the lack thereof.

An idea Rae had considered before suddenly returned. What if Audrey's silence had something to do with her assault? Maybe the missing link was her past and Audrey was protecting someone. Rae hated to stereotype, but circus folk were a rare breed, unusual, often foreign and transient. Every couple of years a modern-day band of gypsies swooped through town like a plague, burglarizing, robbing, and vanishing. It was a documented fact based on police statistics, not a generalization. She conceded gypsies and cirque performers weren't the same. However, it did alter her suspect base. She was officially off Audrey's assault, but she wasn't a quitter. Something about the case bothered her—beyond her desire to play hero.

Rae hurled another dart swift and sure to the heart of the dartboard as a soft tap sounded at her door. The knock was almost inaudible, broadcasting Audrey's uncertainty about being here. Hopefully, Rae could reassure her. She smiled and opened the door.

Audrey looked as if she might run, her body tensed for flight. Her expression relayed questions and indecision. "Please come in." She wore a tailored cream suit and deep-blue blouse that complemented her sparkling lapis eyes. Her wispy blond hair feathered adorably toward her face, and Rae almost reached up to smooth the ruffles back. "I'm glad you came." She motioned toward a chair.

"I'd prefer to stand, at least until I know what this is about. Why am I here, Rae?"

Audrey wasn't making this easy for her. "I wondered if we could talk more about the other night—what you told me."

"Apparently not. You can't even bring yourself to say the words, can you?"

Rae breathed through her frustration. She wanted desperately to understand, to accept. If she still doubted herself, she should've waited longer before talking with Audrey. "Would you at least concede this is hard for most people? Surely, I'm not the only skeptic."

"No…" Audrey paused as if weighing her next words. "But I'd hoped your *interest* in me would've made you more open."

Audrey's gaze made Rae feel completely transparent. Heat rushed up her neck and across her face. Audrey knew she cared for her, and she hadn't been the woman Audrey needed. Why did she feel her disappointment so acutely? "You're right."

"About which part?"

If she hoped to salvage even a friendship with Audrey, Rae had to be as open as she had been. And after three days without contact, Rae knew she wanted more than that. "Both. I should've been more objective…and I do care. I've thought of little else since."

"And what have you come up with?" Audrey's eyes penetrated as if to mine any hidden inference or agenda.

"Will you please sit down?" Rae moved to the small settee and waited for Audrey to join her. When she did, Rae took her hands. Audrey's skin was soft and supple, and energy surged between them. Rae felt intuitively that her decision to believe in Audrey was the right one. Could she trust her instincts on something so vital, or was she only responding to their physical connection? Whatever was happening, she couldn't stop now.

"It must've been difficult for you to tell me about your past and your gift. I haven't been your greatest supporter. I grilled you about your life, questioned your motives, and refused to stop investigating your assault. You might say I've been a true pain in the ass." Audrey didn't disagree but didn't pull away either. "It must be hard to know what to do with so much unwanted information. You probably feel terribly alone and scared sometimes."

Audrey thumbed the backside of Rae's hand. "Yes. It feels like I'm in a minefield with no map—one wrong move and I destroy myself and everyone around me."

"I'm sorry for not being more understanding and supportive. The concept of psychics goes against everything I've been taught to believe."

"Then why are you trying?" Audrey's eyes had lost some of the cold edge they held when she arrived. The stormy blue calmed into a softer sky hue and seemed to penetrate Rae's soul.

"For the last eight months I've been too preoccupied with loss and betrayal to consider anything else. I thought Janet and I would be together forever. When our relationship started falling apart, I withdrew. I blamed the breakup on her affair and disloyalty."

Audrey edged closer to Rae on the sofa and stroked her hand. "That's a natural reaction. You expect your mate to be faithful."

"It was my fault too, and instead of facing it head-on, I worked more and refused to take any responsibility. Police work is a great way to lose yourself. It's a demanding job that absorbs every ounce of emotion you'll allow, leaving nothing for your personal life."

"You obviously wanted more," Audrey said.

"Yeah, but I took the coward's way out. You're not the only one coming to terms with the past. To answer your question, I want to believe you because disbelief is too limiting. It siphons the joy and possibility out of life."

"Brilliant. It sounds like you have done a lot of thinking." Audrey kissed her lightly on the cheek and looked at her as if she'd said the most important words in the English language. "If we kept our childhood wonder and belief alive, we'd be much happier. And…I accept your apology."

If the smallest speck of skepticism still existed inside Rae, she'd endure it forever and never speak of it again—as long as Audrey looked at her the way she did right now. Rae's heart almost burst. Her cheek burned where Audrey's lips had touched and heat spread through her. She bridged the distance between them, wanting desperately to connect, afraid of overstepping. It was more important that Audrey know she believed her than to know how much she wanted her.

As if reading her mind, Audrey turned into her arms and brought their lips together. They joined tenderly, teasing and testing, parting and reconnecting, breathing and not. Rae felt the initial surge of desire, the immediate heat between them, and moistened Audrey's lips with the tip of her tongue. Sweet and savory tickled her taste buds.

Audrey raked her fingers through Rae's hair and brought them closer, deepening the kiss. Her lips parted and Rae explored the wet softness. Her body hummed like current along a live wire, and she drew Audrey tighter. Rae probed with her tongue, drinking, inhaling, and absorbing Audrey's essence like a parched traveler. Sliding her hand up, she cupped Audrey's breast in her palm. It felt as if someone had squeezed her sex, flooding her with arousal.

Rae wanted Audrey to understand her feelings, not only her desire, so she moved slowly. The pull between them was strong, but it wasn't just sex; it was Audrey. She felt bewitched, drained of resistance, open to every stimulus. Her insides burned and her body shifted of its own accord. Her hips jerked each time she closed her fingers around Audrey's breast. Rae could almost taste the soft flesh in her mouth, imagine the suck and release on Audrey's erect nipple as she teased it with her tongue and teeth. She worked her hand down the length of Audrey's body toward her waist.

"Please stop." Audrey backed away, her breath coming in spurts. "We can't do this."

"Why?"

Audrey didn't have a chance to answer. At that moment the picture window facing the garden side of the condo exploded. Rae instinctively covered Audrey, shielding her from the shards of flying glass. When no second volley occurred, she held her at arm's length and checked for injuries. "Are you all right?"

"I think so. What happened?"

Rae leapt from the sofa. "Wait right here. Don't move." She ran out the back door and toward the garden. As she rounded the corner, out of the darkness something slammed into her head. Rae hit the ground, momentarily stunned. She tried to sit up but felt dizzy. Grabbing her forehead, she felt the warm sticky blood trickle into her eyes. *Audrey.* Adrenaline kicked in. Rae stripped her T-shirt over her head, wiping her face as she made her way to the back door. She had to make sure Audrey was safe.

Audrey had risen unsteadily to follow Rae but paused at the back door, staring into the darkness. She felt drugged, her senses overwhelmed by their physical interaction. Rae's kiss stirred things Audrey had never experienced—raw sexual desire and emotional longing. The exhilaration was nearly as heady as the kiss itself. The layers of protection fell away from her heart, and she ached for more. How could one kiss reveal so much yet cause such confusion? These feelings were too new, too intense, and she wasn't adjusting quickly.

As she waited at the door, another wave of sensation obliterated her euphoria like a blast of foul air—something sinister. Rae was in danger. Audrey flipped the switches by the door but nothing happened. She fought the panic, trying instead to focus on what threat awaited Rae in the night. She and Rae had been so close seconds before and now she'd disappeared. "Rae. Where are you? Can you hear me?" No response.

The minutes seemed like hours until Audrey heard a faint voice calling her name. Audrey stood in the doorway, waiting until she saw Rae illuminated in the patch of light from the kitchen. Then she ran to her, fear giving way to a need to protect. "You're bleeding." She helped Rae to a chair.

Audrey knelt in front of Rae and lowered the crimson-stained T-shirt from her forehead. Blood wasn't her thing, and she fought the urge to gag as the gaping wound flowed freely. She quickly replaced the T-shirt. "Hold that while I get some ice."

Rae's face paled and she looked like she might pass out. Audrey wasn't a violent person, but she would consider changing if she knew who had hurt Rae. For the moment, she had to tend Rae's injuries and keep her conscious. *Get her to think like a cop*. "Do you have any idea what happened?"

"No, I…I don't know…" Her soft voice sounded confused.

"What do you think? Best guess?" Audrey asked as she filled a dishcloth with ice and twisted it into a bundle.

Rae seemed to regain focus when she looked up and saw Audrey. "Neighborhood kids, maybe. We've had some vandalism. I'm sure I don't have any enemies." Rae smiled weakly.

"What about someone from your past…an ex-lover, maybe?" Audrey grinned when Rae opened her mouth to speak then stopped.

"Touché."

"We have to cover all the bases."

"I'm bleeding to death, and you're making jokes. Perfect."

Audrey stroked Rae's back and placed the ice on her forehead. "At least I know you're thinking clearly."

"This doesn't make sense. The vandals we've had in this area were mostly bored school kids, never anything violent or personal."

The strange feeling Audrey experienced earlier returned. She looked toward the open back door, convinced someone was watching them from the darkness. Then she heard it—that vacuous white noise—a high-pitched mechanical whine full of raging energy and hatred, almost an angry whisper. Her hand shook as she tried to block the invasive sound. She'd heard that noise before, almost a week ago at the mayor's press conference. *He* had been in the crowd. Who was he, and why was he here now?

"Audrey, are you all right? You're shaking." Rae took her free hand and cupped it in hers. "You look a little pale."

"Don't like blood." She removed the ice pack from Rae's forehead and examined the injury. "The bleeding has almost stopped. It doesn't look as bad as I thought."

"Head injuries always bleed a lot. I have some Band-Aids in the bathroom if you wouldn't mind. I'm sure that'll be fine."

Audrey relinquished the ice pack, closed the back door, and gladly retreated to the bathroom. She clung to the sides of the sink and looked in the mirror at her stark-white face. She still felt as if someone was inside her head, taunting her, and she couldn't get a fix on him. Maybe her instincts were simply warning her to stay away from Rae. What if it was more? What if something or someone from her past had returned to threaten her present? If that was it, she'd stay away from Rae until she figured it out. She wouldn't be selfish enough to put her in jeopardy, no matter how much she wanted her.

She retrieved the Band-Aids, alcohol, and antiseptic from the cabinet and returned to Rae. "I'll have you fixed up in a jiffy. Then we'll get that window patched before I leave." Audrey removed the ice pack, relieved to see the bleeding had stopped. The jagged cut across Rae's forehead measured about three inches long just below the hairline. After she'd applied the Band-Aids, she fingered Rae's wavy auburn bangs back in place. She could barely see the damage. "Good as new…almost."

Rae waited until Audrey finished her nursing duties and stepped back. "Now, what is this about you leaving?"

"It's getting late, and I want to help you fix the window." She couldn't meet Rae's gaze.

"You've sensed something. I haven't seen that look before."

Audrey considered denial. The only two people who had ever been able to tell when she had extrasensory flashes were her mother and Yasi. She was excited and terrified that Rae had picked up the signs so quickly. "Yes, but I don't know what it is…only that it's dangerous."

"For you?" Rae rose at Audrey's side.

"Actually…for you. I get the sense that it's a warning for me and serious risk for you."

"Then I'm not worried. Let's fix that window."

Audrey grabbed Rae's arm as she started to walk away. "This isn't a joke, Rae. I'd appreciate it if you didn't treat it like one."

"Is that what you think? That I'm making fun of you?"

Audrey nodded.

"Well, I'm not. I'm trying to accept this gift of yours. Besides, I like advance notice about danger. It could come in handy in my line of work. I'm not discounting your intuition, but you have to let me decide how it figures into my life. Risk is part of my job."

"Rae, this isn't a hunch, it's a warning. I'm almost certain that what happened tonight wasn't random." She couldn't explain the strength of her knowing. To outsiders, it probably seemed like a woman's hysteria for someone she cared about. Rae was too dedicated to stand down for even an overt threat, much less the *perception* of one.

Rae pulled Audrey into a close hug. "I appreciate your insights. More than that, I believe them, but I'm not sure what I'm supposed to be afraid of. Is it something I'm working on, you, us? Can you be more specific?"

"No," Audrey mumbled into her chest.

"Then you understand that I have no choice but to continue with my life…and I hope that will include you in some form."

"What if this is about me? What if it's a warning for us to stay away from each other?"

"Is that what you think or are you feeling emotionally vulnerable?"

Audrey didn't have the answer. Her feelings for Rae were untested. Possibly her defenses were simply clicking into place for her protection. She'd never dealt with her gift in the context of an intimate relationship. Perhaps two such intense sets of feelings would cancel each other out. If that was true, why did she have a sense of foreboding? "I'm not sure."

Rae tilted Audrey's face and kissed her lightly. "Let me worry about the risk. And if you sense anything else, we'll re-evaluate. Now, help me secure this window."

They closed the hole in the window with heavy plastic and carpet strips while Audrey reviewed their tacit agreement. This was one of the few times in life when her blasted gift would've actually been useful, but it seemed stuck in an emotional loop. At one end her growing feelings for Rae loomed, and an almost tangible fear of the unknown lurked on the other. If she could read Rae more clearly, perhaps she could make a more informed decision.

Her mother had told her that reading loved ones was not only cheating but often times impossible. She reckoned it was the universe's way of ensuring everyone experienced true love…even psychics. Right now it was just another obstacle.

"Audrey, did you see something?" Rae stared at her, the green of her eyes almost black.

"Nothing else. You'll probably be safer when I'm gone. And I should be getting back. Cannonball will claw the stuffing out of my sofa if I'm much later. The little devil has started venturing out while I'm away."

Rae followed her to the door, disappointment obvious on her face. "I wish you'd stay…at least a bit longer. What if I have a concussion and need a nurse?"

Audrey kissed her on the cheek, lingering momentarily to consider her options, and said, "Call an ambulance or go to the hospital. You'll be fine."

"Will you come back tomorrow?"

Audrey's heart pounded at the suggestion. "To check on you?"

"To spend time together."

"I thought psychics and police didn't mix."

"There's a first time for everything…tomorrow?"

Audrey should've said no but heard herself reply, "Okay. I'll bring lunch and that pesky kitten. She can shred your furniture for a while."

"Excellent."

Rae opened the door and Audrey stepped outside into the cool evening air. She immediately sensed something was wrong. The feeling wasn't as strong as earlier, and as she walked toward Rae's blue SUV parked in front of the condo, she understood why. The front and back tires were flat, with huge gashes in the tire walls. She walked to the other side and saw the same thing.

"What the hell?" Rae almost came to attention and scanned the area like a sentry on duty.

Though no longer visible, the culprit lurked close by. He wouldn't reveal himself. Now Audrey understood. This person was very real, not a product of her conflicted emotions or imagination, not some malevolent energy in the universe. And he was fixated on her and those around her.

"I can't come over tomorrow, Rae. It's too dangerous."

"But—"

"I won't do it." She left Rae standing in the parking lot staring after her.

CHAPTER TWELVE

The next morning Rae checked the area around her car for signs of the vandal. She didn't find any indication he'd touched her car as he slashed the tires. He was certainly brazen. Light flooded the parking lot at night, and anyone who was looking could easily see an intruder. Usually no one was. People in the relatively safe neighborhood minded their own business.

She moved to the back garden. The bloody rock used to assault her lay near the kitchen door. In the mushy ground around the side window, she saw two footprints that bore no distinguishing marks. She snapped a couple of quick photos of the window damage on her cell phone and texted them to her insurance agent. At the last minute she took one of the prints too. Might as well be thorough.

While Rae waited for AAA to replace her slashed tires, she called the forensics weapons analyst on contract with the department. Barry Hewitt answered on the first ring.

"Barry, it's Rae Butler. I know it's Saturday, but—"

"You've got something that can't wait, right?" Barry's gruff tone belied the gentle giant who lurked beneath the surface. His stare alone was enough to quiet the most boisterous recruit in his forensics segment at the academy. He and Rae had a great working relationship based on dedication and a respectable dose of perfectionism.

"Actually, no. I wanted to get on your schedule. I'd like you to look at some injury photos and see if you can narrow down the type of weapon. It doesn't have to be today."

"I understand. Where are you? I can be there in fifteen minutes."

The light bulb went off in Rae's head. "I'm at home…oh, I see. Susan has you looking at wallpaper and paint for the nursery renovation, doesn't she?"

"Exactly, see you there."

A few minutes later, Barry whipped into the parking lot like he'd been on a high-speed chase. "I'm glad you called," he said as he lumbered to her door. Barry was over six feet tall with a hefty build that hadn't seen much exercise. As he walked by her car, he looked at the tires then back at her.

"Vandals," she said in response to the implied question.

"Case related?"

"Nah, kids, I think."

"Sucks."

Cops had a way of saying exactly what needed to be said with the least amount of exertion. One word with the proper inflection, facial expression, or body twitch spoke volumes. Others often found the language clipped and abrasive. They understood each other perfectly.

"Is Susan pissed?" Rae asked.

"Yeah, she'll get over it." The cavalier attitude didn't fool Rae. He adored his wife and went out of his way to give her everything she wanted. Indifference to emotions and all things domestic seemed a trademark of male cops, especially with each other. "What you got?"

Rae led the way to her study and pointed to the wound photos tacked to her case board. "Four assaults, same suspect, occurred over a year's time. The victims all survived." Rae knew Barry preferred minimal details so no one else's opinion would color his interpretation of the evidence.

He studied the pictures for several minutes, took them off the board, and examined them with a magnifying glass. "Jesus, look at the haphazard slashing. I don't see a pattern. All sharp-force injuries obviously ante-mortem. It's always easier to make these determinations if death resulted. It diminishes the skin's elasticity and captures the weapon's imprint in the flesh."

Rae cringed as Barry continued. “Incised wounds—as if someone drew the weapon across the skin in a parallel or tangential manner. Wound margins are sharp with no abrasions or contusions, which is unusual considering the wild cutting.”

“What do you mean?” Rae wanted to understand every detail.

“I would expect to see more physical contact with the body during the cutting. If he’s out of control, he’d normally bruise or tear it, maybe even stab it inadvertently.”

“And what does that tell you?”

“Well, I’m no shrink, but based on my experience with wounds, I’d say this guy is extremely controlled during these acts. At first glance, it appears he was in a fit of rage and cut randomly. On closer examination, I think he intended each cut exactly as you see it. If he ever loses control, it isn’t during the assaults. It’s almost like he’s sending a message.”

“A message?” Rae was having trouble interpreting Barry’s information. A raging controlled maniac who slashed nonsensical patterns to send a message?

“Your guess is as good as mine. He intentionally keeps the victims alive by controlling the depth of the cuts. He didn’t cause any major damage to the underlying muscle or organs. Is that right?” Rae nodded. “He must have at least a basic knowledge of anatomy, maybe more extensive.”

“Some type of medical training. That would make sense, because he has to use something to initially incapacitate the victims in order to move them.”

“Are the victims awake during this?” Barry asked.

“How did you know?”

“It fits the control-and-domination scenario. If you figure out what he’s trying to say with the cuts, I’ll bet it does as well.”

The only message Rae could fathom was that some sick person got off torturing women and hearing them beg for mercy. The image turned her stomach as she envisioned their pain and terror. She maintained focus by believing she would find this man and put him away forever.

“And the weapon?”

Barry used the magnifying glass again. "The angles of entry are sharp, but smaller superficial, incised wounds extend from the larger ones in some areas." He put the glass down, turned toward her, and nodded with satisfaction.

"In English, please, Barry."

"He most likely used an extremely sharp knife with a serrated edge, which I find interesting."

"Why?"

"He's obviously very skillful because serrated edges often rip instead of cutting cleanly."

Audrey's words flashed through Rae's mind: *She was cut, probably with a very specific type of knife.* "Not a scalpel?"

"Definitely not. The smaller parallel wounds are specific to a serrated edge. Anything else?" Barry walked toward the front door.

"That's it, thanks a lot."

"No problem. Guess I better get back before the wife sends out a search party. Good luck with this one. You'll need it. He won't make many mistakes."

Many? Rae would settle for one. She had nothing except a psychic's prediction that the suspect had used a knife and a weapons expert's confirmation. Not exactly the kind of evidence one took into a court of law—at least not the former.

Rae had a nagging curiosity about the extent of Audrey's abilities. She couldn't actually use her in the investigation, but she could test her skills to see where they led. If Audrey unearthed anything interesting, she'd do the requisite legwork and convert the details into a valid clue. Would she be using Audrey? She wasn't totally convinced the whole psychic thing was on the up-and-up, but she wanted to believe in *Audrey*—to trust her.

She picked up her cell to phone Audrey and remembered their exchange from the night before. Audrey had seemed determined not to have contact, certain Rae was in danger because of her. Had Audrey seen something or was she still holding back? As much as she wanted to make that call, Rae placed the phone back on the counter. She'd taken a giant leap of faith by accepting Audrey's psychic ability. If they were to trust each other, they'd have to meet at least halfway. It was Audrey's move.

❖

Audrey woke to the screechy scratching of sharp little claws on Sheetrock. “Cannonball, stop that. You’ll get us evicted.” Her new pet had been trying to climb the walls recently and leaving behind unmistakable evidence. The hallway between the bedroom, living area, and bathroom looked like a tree trunk with claw marks as far up as her short legs could reach. Audrey didn’t understand the recent urge to score and claim her territory, but so far CB had limited her activities to the hall and the furniture.

When she got Cannonball, she had jumped, rolled, and swatted playfully. Maybe her bundle of joy wasn’t quite as happy in her new surroundings as Audrey thought. The wall etchings and hole digging in her sofa had developed recently. She seemed to become progressively more anxious, her behavior indicating discomfort or irritation.

Maybe the cat picked up on Audrey’s disturbing psychic energy. Animals were very attuned to their owner’s moods and feelings. Audrey vowed to be more calm and affectionate with CB because she refused to give her back to Yasi. After only a few days, she couldn’t imagine her life without the wiry-haired vixen.

“Cannonball, come here.” Miraculously the kitten stopped scratching and looked from Audrey to the wall as if trying to decide which she preferred. She bounded onto the foot of the bed, climbed Audrey’s body, and settled on her chest. Her mismatched eyes seemed to convey conflicting messages—the green one suspicion and the yellow mischief. “What’s going on with you?” Audrey stroked the kitten’s back and heard a contented purr. “I wish you could tell me.”

Audrey settled into a semi-slumber, stroking CB and enjoying her appreciative whirrs. When she touched Cannonball and listened to her satisfied purring, Audrey could block out the invading sensations of the outside world. She was a true gift, and Audrey silently thanked Yasi again for her thoughtfulness.

Suddenly the old apartment building groaned with a loud settling creak and Cannonball projected herself off the bed and into the hallway. She clawed the walls again and looked back toward Audrey as if asking for help.

"Settle down, darling. It's this place. It makes noises. Come with me. We'll do our faux paper fetch." The only time Audrey wished CB was a dog was when she wanted the morning paper brought to her bedside. Still, even that wasn't enough to make her trade her newfound gem of a pet. She loved cats, and once a cat person, always a cat person.

Audrey opened the front door and looked out on the courtyard surrounded by small single-story apartments. The beautifully manicured garden with its variety of plants and flowers had drawn her when house hunting. Unlike most apartment complexes, this one provided parking spaces in the back and this scenic view of nature out front. The comforting setting had immediately won her over. She inhaled the fresh morning air and retrieved the newspaper. CB scurried past and dipped her front paws in the dew before running back inside.

Audrey made a cup of coffee and settled on the sofa with the newspaper and CB. When she opened the paper, a sheet of folded white stock fell onto her lap. She started to put it in the discard pile, but noticed the bold type: ***Stay away from the cop or face the consequences***.

Dark, threatening sensations pricked her fingertips and crawled up her arms into her chest. She dropped the note like it was hot metal and watched it flutter to the floor in slow motion. Cannonball leapt off the sofa and into her cage. It was *him*.

She felt his presence as clearly and coldly as she had last night at Rae's condo. Audrey focused all her energy, trying to draw him to her so she could picture his face or place their connection. She picked up the note, hoping for another flash. Usually touching something a subject had handled would give her an image. This man was different. He seemed to understand her gift and purposely blocked or avoided it.

"Where are you? Why won't you show yourself? What do you want?" In response to her frustrated questions another settling moan came from deep in the building's framework. She wanted to run as the sound blanketed her like an oppressive odor. The walls suddenly felt confining, the noises hostile. Her homey apartment had become uncomfortable and unsafe.

Audrey left the house in minutes, Cannonball in one hand and the note in the other. As she drove out of the complex, she tried to decide where to go. She wanted to see Rae, but the note was specific. Her hunch from last night had become more concrete. Rae had the right to know she was in danger. Shouldn't she have the chance to find out who was threatening them both? Audrey struggled with the decision, trying to separate her selfish needs from her responsibility. Maybe for once desire and need could serve the same master.

She timidly knocked on Rae's door, unsure of her reception. Rae valued stability, not the capriciousness that surrounded Audrey. Even she often found the fluctuations of emotion and energy in her life hard to handle. How could she expect someone as grounded as Rae to understand and accept her? Last night she'd been adamant that they not see each other, yet here she was less than twelve hours later.

When Rae opened the door, she didn't seem surprised. She took Cannonball, stuffed her inside her worn sweatshirt, and waved Audrey in.

"Coffee?"

"Please." Audrey looked at the newspaper scattered across the settee and the substantial coffee cup on the end table. It felt so welcoming. "Is it okay that I'm here? I know I said that—"

"I was hoping you'd come." Rae handed her a cup of coffee and they settled on the sofa. Cannonball peeked out of the collar of Rae's sweatshirt, then scampered onto Audrey's lap. "You're upset. What's happened?"

Audrey caught her breath. Rae's eyes never left hers, which distracted her. "I'm not used to this...someone reading me for a change."

"Then I'm right?"

Audrey nodded.

"It's nice to know my intuition still works. It can seem invasive or intimate, depending on who's doing it, don't you think?"

She'd never thought of her gift in that context, but it certainly made sense. Maybe Rae understood more than she gave her credit for. Audrey's insides warmed and for the first time she wanted to tell Rae everything. "I got a note this morning in my newspaper, actually a threat."

Rae subtly shifted into cop mode. "Did you bring it?"

Audrey produced the sheet of paper, and Rae carefully unfolded it, using only her fingernails. "Your instincts were partially right."

"How do you mean?"

"This isn't a warning to you and a threat to me. Someone's threatening both of us. I'll have this checked for prints, but I won't hold my breath. Any idea who left it?"

"No, not really."

Rae moved closer and took her hands. "Please, Audrey. You can trust me."

Audrey didn't know how to say what she needed to. "It's not about that." She paused, organizing her words. "Someone assaulted me a year ago, before I came to work for the mayor. I didn't report it. I didn't tell anyone, and I have no idea who did it."

Finally someone besides Yasi knew about the attack. She felt as if a third person was giving the account, a reporter broadcasting the latest entry on the police blotter. She watched, waiting for Rae's reaction, expecting disapproval.

Rae seemed to be trying to put pieces together. "I'm so sorry. It must've been awful to go through that alone." She stroked the back of Audrey's hands with her thumbs, but asked no cop-like questions, just the perfect amount of encouragement for her to continue.

"He cut me…not badly."

Rae paled. When she spoke her voice was barely audible. "You never reported it?"

"No, I left the area. I imagined he was everywhere, and I couldn't remember."

"Do you remember now?" Audrey shook her head. "Amnesia?"

"I think I've purposely blocked it. When images resurface, I push them back down. I've done that so long, I probably couldn't recall if I wanted to…and I don't."

"My God, how we've failed you." Rae's eyes filled with tears.

"Who?"

"All of us—your friends, the police, the system, society. If you didn't feel comfortable sharing the pain of something so awful then obviously we all failed. No wonder you haven't been able to open up about this latest incident."

Compassion and a strong undercurrent of sadness radiated from Rae. She hadn't understood until now that Rae would take personal responsibility.

Audrey placed CB on the floor and hugged Rae. "It's not your fault. I chose to go it alone, but thank you for caring. It means a lot."

Rae slowly pulled away, eyes full of questions. "And your… gift? You never got any information, hits, leads, whatever you call it, about your attacker?"

Audrey shook her head. "And it's so frustrating. It's like a therapist trying to handle her own emotional issues—it's not as easy as dealing with someone else's."

"When it happened…nothing either? I hate to bring up bad memories. I'm trying to understand how it works."

"That's the strange part. During the assault, I was blindfolded. I tried to focus on him, to get some kind of reading, but it was like staring into a black hole, darkness and—"

"What?"

Audrey felt a stun gun had zapped her again. Her system hummed and she reviewed a series of memories like flash cards in a whirlwind. "Oh my God. Oh. My. God."

"Audrey, what is it? You look terrified."

"All I could read about him was darkness and white noise." Audrey's stomach lurched. She thought she might be sick as another recollection slid into place. "The guy at the community center—again, nondescript noise—when it happened and later at the press conference. He was there, I'm certain of it."

The surprise was evident on Rae's face. "Are you saying the same person attacked you both times?"

Audrey didn't want to believe in coincidence. The thought that the two events were remotely related, much less committed by the same person, gave her chills. She'd inexplicably pursued her recent attacker more than a normal victim would.

"Is that why you insisted on finding the stun-gun guy yourself?"

"These bits are surfacing for the first time. I can't jump to conclusions. Right now they're only flashes, maybe of absolutely no use. That's how this gift works."

"Have you encountered anybody like this before, a void-and-white-noise person?"

"Not that I remember. Obviously I've been trying to protect myself and—" She stopped, suddenly aware of what she was about to say…*and possibly one of my closest friends.*

Rae pulled back. "And what? Were you protecting someone else?"

She'd come too far not to trust Rae with everything. "It crossed my mind that it might've been someone I knew. But I would've sensed that at some point." She felt good, but also a bit disloyal purging the conflicting thoughts that had plagued her for over a year. It pained her to admit she'd actually considered one of her cirque family as a suspect in the initial attack.

"How can you be sure if no one ever investigated?"

"I just know."

"You're that certain of your abilities?"

Audrey considered her answer carefully. Until recently she'd have bet her life on her instincts. When she met Rae, things changed. She could discern Rae's moods, but the tremendous physical attraction between them distorted deeper readings. Perhaps the intense emotional response to her attacks also affected her psychic ability. Why hadn't she picked up anything from the assailant in either case? It was easy to understand how the betrayal of Rae's partner had shaken her confidence. Audrey hoped she sounded more convincing than she felt. "Yes."

"Then I believe you."

Rae's sincerity rushed straight to her heart. "Thank you." She relaxed against Rae and savored the sweet freedom. This felt right.

Audrey placed her ear to Rae's chest and listened to her heart's steady thump. Rae would be as true and devoted as it was, once she committed to something or someone. Audrey slid her hand up Rae's arm, and her heartbeat quickened.

She wanted to share one more truth with Rae before she lost her nerve. It was vital if they were to move forward. "I've only been with one woman in my life. Actually a girl, right after college. We had no idea what we were doing."

Their nervousness had prohibited a real connection. She'd been amazed when they actually kissed, which happened only twice. Audrey had craved more since then but hadn't met anyone who attracted her strongly enough. For her, intimacy was all or nothing. She sensed the same need in Rae.

Rae's arms tightened around her and her voice held a hint of a smile. "And you're telling me this because?"

Audrey tilted her head and looked into Rae's sexy eyes. She remembered their first kiss and tried not to look at her lips. "Because I'd like to be with you, and I'm terrified. I've never felt this way before."

"You mean terrified?"

"No. I mean yes, and also excited, physically turned on to the point of distraction. It's new to me. When I'm around you, my psychic compass goes haywire and my hormones are all over the place."

"Don't worry. I'll take care of you."

Audrey believed Rae and for the first time in her life felt physically safe and totally defenseless. All her secrets were out, and Rae hadn't judged or rejected her. She'd exposed herself emotionally, but could she be as brave about her sexual needs? Her instincts told her she could trust Rae completely. "Can we go to bed?"

"Now?" The surprise in Rae's voice was apparent. Maybe she should've taken it slower. Her lack of experience would've shocked anyone with a normal history.

Audrey pulled away from Rae's embrace. "Sorry, I'm being too forward."

Rae stood and offered her hand. "Not at all. I like a woman who asks for what she wants." She looked at Cannonball, asleep on the carpet beside the sofa. "Will she be all right?"

"Looks fine to me."

"Maybe we should leave her something familiar in case she wakes up." Rae grabbed the tail of Audrey's sweatshirt, waited for the okay, and shucked it over her head. She dropped it on the floor next to the sleeping kitten. "There, that should do nicely." She reached for the waistband of her baggy sweats, but Audrey stopped her.

"I think that's enough."

"Not nearly." Rae guided Audrey into her bedroom and onto the side of the bed. "Now…can I take them off now?"

"You first."

Completely at ease, Rae removed her clothing one piece at a time in a slow burlesque that teased Audrey with each motion. She slid her arms out of her sweatshirt, then lifted it inch by inch over her head, revealing an expanse of ivory skin that Audrey ached to touch. Her small breasts were free, and the darker nipples puckered as if Audrey's gaze were a caress. Rae skimmed her sweatpants down over slender thighs and kicked them away. The triangle of auburn hair between her legs glowed in a patch of sunlight like a slow-burning ember. Rae stood nude in front of her.

Audrey had fantasized seeing a fully developed woman completely undressed, imagined what she'd look like, wondered about the similarities in their bodies. She'd only groped the slight curves of a teenager through clothing, never actually seen her lover naked. Now she stared at Rae, appreciating the distinct and subtle attributes of a woman.

Rae was tall and lean, her almost-translucent skin following the cut of feminine muscles. Her squared shoulders were strong and the curve of her hips slight yet seductive. The swell of her breasts, the taper of her waist, and the slight bulge above her pubic mound screamed *woman*. Audrey felt embarrassed as the moments passed while she continued to stare.

"You are so gorgeous, Rae. May I touch you?" The self-assured woman in front of her shifted from side to side and her ivory skin flushed. "Did I say something wrong?"

"I'm not used to somebody asking before they touch me." Rae stepped closer. "You can do anything you want."

Audrey's hand shook with excitement and years of anticipation as she stroked the side of her face, watching Rae's eyes spark with passion. Rae's skin was hot against her palm and the feeling coursed through her, welcoming and right. Sliding her hand down the middle of Rae's chest, she covered the beating pulse and savored the feel beneath her fingers. The beat accelerated and the tempo became her own. Her body ached with the fullness and newness of sensation. She never imagined a simple touch could be so intimate yet so full of vitality and desire.

"This is so…I can't find the words." Audrey gently stroked Rae's breasts and licked each nipple, watching them pucker from her efforts. She cupped a breast, sucked it into her mouth, and kneaded the malleable flesh with her tongue. Rae's moans of enjoyment made her wet, and she wanted more than life to please this woman. She prayed her lack of experience wouldn't disappoint Rae.

Audrey kissed Rae's taut abdomen and rested her cheek against its smooth surface. This was how a woman's body should look and feel—an exquisite, unaltered, welcoming path. She raked her fingers through the short patch of hair between Rae's legs, rewarded with a sharp intake of breath and the scent of arousal. She wrapped her arms around Rae's waist and hugged her tight, unwilling to let go and unsure what to do when she did.

"I can't stand much longer if you keep touching me," Rae said.

Audrey reluctantly released Rae and looked around the cozy room filled with morning light. She suddenly felt terribly shy, inexperienced, and exposed. Her full breasts bulged from the skimpy lace bra and her nipples dimpled with excitement. Then she remembered the final skeleton in her closet, the one that hadn't seemed at all important until this moment. It lay hidden beneath two layers of clothing and a film of self-consciousness.

She couldn't tell Rae, afraid of rejection. This secret seemed even more personal than the others, more damning. It broadcast a failure of autonomy, of her very character. How did you come to grips with the inability to protect the soul's sacred temple? Audrey hadn't yet. "Would you mind closing the curtains?"

"I'll do better than that." Rae lowered a blackout blind over the window and pulled the curtains. The room was almost completely dark. "I want you to be comfortable."

"Then kiss me."

Rae knelt in front of where Audrey sat on the bed and gently separated Audrey's knees with her hands. Her skin was hot as she slid between Audrey's legs and brought them closer. Rae's warm breath signaled their proximity seconds before their lips met.

Audrey drank in the cushiony softness as Rae traced her lips with the tip of her tongue. Heat swept through her and pooled between her legs. Teenage kissing had been all about animalistic desires, not this intimate physical urging. She opened to take Rae in, sliding and stroking her tongue against Rae's, savoring the promise of it.

Rae released the clasp of Audrey's bra and cupped her breasts in her palms. Audrey concentrated on the touch. She wanted to isolate and memorize the coarse feel of Rae's thumb as she dragged it across her nipple. The sensation spread from the point of contact, twirled to the base of her breast, and spiraled down her abdomen. Several hands seemed to massage and manipulate her at once. She moaned and gasped for breath, the intensity almost unbearable.

When Rae slid her fingers into the waistband of Audrey's sweats and inched them down, she didn't object. She hoped it was dark enough. Audrey felt only need, deep and demanding. Skin smoothed against skin, cool at first, then hot and damp as Rae eased her back onto the bed and settled on top of her. Their next kiss liquefied her insides. Unable to capture a full breath, Audrey pulled back. She wanted the visual of Rae Butler wedged between *her* legs, head resting between *her* breasts, face flushed with desire, desire for *her*.

Audrey felt Rae's slick arousal against her leg as she shifted sideways and rubbed herself along her length. She wanted to dip her fingers into the depths of her, but was too mesmerized by Rae's hands on her flesh. Rae teased Audrey's breasts, flicked her nipples playfully, and gently caressed her sides before reaching lower. Rae feathered light touches around Audrey's thighs, darted closer to her sex, swept across her stomach, then suddenly stopped.

Chapter Thirteen

"Oh my God," Rae whispered.

She had slid her fingers over the irregular raised scar on Audrey's abdomen and had spoken without realizing it.

Audrey immediately interpreted her words as rejection. Sliding out of her embrace, she drew her knees to her chest like a frightened child. Even in the dim light of the room, Rae could see the pained expression on her face.

"It's hideous," Audrey said. "The doctor wasn't exactly a reconstructive surgeon. I paid him for his silence, not his expertise. It's a bit like a jigsaw puzzle, isn't it?"

"Please don't do that." Audrey's attempt at humor was more telling than her tormented body language.

"Do what?"

"Try to make light of this. Audrey, I—"

"You don't have to explain, and you certainly don't have to touch me again."

Rae scooted gently toward her. "I'm sorry. I didn't expect it." She raked her fingers through Audrey's hair and looked her in the eye. "I very much want to touch you again. You're a beautiful woman and nothing he did can change that. If anything, I want you more. Please believe me."

People responded to traumatic events differently. They even remembered things inconsistently from one conversation to the next. Rae had seen everything from hysterical laughter to complete emotional meltdowns. Audrey had obviously chosen to deny and suppress the details of her assault. The scarring most likely constantly reminded her of what she perceived as personal failure, an inability to protect herself. For someone as independent as Audrey, that would cut as deeply as the wound.

"Will you hold me for a minute?"

The despair in her tone ripped at Rae's heart. She wished she'd been there for Audrey during those awful times. Apparently no one had been, or Audrey hadn't allowed anyone in.

While Audrey rested against her chest in silence, Rae pieced together the details of her initial attack, becoming increasingly more uncomfortable. Should she share her suspicions about a connection in the cases? She cared too much to cause Audrey any more pain. She hugged Audrey tighter against her chest, trying to shelter her from the unknown.

"I can't breathe." Audrey placed her hand between Rae's breasts and stretched back to look her in the eyes. "Are you sure you're okay with this…?" She glanced down at her body. "I don't want you here because of some sense of misplaced duty or pity."

"Oh, Audrey, the last thing I feel for you is pity. You're the most resilient, amazing woman I've ever met, not to mention sexy, desirable, gorgeous, hot—"

"Enough with the flattery. Kiss me before I change my mind."

Rae claimed Audrey's lips and again intense feelings flooded her system. She arched to meet Audrey's stroking hands, hungry for her touch. Its delicacy reminded Rae of her confession, of her inexperience.

She slid down on the bed, taking Audrey with her until they lay facing each other. "Relax. You don't have to do anything." Audrey's eyes shone with gratitude and desire that spoke to Rae's deepest need. She'd been many things to women in bed, but never a teacher. The role excited her more than she could've imagined. Few people received the gift of innocence and virtue in an age of sexual freedom. Audrey hadn't given her trust easily; she'd exhibited true courage and Rae wouldn't take it lightly.

"If I do anything you don't like, tell me." She cupped Audrey's face and encircled it with light kisses, savoring her delicate scent. Audrey's skin warmed as Rae painted a path with her lips across her forehead from eyelids and high cheekbones to the tip of her chin, over and over. Their bodies touched only there, and the tension built inside Rae with each gentle kiss.

When she finally allowed herself to taste Audrey's lips again, she feared she'd lose control. Audrey sucked hungrily on her tongue, and with each pull Rae felt the tender tug at the base of her clit. She clamped her legs together. Surrender would be so easy, but she wanted to be fully present and totally aroused as she satisfied Audrey. She refused to allow her own pleasure before Audrey's.

More than anything, Rae wanted Audrey to feel beautiful, desirable, and special. She wanted her to know the hunger she evoked, the pure sexual need. Even with all her experience, Rae felt incapable of proving to a novice the depth of her feelings. Simple words and the basic act of lovemaking seemed indelicate for a person as sensitive as Audrey. The act itself was what it was. She had to infuse it with emotion and bring it to life.

She slid her hands over Audrey's breasts, down her sides, and up her legs, etching the peaks and dips into her tactile memory. When she touched Audrey's abdomen, she paused and raised her head to reassure her. She then pressed her lips to the scarred tissue and kissed every inch with all the reverence she could impart. With each kiss she exorcised the evil intent that caused the horrendous injury. She licked and kissed the area until the muscles relaxed and Audrey moaned with pleasure.

"Thank you." Audrey spoke just loud enough to be heard. "I never thought anyone would want to touch me."

When Rae looked up, Audrey's eyes shone with tears. She inched up, wrapped her arms and legs around her, and cradled her into the protective cocoon of her body. "You're a gorgeous woman, inside and out, and no one can ever take that from you."

Audrey snuggled deeper into her embrace and Rae sensed the need for unconditional solace. As Rae held her, Audrey alternated between quiet sobbing and the gentle rocking. Rae occasionally kissed the top of Audrey's head and whispered reassurances, thinking only of giving Audrey what she needed. Everything else was irrelevant as she allowed Audrey to set the tone and pace of their time together.

When she relaxed against Rae's body and sought a kiss, Rae could barely breathe. The smoldering desire that their intimacy had stoked flared to full flame. Her body ached and her clit throbbed. She thrust her pelvis forward in an almost involuntarily motion and quickly jerked back. "I'm sorry. I didn't mean to—"

"Don't apologize. Come here," Audrey said as she shifted her weight and tucked Rae's leg between her own.

"Are you sure you're ready?" Even as she asked the question, Rae slid her center along the strong muscle of Audrey's thigh.

"Totally." Audrey's gentle rocking of earlier changed into a steady, demanding rhythm. "I want you, now."

Audrey guided Rae's mouth to her breasts and gasped aloud when she claimed them. Her flesh was so soft and pliable, her nipples a juxtaposition of rigid protrusion. Rae massaged the soft tissue and sucked the pebbled tips as their pelvises found each other again and again. She wanted to make love to Audrey leisurely the first time but was losing control.

"Wait. I wanted to go slowly."

"Can't wait…this time." Audrey pressed her breasts against Rae's and lowered her hand between Rae's legs, penetrating her with a slow, firm stroke. "You feel so good. Come for me, Rae. I want to feel you in my hand."

Audrey's urging and the unrelenting pace of her humping chiseled at Rae's resistance. She wouldn't last much longer yet she was determined to satisfy Audrey first. Rae wedged her hand between them and found Audrey's rigid clit. Sliding her fingers along the sides, she milked it into a tighter bundle of nerves, then slowly stroked it with the pad of her thumb until Audrey trembled.

"Oh, yes. More," Audrey pleaded, and Rae complied. "Again." Audrey pumped against Rae's hand until her entire body stiffened and her clitoris softened. "Oh my God!"

Audrey's cry shredded the last of Rae's self-control. She rubbed herself with one long, finishing stroke along Audrey's thigh and emptied into her hand. Tremors wracked her body as she jerked and released until she was sated and exhausted.

Rae rolled onto her back, taking Audrey with her. She'd never felt so amazingly and totally satisfied…and by a sexual novice. What Audrey lacked in experience she made up for in enthusiasm. She couldn't fake responses like those. Audrey's eagerness and willingness to open herself completely turned Rae on. She might not survive a more experienced Audrey Everhart, but she was willing to try.

Audrey collapsed against Rae's chest, unable to control the spasms still rumbling through her. "Jeez…that was…"

"You like?" Rae asked.

"Nope, I love." Audrey felt physically fatigued yet emotionally and sexually energized. When she'd blurted earlier that she wanted to be with Rae, she had no idea how much she wanted it. All her primal energy had been locked down until Rae touched her.

Rae's touch, and also her sensitivity, had aroused something wild inside her. "More?" She placed her hands on the pillow beside Rae's head and lifted her upper body, careful to maintain contact at the aching point between her legs.

When Rae started to answer, her cell phone rang, followed shortly by the muffled sound of Audrey's buried underneath her sweatpants. She found it and flipped it open. "Hello?"

"Sanjana." Sam's deeply accented voice commanded Audrey's immediate attention.

"What is it, Sam?" As she waited for him to deliver the bad news, she could tell by Rae's expression that her news was also not good. She'd already started getting dressed.

"It's Yasi. Come to the Kramer hospital, quick."

"What happened?"

"Come quick."

The line went dead and Audrey collapsed onto the foot of the bed, grabbing her clothes as she fell. "Oh, God, no."

Rae was dressed and standing beside her. "I'll drive. And I've already put in a request for a protective detail for you."

Audrey obviously wasn't thinking clearly. Yasi was in the hospital but Rae was talking about protection for *her*. "I don't understand."

"We'll talk later. Let's get you to your friend."

❖

She had surely been corrupted. Even after his warning, she disobeyed him. Arya followed her once again to the cop's residence. Detective Butler was an excellent investigator and highly revered member of the police force. Too bad. Arya appreciated competence and loyalty, but she'd stepped over the line. No cop, especially a woman, could invade his turf.

Standing outside the broken window at Butler's condo, he watched the cop put her hands all over his beloved. Perhaps she was coerced, tricked in some way to take part in this vile exhibit of depravity. She offered no resistance as Butler removed her shirt and slid her filthy hands lower. Irritation gave way to anger, then rage. *And she let it happen.*

How could he have been so wrong about her? Their initial encounter had been his first, pure and promising. She was his hope and his salvation. He hadn't needed to verbalize his plans. She could read his thoughts. Their connection had been deeper than words and beyond the comprehension of others. Now it seemed she had lost faith, abandoned him, and turned to another—to a *woman.* Her betrayal was the most humiliating and disrespectful insult. No other man was worthy of her, and certainly no woman.

The images in front of Arya glowed in a red haze and his vision momentarily blurred as the two women disappeared into the bedroom. His mounting fury jeopardized logical, precise thinking and he struggled to contain it. Fire burned in his lower body, arousing desires he could not yet satisfy. He clutched himself, squeezed, and immediately doubled over as the pain exploded. He bit his tongue until he tasted blood. Sweat drenched his body. Very soon someone would pay for this betrayal. While they writhed and groped in their perverted pleasure, someone she cared about would cry and beg in agony.

Hours later, secreted in the shadows, Arya waited patiently until the woman was alone and away from the streetlights. Her best friend would be the perfect target and would carry his message of disapproval back to her. She would acknowledge her horrible mistake and seek his forgiveness. Maybe he could still save her.

Arya smiled as he approached her from behind, the soaked handkerchief in one hand and his KA-BAR knife in the other. She squirmed in his powerful arms before going slack. He would receive no pleasure defiling her perfect body any more than he had with the others. The ritual was part of the process necessary to bring them back together. This particular act of retribution would have the bonus of taking place in Middleton, where it all began a year ago. He had indeed chosen well.

Chapter Fourteen

When Audrey walked into the stark hospital waiting area, her cirque family appeared to already be in mourning. Melvin and Tony huddled together holding hands in an uncustomary display of emotion. The girls' alabaster complexions were streaked with tears, and they paced in a symmetrical pattern around the room. Her dear friend Sam stared out the huge plate-glass window, still as an acacia on a breezeless African night. She ran to him first, in need of his courage and physical support. Her insides ached for them, and while her mind screamed for news of Yasi, her heart railed against it.

"How is she?" Audrey asked as the others gathered around.

"No one has spoken with us yet," Sam answered.

"What happened?"

Each member of the group looked at Sam, all of them either unwilling or unable to speak. "We do not know."

"How badly is she hurt?"

Sam's charcoal features twisted into a tortured mask, and when he tried to speak, only a choked cough emerged. He simply shook his head, unable to meet Audrey's stare.

"Where was she?" Audrey tried again to get some useful information.

"Near the venue in Middleton."

She felt as if she'd been sucker punched. Not *that* place. Though it was only a short drive from Kramer, Audrey associated its proximity to the distance in her memory. It felt light years away. Sam had no idea what had happened to her there, but he'd always been sensitive to her responses, overt and subtle. Their connection had made them an impressive performance act. She gave him her best attempt at a smile and started to ask another question.

Rae stepped forward, and Audrey read her impatience. Her cop face said the cryptic back-and-forth wasn't working. "Somebody tell her what's going on? How was she injured? Is it serious? Was she attacked or was it an accident?"

Sam was obviously unsure if he should speak freely in front of Rae. He knew better than most the complications involved in sharing cirque matters with the outside world. Audrey nodded for him to continue. "We were meeting for a drink. She didn't come. Tony found her…later…in an alley near the stadium. She had been assaulted. This was the closest hospital."

As Audrey heard the similarities to her own assault, her queasiness increased.

"Did you call the police?" Rae asked.

Melvin responded, his tone adding another layer of disapproval to his words. "*We* didn't, but you're obviously here."

This isn't about you. Focus on Yasi. "Guys, please," Audrey said. "Rae is trying to help. What *do* we know?"

One by one her friends shook their heads and looked away. They had no idea what happened to Yasi. They'd found her, brought her here, and now they waited for news of her condition. Unlike Rae, they weren't trained to look for clues at the scene, to preserve evidence, or to think about an eventual arrest or prosecution. They were concerned only for Yasi's welfare.

"I have to see her." Audrey turned toward the nurses' station as a doctor rounded the corner and headed for them. "How is she? Can I go in?"

The gray-haired man scanned the gathering and settled on Audrey. "She has asked to see Audrey. Is that you?"

She nodded.

"You can go in, briefly. She is stable but very heavily sedated. Don't expect her to make sense."

"I'm a police officer. May I see her as well?"

"She is *sedated*. No questioning at this time. I'm sorry, Officer. You'll have to wait."

Audrey took Rae's hand. "She's with me. I promise she won't ask any questions. I need her." Audrey felt she might collapse without Rae's confidence and control. If she did fall apart when she saw Yasi, Rae would take care of both of them. She hadn't been that sure of anyone since…since Yasi. The thought elicited a fresh flood of emotions. "Please, Doctor."

"Be brief. Room 222."

Audrey looped her arm through Rae's as they walked toward Yasi's room. It was hard to believe that minutes ago they were lying exhausted after their first lovemaking session. Now they walked another path with potential to change their lives yet again.

Yasi had always been important to Audrey, and she'd hoped she would be to Rae as well. If they had a future, the two worlds she'd tried so desperately to keep separate would have to blend into one. She tried to imagine Rae in her cirque family and vice versa, but horrific scenes of her best friend in the clutches of a maniac cluttered her mind.

As they approached Yasi's room, Rae placed her hand in the small of Audrey's back and massaged small circles. "Are you ready for this?"

"I don't think anyone is ever ready for something like this." Audrey told herself no matter what she saw when she crossed the threshold, this person was still her best and dearest friend. She willed herself not to react as Rae pushed the door open and stepped aside.

Yasi looked like an angel with a halo of dark, flowing hair. Her usually fair complexion was milk-white, blending into the bedding that encased her like a cocoon. A sheet covered her to her neck and, except for the small tubes snaking underneath its edges, she might've been asleep in her own bed. Audrey saw no marks on her porcelain skin, which she found strangely comforting. She wasn't ready to know how her friend had been violated or to what extent. Even though Yasi would never be the same again, she still looked the same. Audrey bent down and kissed her forehead. "I'm here."

"No!" Yasi's eyes flew open and she screamed, "Get away." Audrey stumbled backward as Yasi flailed her arms in a self-protective sweep.

Rae steadied her from behind. "Let her get her bearings."

Audrey couldn't bear the terrified look in Yasi's eyes. She'd seen that expression in the mirror many times after waking from her own nightmares recently, accompanied by disorientation and total helplessness. Her heart ached as Yasi's movements slowed and her unfocused gaze scanned the room. When she spotted Audrey, she stopped completely. "Aud?" She squinted in Rae's direction. "Detective Butler?"

"Yes, darling, it's me…and Rae." Audrey returned to her bedside but hesitated to reach out again. "It'll be all right. I'm here now." Audrey wanted desperately to return normalcy to Yasi's world. She'd never seen anything except love in her friend's eyes. Tonight their sable depths burned with panic and questions.

"How did I get to the hospital?"

"The gang brought you in. Don't talk now, darling."

"Had to see you. Wanted you to know…I'm all right."

Her words filled Audrey's heart. Yasi always worried about her, even at a time like this. She placed her cheek against Yasi's and whispered in her ear, "I love you so much. Don't worry about me. Get better because we have things to discuss." She pulled back and winked at her friend before inclining her head slightly toward Rae.

"You devil." Yasi's attempt to smile turned into a wince. "Need to talk to her." Yasi shifted in bed and grimaced with pain. "Alone."

"Alone?" Audrey suddenly realized she wasn't sure why Rae was here beyond providing emotional support. When they left the condo she'd been too distracted to ask about Rae's phone call. Was she on duty? Had she been assigned to Yasi's case? Even so, Yasi wouldn't know that. So why did she want to talk with Rae and what couldn't she say in front of her? They didn't keep secrets from each other. Maybe she was concerned about the new turn of events between her and Rae. That could definitely wait until another time. "Yas, you don't need to do this now. There'll be time to grill her later."

"Have to talk to her now…before I sleep again."

Yasi was holding something back. Audrey's senses tingled, but she'd been too preoccupied with her physical condition to focus on her emotional one. "The doctor said you weren't to talk much or be questioned."

Yasi nodded. *"Please."*

"Okay, Yas. I'll go fill the others in. Don't tire yourself." Audrey gave Rae her best take-care-of-my-friend look and stepped out of the room.

Rae pulled the straight-back chair closer to Yasi's bed and sat down. She never got used to the haunted look in victims' eyes. It conjured up an empathic ache. Everyone expected her to have answers for an unexplainable event, needed reassurance they weren't to blame and guarantees that someone would be held accountable.

Rae's job frustrated her. When she arrived, the crime had been committed, the victim irreversibly altered, and the suspect was usually gone. She had to console, investigate, and apprehend. Sometimes she felt like an overpaid sanitation worker cleaning up after the fact, no chance to amend anything or solve the real problem. She was particularly disappointed this time because she'd met, liked, and hoped to know the victim better.

Yasi drifted between sleep and semiconsciousness, and Rae waited until she felt strong enough to begin. Yasi probably wouldn't be able to give her best answers at this point. As she flipped to a clean page in her notebook, she remembered the earlier phone call and jotted down the time and particulars she'd received.

A nurse in the ER had notified Kramer PD about the assault, and an astute dispatcher familiar with the Whisperer MO called Sergeant Sharp directly. The incident occurred in Middleton, technically the county sheriff's jurisdiction, but they often called on Kramer for assistance in major cases. Not So had sent Rae directly to the hospital for the interview and patrol officers to secure the scene until she arrived. He wasn't about to pass on this fresh opportunity for publicity. Yasi stirred and Rae closed the notepad.

"We don't have to do this now."

"You have to know." Yasi took a labored breath. "Can't tell Audrey." She obviously had to dredge every statement from deep in her soul. "He wanted her." She fell back against the pillow, tears streaming down her face. "Said she was *spoiled* now."

The room closed in around Rae, and she stared at Yasi as if she'd spoken in a foreign language. For the first time in her life she felt real fear—not the adrenaline-charged surge she experienced in dangerous situations. This malicious force burrowed into her private life, gnawing on her newfound connection to Audrey. A sensation of misfiring nerves crackled up her spine, but if she hoped to help, she had to focus and do her job.

Rae opened her mouth to speak. Nothing came out. She tried again. "Tell me."

"He said it was her fault, that she didn't listen. He whispered, this sick, spooky whispering. Then he cut me." She pulled back the covers and motioned to her abdomen. "It was the same man who hurt Audrey, wasn't it?" The effort clearly exhausted Yasi, but she seemed determined to continue. "You can *not* tell her. She doesn't remember what happened to her, and she will blame herself. Promise me."

Yasi's request reinforced Rae's earlier dilemma. She was in an impossible position: tell Audrey her suspicions about her attacker or remain silent and hope she didn't find out. If she told Audrey, it could jeopardize her mental stability, force her to confront a situation she wasn't ready for. If she didn't tell her, Audrey could be in physical danger. And the secret would put them at odds with each other.

Yasi insisted. "Promise me, Rae."

"I don't want to keep things from her. It's not how I operate."

"Only until you catch him."

"When she sees your injury, she'll know anyway. You can't hide that from her."

"I can try. Please…until you're closer to finding him."

"The others—they've seen. They brought you in." Rae believed in the old saying that three people could keep a secret only if two of them were dead. Eight was impossible and an intentional conspiracy.

"Talk to them. Tell them I need their help. They'll cooperate."

Yasi's bandages extended below her breasts to her lower abdomen. She could keep the nature of her injury from Audrey for a while, but one of the others would slip up. The whole cover-up was a disaster waiting to happen. And Rae would be on the clock to arrest a suspect she hadn't even identified yet. The longer it took the more danger Audrey was in and the longer she'd have to keep the truth from her. If she agreed, she'd not only need a lot of help, but divine intervention as well. "Can you tell me *anything* about this guy? We've got nothing so far."

Yasi suddenly seemed even more damaged. She shook her head as fresh tears streaked her cheeks. "He drugged me, something over my mouth. I was blindfolded. It was horrible."

Rae's hopes sank as she listened to the MO she could've recited from memory.

Yasi's eyelids drooped. "Anything else?"

"Kept whispering that I was a traitor over and over. He knows—"

Yasi's room door burst open and the doctor entered. "All right, that's enough. I told you no questions. Out, now."

"Could I ask one favor, please, Doctor?"

"As long as you don't continue questioning my patient. She needs rest." They both looked at Yasi, who had already fallen asleep. He nodded at her to emphasize his point.

"Would you have the lab run tests on her blood? I'm looking for some type of anesthetic, anything that could temporarily incapacitate."

The doctor scratched his head as if the gesture were a side effect of deep thought. "That's a pretty broad request. Can you be more specific?"

Rae scrolled through the case notes she'd committed to memory. "It has a pleasant, even a sweet smell. It will also be short-lived in the system. Our tests only a day after the assault didn't show anything unusual."

"Do you know how it's administered?"

"By something placed over the nose and mouth, and it irritates the eyes and skin."

"Inhalation. Hmm, my first guess, and it's only a guess, would be chloroform. It's relatively easy to use, leaves no marks, and disappears quickly. Someone would have to know what they were doing because it can be lethal." His voice held the slightest hint of admiration. "I might not be able to help you."

"Why's that?"

"If it is chloroform, it may already have been assimilated into the system. It's a breakdown product of other chemicals in the body, so a low concentration wouldn't necessarily indicate an intentional introduction. We'd need a high reading." He turned toward the door. "We better get busy. We're wasting time."

As they walked out together, Rae said, "Thank you, Doctor."

"Thank you for what?" Audrey asked as she approached from the waiting area.

"Taking such good care of our friend." Rae knew her answer sounded weak.

"Doctor, may I sit with her tonight if I promise not to talk?" Audrey asked.

The doctor looked at Rae and must've read something in her face. "No, I think not. You can look in on her, then come back tomorrow when she's had a good night's sleep. She'll be here for at least another day." Before Audrey could object, he hurried down the hall.

Rae sighed with relief. She didn't need Audrey to have a psychic episode with Yasi and discover their secret. She looked into Audrey's eyes and saw pain and questions she couldn't answer. As much as she wanted to comfort and reassure her, Rae had to talk to the others and then go to the scene. She sucked at hiding the truth.

"Audrey, I'm so sorry. I have to go."

"I don't understand. Are you working Yasi's case? Why would you be assigned an assault? Special Victims Unit handles sexually oriented crimes. Was she—?"

Audrey couldn't say *raped* aloud and Rae understood why. The word carried such connotations that its introduction changed the entire tenor of a conversation. "No, Audrey, I swear, it's nothing like that. I have to go to the scene. We'll talk later."

"That's what you said when we left the condo. I need you to be honest with me."

"Later." She kissed Audrey on the cheek and reluctantly pulled away, her heart aching. They'd made love for the first time, and she wanted desperately to hold her again. She couldn't bear to have Audrey think she didn't matter or she was just a one-night stand.

"Where will you be?" If she knew Audrey's whereabouts and that she wouldn't be alone until the guard detail arrived, at least she'd be able to concentrate on work.

"I guess I'll take everybody to my place. We won't sleep anyway. Will you come by?"

"As soon as I can." She made eye contact with Audrey and held her gaze. "I care about you, a lot." She hugged Audrey again, then sprinted down the hall to find her cirque friends.

Rae found them still in the waiting area, chatting quietly. As she approached, they stopped but no one acknowledged her—an outsider and a cop. Audrey had already told them about Yasi's condition so she didn't have anything new. She'd had enough experience with tight-knit groups and closed societies to know the signs. But she needed their help and not only as a cop.

"I think she'll be all right. She's resting now." She waited for someone to respond. Sam made eye contact. From what she'd seen, Yasi was their informal leader, but in her absence, Sam had assumed the role. She addressed him directly. "Yasi and Audrey need your help—actually *our* help." Suddenly she had their full attention.

Rae couldn't tell them about Audrey's assault because she would violate personal and professional confidences. The other option was a half-truth that she had difficulty verbalizing.

"The man who assaulted Yasi implied that he was going after Audrey next. Yasi has asked that all of us keep this information from Audrey for the time being." Rae could see the conflict on their faces. She tried again to win them over.

"Yasi is afraid Audrey will blame herself, then try to go after this guy alone. She can apparently be pretty stubborn and independent." Each person nodded in acknowledgment and looked to Sam for guidance. She apologetically asked for their silence until she could make headway in the investigation. One by one they consented.

She addressed Tony next. "Did you see anything that might be helpful when you found Yasi?" He shook his head. "Were you alone? Where had you come from?"

Rae didn't hear Audrey come up behind her. "What do you think you're doing?"

When she turned, Audrey stood with her hands on her hips, anger sparking in her eyes. "I'm—"

"Don't bother. You're obviously interrogating my friends because they *have* to be involved in this, right?"

"That's not what—"

"Sure it is. You're a cop first and a human being later. And who better than a bunch of transient circus people to lay the blame on. Isn't that the way you people think?"

"You people?" The sharp-edged comment cut deeply, especially after what they'd shared earlier. Rae wanted to defend herself but Audrey was too emotionally distraught to hear her right now. She needed the security this group provided much more than she needed to trust Rae. "I was only doing my job. Sorry." She turned away, the sudden distance between them gutting her.

This wasn't the time to appeal to reason or remind Audrey that *she* had expressed doubts about her friends after the first assault. Rae would have someone check out Audrey's cirque friends, their backgrounds and locations during the previous attacks. Audrey would defend her adopted family no matter what, particularly since one of their own had been attacked. She had shifted from intimacy to suspicion, and though Rae understood the delicate nature of trust, Audrey's attitude still hurt.

On her way out, she stopped by the nurses' station, praying one of the more-experienced nurses was on duty. A seasoned medical professional often took pictures of a victim's injuries before the doctors performed their magic. She got lucky tonight because the head ER nurse was an acquaintance. After a brief exchange, she pulled an envelope from under the counter and handed it to Rae. As she headed toward the parking lot, Rae hoped the pictures would give her a clue. All she had was more questions and pressure to produce answers.

Yasi had delivered a threat from a deranged man aimed at the woman Rae cared about. Because this inquiry had become even more personal, she should relinquish the case. Not happening. She wouldn't trust anyone else with Audrey, Yasi, or the other Whisperer victims.

They weren't victims in some routine case. A psychopath had torn their lives apart for his perverse enjoyment, and she was determined to find him. As she made the short drive to Middleton, she wondered about Yasi's comment, "He knows." It could be a vital piece of information. She added it to the growing list of things *she* didn't know.

The next four hours Rae sifted through every piece of debris, garbage, food, and feces lining the narrow alleyway where Yasi had been found. The local fire department had erected lights to illuminate the site while she worked, and Rae processed the scene completely alone. If she found anything, she called the crime analyst forward to collect it. As she gathered each item, she assessed its evidentiary value. The Whisperer had never made a mistake, never left hair, fibers, bodily fluids, or fingerprints at the scene. But she had to follow procedures and explore every possibility.

When she finally reached the end of the alley and stretched her aching back, the sun was cresting the horizon. Rae took the beautiful red-sky dawn as an omen of better things to come. She motioned for the crew to clear the scene and thanked them for their patience as she walked to her vehicle. One of the CSIs handed her a cup of hot coffee, and she took several sips before reaching for the envelope she'd collected at the hospital. She instinctively knew the contents wouldn't improve her mood, but she had to look.

The first image of Yasi's gray, blood-encrusted body made her stomach lurch. How close had Yasi and the others come to being a corpse? She fought the rage that surfaced. If she gave in to it, she'd be professionally useless. She sipped her coffee and watched the sunrise for a moment, appreciating the wonder of life juxtaposed with the specter of death. The next photograph illustrated the suspect's trademark slashing. Random zigzag cuts sliced Yasi's tender flesh across the width of her abdomen with no apparent pattern or logic. How could someone capable of this type of damage possess logic, as Barry had suggested? Rae slid the photos back into the envelope and started the car. She wanted to get to the hospital this morning before anyone else. If she arrived first, she might get an official statement from Yasi and catch an hour of sleep before she faced Audrey again.

The facts of the Whisperer case surfaced in her mind and blurred with the snippets of recollection Audrey had provided. The scar added a final, undeniable element.

Rae didn't want to believe any of it. If the Whisperer had assaulted Audrey, why had he returned to do so a second time, why had he waited a year, and how had he failed? Audrey had been alone at the community center, an easy target. She cautioned herself about jumping to conclusions. Audrey's inability to read either of her assailants didn't mean they were the same person. She needed real evidence.

If the Whisperer attacked Audrey both times, he was obviously fixated on her. And if Rae had the timing worked out properly, Audrey would've been his first victim, not Carol Flynn, as she initially thought. That could account for the threatening note. He wouldn't want Audrey talking to the police or even socializing with anyone too often. He would see the object of his attention as his exclusive property. The scenario spinning into an active theory in Rae's head disturbed her.

Audrey had already considered that the same person had attacked her both times. Could she handle any more? Maybe this one little detail didn't have to come out yet. If Rae stated that Audrey might be a victim of the Whisperer, the shock could be traumatic. Rae was no good at psychology, but telling Audrey about her suspicions could present more problems.

Audrey might embark on another personal investigation, and the Whisperer wasn't the kind of case for a civilian to poke around in. Even without definite proof, Rae already wanted police protection for Audrey but wasn't sure she could get approval because of financial constraints. If she could, it would be more difficult without Audrey's knowledge or cooperation.

Rae still wasn't sure what she'd say the next time she saw Audrey—truth or consequences?

Chapter Fifteen

When Rae walked into Yasi's room, a nurse was re-dressing her injuries and the strong smell of antiseptic and blood prickled her nostrils. "Sorry, I'll come back later."

"Don't go, Detective," Yasi said. "You probably need to see this anyway."

Rae stared at Yasi's abdomen as the images in her head came to life. She preferred the matte-finish photos; they didn't convey the pain as clearly as a live victim, and she could slightly detach. In some areas where the knife had cut more deeply, careful stitches pulled the wound together, in others Steri-Strips traversed the injury like railroad ties beneath rails. Yasi would never look at her body the same way again. The once-smooth, unblemished flesh would never casually welcome a lover's touch. She thought about the self-consciousness Audrey's injury caused her and wished she could spare Yasi the same fate.

"All done. Ring if you need anything, dear." The nurse added the final touches to the bandage and left.

Yasi took Rae's hand. "It's all right. Everything is still pretty numb right now, which is probably a good thing. You need to toughen up or learn to hide your feelings better. Your eyes give you away."

Rae felt her skin flush. "Sorry, I should be comforting you, not the other way around. How are you feeling?"

"Numb below the waist and a bit disoriented above. It's hard to wrap my head around what happened." Yasi stared at Rae for several seconds, taking in every detail of her face. "Did you sleep at all last night?"

"Yasi—"

"I know. You're uncomfortable and we need to get back to business, right?"

"Is all your cirque family psychic or just you and Audrey?"

"I'm glad she told you. Audrey is the only one with that particular gift, but we all learn to read people. It's part of our professional and personal survival, sort of like cops."

Rae acknowledged Yasi's astute observations with a simple nod. She understood why Audrey loved her. She was brave, caring, and selfless in the face of tremendous personal adversity. Her courage would be vital in the days and weeks ahead. As Rae mentally prepared her list of questions, she was glad Yasi seemed more alert and focused. Her friends would be here soon and she'd need all her faculties to distract Audrey.

"I assume our little secret is safe?" Yasi asked.

"For the moment. The others agreed to help." The reason she was avoiding Audrey tweaked her again and she brushed it aside. "Do you feel like giving me an official statement?"

The easy smile that brightened Yasi's face disappeared. She clasped her hands together as if drawing strength from the joining. "I was walking from the venue at Middleton to a small bar in town to meet the group for a drink. I cut through an alley—stupid, I know. As I turned onto the main street someone grabbed me from behind. He put a cloth over my mouth. It smelled nice, sort of sweet. I struggled, but the next thing I knew I was restrained, gagged, and blindfolded, lying on cold plastic."

"Did you detect any taste to the substance on the cloth?"

She shook her head. "It burned my eyes and skin for a few seconds before I passed out."

"What did your bindings feel like?"

"Definitely soft, some type of rope, very tightly bound around my hands and feet. The blindfold didn't let in any light at all. The plastic under me felt thin, not substantial, maybe like the plastic used to wrap clothes at the dry cleaners."

Carol Flynn had mentioned thin plastic, but Yasi's impression gave her a possible lead. "And the space you were in, anything about that?"

"It was definitely small, tinny sounding. When he whispered, I heard a slight echo. If I had to guess, I'd say we were in a van or vehicle of some sort. I felt movement underneath as he—cut me—like the rocking of a car."

Rae jotted notes as Yasi spoke. No one had mentioned a vehicle, another detail she could follow up. "Tell me what he said to you, how he spoke, in as much detail as you remember."

"He whispered, always this urgent whispering, spooky. He's educated, though, speaking in grammatically correct phrases. And I detected a hint of an accent that he used at will. I couldn't tell the specific region of origin. It sounded acquired, not native."

"How would you possibly know that?"

"I've spent my entire life in the cirque. We employ people from all over the world. I have a pretty good ear and I listen to how people talk. It's sort of a quirky pastime."

"Very nice skill to have, especially in this case." Yasi was an excellent witness. Rae hoped one of these little fragments would lead to a suspect.

"Some of the phrases he used…they seemed familiar. Spoiled. Cleansed. Those aren't the kind of words you hear every day in this part of the world. They're reminiscent of my childhood in Morocco—sort of that region."

Rae felt a momentary pang of guilt and irritation. Why hadn't she picked up on that before? She thought back to the other victims' statements. The Whisperer had spoken only one word to them over and over again, never sentences or phrases. It hadn't been enough. "Go on."

"He called me a traitor several times. Each time, he slashed my abdomen again. I passed out a couple of times, but he revived me with cold water and told me to pay attention." Yasi stopped and closed her eyes for several minutes as tears trickled past her temples into her hair.

"We can finish some other time if you want," Rae offered. "I know this is difficult."

"I remember something else. When he whispered in my ear, I felt fabric against my skin. When he touched me, he was definitely wearing gloves, rubber gloves."

Rae noted every detail exactly as Yasi described. This was new information and it certainly fit the lack of evidence. For the first time since she'd gotten the case, Rae felt a slight tug of enthusiasm and possibility.

"Did he say anything else?"

"He said Audrey disappointed him and she was spoiled."

"Did he explain what he meant or how she'd been spoiled?"

"Not exactly." Yasi suddenly seemed reluctant to answer the question directly.

"What do you mean, 'not exactly'? You said yesterday 'he knows.' What does he know?"

Yasi looked at Rae with what could only be described as sympathy and regret. "He knows about you and Audrey. I think he's been watching her. He said you, *that cop,* spoiled her and she has to be *cleansed.*"

A knot of nerves twisted in Rae's gut. She remembered their first kiss, the damage to her window, and her assault. Now it didn't seem random or a juvenile prank at all. Rae imagined the suspect lurking in the shadows, spying on their most intimate moments, their lovemaking. She wouldn't share those details with anyone, not even her closest friends. Having a potential killer witness them made her nauseous. She was responsible for his violent escalation. She'd pursued Audrey and as a result put her directly in harm's way.

"I'm sorry, Rae, you had to know. I don't want you to blame yourself."

"But I *do*. I should've left her alone, especially after the warning note."

Yasi took her hand again. "No, *he* is to blame, only him. He's been after her since the first assault last—"

"What?" Rae's voice sounded urgent, and she reframed the question. "Did he say something about that incident?"

"He said he'd waited a year to get her back and he was almost ready."

His statement could be potentially damaging but hardly evidence. The nature of the injuries inflicted on Audrey and the subsequent victims certainly pointed to this suspect. Had he also been responsible for the assault at the community center? Rae heard voices in the hallway and turned her attention back to Yasi. "Is there anything else?"

"This man is desperate, Rae. I heard evil in his voice. He's looking for something that doesn't exist, something in his mind. If he ever had it all together, it's come apart. He's more dangerous with every day that passes…but you know that."

Rae couldn't meet her gaze. Yasi had already seen too much in her eyes. Rae's concern would only upset her more. "Thanks for your help…you *have* helped."

Rae turned to leave, but Yasi stopped her. "You care about Audrey. I see it when you look at her. Don't ever be sorry for that. Find this man before he hurts her again."

She tried to give Yasi a reassuring smile. "I need to get going before the gang shows up."

"Yep, you can bet there's been a curtain call."

"Pardon?"

"Sorry, our way of calling a meeting when one of us needs help. Performers, you know."

Rae smiled at the thought that every profession probably had its own specific lingo. "Please don't tell Audrey I was here this morning." She took the back stairs out of the hospital and drove to Sergeant Sharp's office. She had to address one final detail before she could rest.

The Whisperer had been cautious not to leave evidence at the crime scenes, but she might have caught a break. He'd spoken to Yasi more freely, exposing his vulnerability and intentions. It sounded like the suspect was losing touch with reality. His verbiage indicated an almost fanatical mindset, a sort of theme, different from usual perpetrators. His insistence that Audrey be cleansed could imply an involvement in or exposure to another culture.

An uncomfortable feeling settled over Rae as she thought about the horrific devastation extremists had caused in recent times. Before she slept, she wanted Audrey's protection detail on the job.

❖

Audrey grabbed her cell phone from underneath the pillow when she woke up and looked at the display. Useless device. No calls, no texts, no messages—nothing from Rae. She'd said she would come by. *As soon as I can*, Audrey reminded herself. Guilt invaded as she thought of Yasi lying in a hospital bed, injured and afraid. She was feeling sorry for herself because her new girlfriend—if Rae could even be called a girlfriend after one round of sex—hadn't checked in. Rae had better things to do than babysit and reassure her. But Rae was essentially her first, and that distinction came with certain privileges of insecurity and anxiety. Add the assault of her best friend to the mix and Audrey broadcast neuroses.

As she showered, she tried to separate the jumble of sensations swirling in and around her. Her cirque family was in the next room upset about Yasi, and they were all humming or going through their acts in their heads. She reasoned they needed the distraction. Audrey worried about getting to the hospital to comfort her friend too, but images of Rae intruded. It was surreal, as if their lovemaking, eclipsed by the attack, hadn't happened. But it had. Her body still vibrated with the intimacy and intensity of their short time together.

Rae's unconditional acceptance of her inexperience and her ghastly injury had touched her deeply. She'd been so convinced a lover would see her only as a victim, and look at her scarred body with pity, that she'd distanced herself from any possible involvements, until Rae. The attraction between them was too strong, the chemistry too compelling to ignore. She'd taken the chance. As she pulled her clothes over sensitive skin and imagined Rae's hands there instead, she knew she'd made the right decision. She hoped Rae felt the same.

"Sanjana, we can go now?" Sam called from the living room.

She opened the bedroom door and joined her friends. The array of makeshift bedding that had been scattered on the floor, sofa, and chairs last night was neatly folded in a stack. "I like guests who clean up after themselves. What time is it?" She'd lost track as she dressed and thought of Rae.

"Almost ten. We go now," Sam answered.

"Don't I even get a cup of coffee?" What she really wanted was a few minutes to ask her friends what they knew of Yasi's assault, how they'd found her, and other details that seemed too insensitive at the hospital last night.

"Ahead of you." Tony waved a travel mug under her nose and led her toward the door.

They packed into Melvin's van for the short trip, and when the door closed, speculation began about Yasi's release. "We can't take her back to our hotel," Hope said.

Charity agreed. "Too noisy and cleaning people, no good."

Tony said, "I'll rent a place and we can take turns watching her."

"We all contribute to rent," Faith said, and everyone nodded agreement.

Her friends were genuinely trying to formulate a plan for Yasi's housing and recovery, yet something was off. When she tried to focus on their feelings, she picked up only humming or another mental rehearsal. "What's going on with you?" They looked at her but she heard only a cacophony of music. "Stop that and tell me what you're up to."

"We are here," Sam announced as they pulled up to the hospital.

Everyone bailed out of the van like they were taking a bow at a sold-out performance. As she led them into the hospital, she decided they were simply trying to conceal the extent of their concern so she wouldn't worry. She'd talk with them after they checked on Yasi.

When Audrey opened the door to Yasi's room, she was sitting up in bed with the covers pulled tight around her neck. Her skin tone was rosier than the night before, but dark shadows marred her wide brown eyes. The pensive expression Audrey glimpsed as she came in quickly changed to a forced smile as they filed by. Audrey scanned the room when she entered, certain that she sensed Rae's presence, disappointed not to find her.

"The world's greatest cirque performers." Yasi's voice was an octave high, an indication of her understandable anxiety. "It's so good to see you."

As Audrey approached, her arms spread wide, Yasi grabbed her hands and kissed the backside of each, keeping her at arm's length instead. "Don't think I'm quite ready for hugs."

The standoffishness felt personal. They always hugged—long, close, and tight. The snub poked at her insecurity, but she attributed it to the attack and subsequent injury. Yasi quickly released Audrey's hands and wouldn't make eye contact. Before she let go, Audrey experienced a psychic flash that nearly took her breath away.

Traitor, traitor, a voice whispered, followed by an excruciating stab of pain. Audrey grabbed the bedrail for support as the ache recurred time after time.

"Aud, Aud, can you hear me?"

Audrey heard Yasi calling in the background but couldn't answer. She was lost in the agony and a sickening feeling that she was to blame for Yasi's injuries. The nightmares that had plagued her recently resurfaced, along with the frustration of not being able to figure them out. Underneath it all, she sensed something wicked and sadistic.

"Sanjana, come back," Sam said.

She focused on his voice and followed the soothing tones back into the room filled with her friends. Their kindness surrounded her, but with it came an equally potent feeling—fear. "I'm all right now."

Nothing could be further from the truth. She concentrated on the feelings of each person, and as she did their thoughts turned to song and work. "I need to know what's going on with everybody. What are you trying to keep from me?"

Sam moved very close but didn't touch her as he normally would. "We are worried for Yasi. It upsets us deeply." No one else spoke.

"You see, even this is weird. When have we ever been able to keep Tony quiet? And the girls…" She pointed to Faith, Hope, and Charity, who stood like statues in the corner. "They're never still. You're afraid to touch me, my best friend won't let me hug her, and I have a feeling that I'm to blame. What *is* it?"

Sam started to answer but Yasi silenced him with a tired wave of her hand. "Aud, you're probably hypersensitive to everything, which is completely understandable. If this could happen to me, it could happen to any of us. We have to stick together. We're all concerned and afraid. I know I certainly am…and I'm exhausted. It wasn't a very restful night."

Audrey suddenly felt very selfish and inconsiderate for demanding answers that Yasi was obviously in no condition to provide. But the nagging feeling that something was definitely wrong clung to her like a flea in thick fur. "You're right. We should probably let you sleep."

"I'll be able to leave tomorrow. Could I come to your place for a few days?"

Yasi's tentative smile almost broke Audrey's heart. She shouldn't have had to ask. "Of course you can come to my place. I insist." She looked at the solemn faces around the room and added, "You might have to come as a package deal. I don't think these guys will let you out of their sight for a second."

"Absolutely." Yasi's response brought smiles to the others' faces as they waved good-bye and stepped into the hallway.

Before she left, Audrey leaned over the bedrail and lightly kissed Yasi's forehead. "I love you, but don't think for a second that love blinds me. Just because you gave me a precious, intelligent, slightly neurotic kitten doesn't mean you have a free pass for life. You're hiding something, and I will find out what it is." She gave Yasi her biggest grin and walked toward the door.

"You're entirely too suspicious of your oldest and dearest friend," Yasi said.

"Maybe I'll ask Rae. I know she was here."

Sergeant Sharp stared at her like she'd dropped in from another planet. "Yeah, I got your request for protection for Audrey Everhart. The answer is no."

"But—"

"It doesn't matter how many *but*s you have or how compelling the argument, the answer is still no. We don't have money for the overtime."

Not So had shot her down without hearing all the facts, and she didn't have the energy to argue her case sufficiently. "She's the target of a serial attacker, certain to be his next victim."

"Do you know who the suspect is yet?" His smug grin indicated he already had the answer.

"No, but I'm closer. The latest victim provided some possible leads."

"What leads? Physical evidence, circumstantial evidence, or hunches?"

Rae reconsidered the information Yasi had given her, viewing it in the most beneficial light.

"If it takes that long to answer, you obviously don't have shit. Sorry, no protective detail."

"You're putting this woman's life on the line."

"I don't see any imminent danger. You have no suspect and no real evidence, aside from a note that a defense attorney could interpret in numerous ways. There weren't any prints on the note, so that doesn't help."

Rae had to appeal to Not So's mercenary self-interest. "She's the mayor's publicist. It won't look good if she's attacked and we had even the slightest indication it could happen." She dropped her bomb and turned to leave.

"Wait. Maybe the mayor would be willing to make a budgetary concession or offer a couple of his private bodyguards." The sergeant stood, stroked the front of his perfectly pressed suit, and reached for the phone. "I'll get back to you on this."

As Rae left she heard him say, "It's Sergeant Sharp for Mayor Downing." Rae usually avoided anything political, but in this case she'd make an exception. Whatever it took to keep Audrey safe.

CHAPTER SIXTEEN

Rae opened the blackout shades in her bedroom onto another dark morning. She had no idea of the time. Her only recognizable sensations were fatigue and hopelessness. The hours had crawled the past two days as she followed up the minor details Yasi had provided. They could hardly be called clues, but she refused to slow down until she'd exhausted all options.

She'd revisited the body dump sites at various times of the day and night and talked to anyone she could find. She found no laundry facilities nearby but plenty of vans—enough to make the task impossible without further details. Disappointed, she thought constantly of how much she missed Audrey.

Rae looked at her list of unanswered phone calls and unopened mail with dread and a healthy dose of guilt. If she returned Audrey's calls or messages, she'd have to lie or at least evade the truth. Audrey deserved better, and right now she was too busy trying to keep Audrey safe to consider what could happen afterward.

Maybe she was being a coward. She couldn't imagine telling Audrey that the same suspect *had* assaulted her twice and Rae was no closer to identifying him. How would she take the news that the man Rae couldn't catch had spent the last year attacking women, the latest being her best friend? Time was running out. The distance swelled between her and Audrey like a malignancy.

As she showered, she thought about her growing feelings for Audrey. It was time to tell Audrey the truth and solicit her help.

With so little to go on, it couldn't possibly hurt to consult a psychic or even two.

Rae dressed and had started into the kitchen for coffee when her doorbell rang. Daylight had barely tinted the eastern sky. Any news delivered this early couldn't be good. She opened the door and Audrey rushed inside as if she were being chased.

"Audrey…are you okay?" She looked as though she'd just woken up or been awake for a very long time. Her hair was wild, clothes a bit unkempt, and her bloodshot eyes weary.

"As if you care. It's been days since we—since—you know what I mean, and you haven't bothered to ask how I'm doing. Why should I—" She stopped as if seeing Rae for the first time. "You look exhausted." She raised her hand toward Rae's face but lowered it before making contact. "Are *you* all right?"

Without another thought, she stepped forward and hugged Audrey tight. "I've missed you so much and I'm sorry I haven't been around. Can you forgive me?"

Audrey melted against her and they clung together like drowning victims to a single life preserver. "I've been so worried… about everything. I needed you, but I know you've been working. Can you forgive me for barking at you in the hospital and being generally selfish?"

"It's all my fault. I should've called, should've told you…" Rae kissed Audrey's cheek and then her lips, hungry for the connection they'd shared three days earlier. It seemed almost like a dream until Audrey responded with equal urgency. Rae's body flared with the same heat, the same consuming need she'd felt when they first made love. Their bond had been and still was very real.

"I've missed you so much. I was trying to protect you, but I have something to tell you." She pulled back, her hands resting on Audrey's waist.

"It's about the attack on Yasi, isn't it?"

"That and more."

"I knew something was going on. Everybody's acting weird, strangers are following me, and you've been missing in action."

Rae feared the Whisperer was already making his move on Audrey. "What strangers?"

"Well, not exactly. A couple of the mayor's bodyguards have been tailing me the last couple of days, trying to be discreet, like that's even possible for men the size of tanks."

Some of the tension in Rae's shoulders relaxed. Not So had come through. "They're the protection detail I asked for."

"But Yasi was attacked."

"Come sit with me, please." Rae led Audrey to the settee in her study, and when they'd settled in, she took Audrey's hands. "I don't like keeping things from you. The only way I could do it was to distance myself. I'd hoped to have good news. I'm afraid I don't."

"Tell me, Rae. Yasi has been at my place for two days and won't even let me hug her. She's too afraid I'll see what she's hiding. The others went back to work. They were driving me nuts with their incessant humming and avoidance. It's nice that you're all trying to protect me, but I need to know what's going on."

Rae kissed the back of Audrey's hands and prayed she wasn't about to inflict unnecessary injury. "I believe the man who assaulted Yasi is the same person who initially attacked you and did so again at the community center." She waited to see if the information tweaked Audrey's memory about what happened a year earlier but saw no indication she remembered anything.

"That doesn't make sense. The first time he used a knife and the second a stun gun. Don't these guys usually follow some kind of pattern? What do you call it?"

"An MO, modus operandi. They usually do, but I have a feeling he deviated this time. Maybe he was in a hurry. Maybe you surprised him and he had to improvise. It's possible he wasn't ready."

"What do you mean? There's more to it, isn't there?"

"I don't have anything to connect the two cases yet, but I believe they are."

"That would explain why I couldn't read my initial attacker or the stun-gun guy. They were both like an indecipherable mass of white noise."

"I think he's obsessed with you." Rae hesitated. Caring, empathic Audrey would undoubtedly blame herself for Yasi's attack and that of all the other women who came before. "He's been following you, spying on us. He told Yasi he wanted you. It's personal in a fanatical sort of way. Don't worry, I won't let him hurt you again. No matter what I have to do." The light of understanding sparked in Audrey's eyes and the color drained from her face.

"Oh, my God. He cut Yasi just like me, didn't he?" Rae nodded. "And this other case you have—the woman I saw that day in the canteen—they're his vict—he hurt them too?" Again Rae nodded as tears welled in Audrey's eyes.

"I think you were his first." As Rae spoke the words aloud their gravity registered in her soul with a sickening dread. The woman she had come to value so deeply was in the crosshairs of a maniac's sights. Rae would do anything to protect her, even risk her own life.

"Why can't I remember, even now?"

Rae tried to reassure her. "It'll come back when you're ready to deal with it."

"If I'd come forward a year ago, told someone, these other women wouldn't have been victimized...and Yasi..." Audrey covered her face with her hands, and her shoulders shook as she silently sobbed.

Rae held her and tried to reassure her but Audrey couldn't be consoled. It was difficult to imagine feeling responsible for the brutal attack of one of her best friends. Rae had enough trouble distancing from victims she didn't know. If her actions or lack thereof contributed in any way to a friend's injury, she'd never forgive herself. Several minutes passed before Audrey spoke again.

"Who is he?"

"I don't know." Rae hung her head in disappointment and shame, unable to meet Audrey's gaze. "I've been working night and day trying to track down clues, but I'm not any closer. He's like a ghost."

Audrey cupped Rae's chin and forced her to look at her. "You can't blame yourself. I know you're doing everything possible. If anyone's to blame, it's me. I should've reported the initial assault."

"You handled it the only way you could at the time. That's all any of us can do. Maybe you can help now." Rae was desperate to distract Audrey from her guilt and to jump-start her investigation.

"How?"

"Would you consider giving me your take on the case? I could sure use it." Audrey twisted her hands nervously in her lap. Maybe Rae still didn't understand how Audrey's gift worked. Perhaps psychic ability couldn't be conjured up at will or on demand. "I'm sorry. You're obviously not comfortable with that suggestion."

When Audrey finally met her gaze, her eyes brimmed with tears. "It's not you. I've always been uneasy with this ability. It was one reason I found it easier to leave the area when the assault happened. My life was a bit us-versus-them—my cirque family that knew I was a freak and the outside world that didn't.

"After the assault, I started over and pretended to be normal—no assault, no gift. You're the only person I've told. I'm not sure I want to engage that part of myself again. Not everybody is as understanding as you. And what if I get it wrong again? Or what if it comes out that you used a psychic on your case? You'll be the new poster child for the Comedy Club, and I'll be labeled a charlatan."

Rae had never considered the emotional turmoil such a gift could cause or the toll it could take. Denying any part of yourself was like denying yourself entirely. She'd tried with Janet and it only created more uncertainty and eventually total separation. The same struggle now played out across Audrey's delicate features. "You don't have to. I understand."

"My mother said someday I'd have to choose to become a part of the real world or hide from it forever. And when I made the choice, I'd have to embrace my gift as part of that reality. The time has come. I owe it to Yasi and all the women before her to help in any way I can. Let's get started."

Rae had never been prouder of anyone. "You're the most courageous person I've ever met." She squeezed Audrey's hand and fought back tears. "So how—"

"You said he's a ghost? Who better to catch a ghost than a psychic? Let's fight one supernatural entity with another." A grin tugged at the corners of Audrey's mouth. "Cops and psychics working together? I do believe you're coming around. I'll help you on one condition." Her mischievous grin blossomed into a smile. "Hold me."

Rae didn't hesitate. She pulled Audrey down on top of her on the settee, her long legs hanging over the side. Audrey settled between her thighs with her feet pointing toward the ceiling. Arousal stirred in Rae as Audrey's soft, hot body rubbed against her.

"I was afraid you didn't want me anymore. I'm not exactly a love goddess."

"Maybe that's one of the things I like most," Rae said.

"You're one of those defilers of young innocents, aren't you?"

"Only you." Rae covered Audrey's mouth and slid her tongue inside. Audrey sucked and matched her probing. Her hips rocked against Audrey's pelvis with an urgent need. Her jeans, which would usually be a hindrance, served as an additional stimulant against her tender flesh. Desire pounded hard and insistently, her pulse peaked, and a light sheen of sweat covered her body. She had never been so fully stimulated so quickly. If Audrey kept touching her, she would come very soon.

Then she slowed, afraid Audrey would misread her interest as purely sexual. "I want you…in every way. Maybe we should—"

"We should do exactly this, for the moment. I need you so badly it hurts. Neither of us will last long." Audrey resumed the earnest pace between Rae's legs, her moans like physical caresses. "Come with me, my darling."

The pending climax bunched and strained inside Rae as Audrey sucked her breast through the fabric of her shirt and wedged her thigh firmly against her. "I'm coming…now."

Later, Rae's feet and legs tingled as they dangled over the side of the short settee, and the afternoon sun warmed the side of her face. Audrey rested with her head between Rae's breasts. They had climaxed together, slept together for several hours, and would soon wake curled together like a real couple. Rae felt more invigorated than she had in days. She could get used to sharing her life with Audrey, but before that could happen, they had a criminal to catch.

"I can hear you thinking. Is it work?" Audrey asked.

"Some of it—and then there's you and us and this." She wiggled seductively against Audrey and nuzzled her ear.

"Stop that or we'll never get to the work part." Audrey pushed up on her elbows and stared down at Rae. "I can't feel my legs."

"Me either." She rolled Audrey carefully to the side and sat up, her own legs like a pincushion. "I need to tell you something else." She already knew she cared for Audrey, maybe even loved her. What if this was the only chance to tell her?

Audrey placed her fingers over Rae's lips. "Don't say it. I feel the same. When I hear the words, I want to know we have a future."

"I won't let anything happen to you." The thought that a maniac could come between her and Audrey filled Rae with sadness, followed closely by anger.

"It's not me I'm worried about. I have a feeling you're the one in danger."

Rae's heart ached to see such uncertainty and pain etched on Audrey's face. "I'll be fine. If you don't worry about me, I won't worry about you." Even as she said the words, Rae knew neither could live up to them.

Audrey kissed her gently and nodded toward the desk. "Let's see what you've got."

"What about your job? Aren't you supposed to go to work shortly?"

"I've taken a few days off to look after Yasi. The mayor is very understanding."

Rae retrieved the file folder. "If you're sure. I'm not crazy about you being mixed up in this any further."

"Rae, I *need* to help. I've let it go too long. If I look at it objectively, without considering myself as one of his—as involved, maybe I can get a better sense of him. He seems to be able to block me directly. If I concentrate on helping someone else, it could work, like sneaking in the back door."

"It's worth a try, but I'd prefer not to show you the crime-scene pictures…power of suggestion and all. And I have to verify any information you provide. Does that make sense?"

"Yes, darling, I understand the skeptical mind of law enforcement, and I appreciate that you need verification."

"So, how do we do this?"

"If I could hold the file, not open it. I get much better readings from physical touching."

Rae handed Audrey a folder and sat on the arm of the settee. "It's a difficult and disturbing case."

Audrey didn't respond. She rubbed the cream-colored folder between her hands, placed it on her knees, then waved her fingers above it. "Is this a joke?"

"Why would you think that?"

"Because these are notes for one of your college exams."

Rae's face flushed and she tried to sound contrite. "I had to be sure."

"I understand." She smacked Rae on the arm with the folder and gave it back to her. "And you passed. If you open your mail, you'll find the test scores. Congratulations."

Rae looked at the pile of unopened mail on her kitchen counter. She wanted to confirm what Audrey said but didn't want to offend her.

"Go ahead. The sooner you stop testing me, the sooner we can get to work."

Shuffling through the stack, Rae found the official-looking brown college envelope and opened it. As Audrey predicted, her grades were enclosed, along with a congratulatory letter. Audrey definitely had a gift, and it simultaneously thrilled and concerned Rae.

If she had any other leads, she wouldn't involve Audrey. She felt like a failure for putting the woman she cared about in danger. "Thank you for indulging me." Rae handed her a thick manila envelope.

Audrey repeated the process from earlier, but this time her hands quivered. "He's done this five times, six counting me." Audrey's expression soured, as if the statement tasted bitter crossing her lips.

Rae had never seen a psychic at work. She wanted to support and encourage her, but knew instinctively to be quiet. Audrey stared out the window, silent and unfocused. Shadows clouded her face and life seemed to drain from her bit by bit. After what seemed a very long time, she spoke again.

"He uses words, soft words to frighten." So far Audrey hadn't said anything she couldn't have learned from any number of sources, but Rae believed in her. "He's a formidable man—strong, well-trained, perhaps even military. He's damaged in some way. That part isn't clear. I smell chemicals, some pungent and some sweet, and I see blue, lots of blue."

Audrey let out a long sigh. Her shoulders sagged and she clenched her hands in tight fists. Rae hadn't understood until this moment how much her gift demanded of her physically.

"Are you okay?"

When she looked up, the file slipped from her hands onto the floor. Her eyes were dull, void of light and animation.

"I'm sorry. I can't do any more right now. His energy is like a black hole."

She hugged Audrey, hoping to provide tangible support. "It's all right. Rest a bit." As Audrey settled against her chest, Rae reviewed what she'd said. Her impression of possible military training could add credence to the forensics weapons expert's description of the knife and to Ken Whitt's instinct about a services connection. She'd need more to narrow the search. Maybe the damaged angle could help, but again she needed specifics.

When Audrey shifted beside her a while later, Rae asked, "Do you feel like answering a few questions?" Audrey nodded. "You said he's damaged. Can you tell if that's physical or emotional?"

"Sorry."

"What about the blue?"

"Nothing more specific. Sometimes I get additional flashes after the fact. Do you have anything I can touch without compromising evidence?"

"I don't want to push you."

"We need to go on. What dead ends have you run into? Surely you can tell me what hasn't worked."

Rae considered the offer and decided it wouldn't violate any departmental regulations or rules of evidence. Maybe she'd been too close to the case for too long to see clearly. "I've been looking for a dry-cleaning business in the area of the dump sites."

Audrey sat up and touched the file again before responding. "Have you been looking at only active businesses?"

The innocent question settled in her gut. She'd violated a prime rule of investigation—never make assumptions. The business *could* be closed and still give anyone access to supplies left behind. She'd also assumed the business would be in close proximity to the dump sites. However, experience had taught her suspects often disposed of victims away from their home turf. How could she have overlooked two such potentially crucial details?

"I can't believe I missed that." Rae added a check of inactive business licenses to her to-do list. She also included a registration check for vehicles of defunct dry-cleaning businesses in the area. Rae pushed for one more identifying feature. "And a vehicle's probably involved."

"I think you'll find that it's an old white van."

Rae stared at her in amazement. "I didn't even know what type vehicle, much less the color. I can narrow the search using both criteria. How do you know things like that?"

Audrey slid her hand up Rae's arm. "I'm only relaying what pops up. It's your job to separate the chaff from the grain, darling." She gave Rae a mischievous grin. "I'm merely an instrument."

"You can be my instrument any time. You're quite impressive." And the information did *sound* impressive, but Rae had to evaluate it objectively. "Anything else come to mind?"

"This sounds over the top, but I'm not sensing feet. It's almost like he doesn't have any—that can't be right. I'm probably getting mixed signals. Can we stop now?"

"Of course. You've given me a place to start, and I appreciate it. Would you like some coffee? I feel like I need it."

Audrey suddenly jumped from the sofa and headed to the door. "Oh, gosh, I forgot about Yasi. She was still sleeping when I left. She'll wonder where I am…or maybe not." She gave Rae a guilty look. "I told her about us. I hope you don't mind."

"Of course I don't mind. She's your best friend." Rae felt a surge of pride that Audrey cared enough to share her feelings with Yasi, then a prickle of guilt as she thought about her own friends. They'd only seen Audrey once. None of them knew what had happened since they met her. Rae hadn't even contacted them in almost two weeks. Her friends always understood how absorbed she got in her work, and they managed to love her anyway. She vowed to call them soon and celebrate passing her final exams. "How is Yasi doing?"

"Better, but she won't be able to work for a while. She's going back to the new cirque hotel tomorrow. Everybody pitched in and rented a suite of rooms so they could be together. They think they can do a better job of protecting her there."

"I hate to admit it, but they're probably right. At least she'll be in a more controlled environment most of the time." Maybe Audrey should go with Yasi to the hotel. It would certainly address Not So's budgetary concerns. Audrey's seven friends had a much better chance of keeping her safe around the clock than she and two rent-a-cops.

But she didn't want to relinquish Audrey's safety to anyone. However, she couldn't properly investigate the case and constantly guard Audrey at the same time. Trust or lack of it was a heavy burden. "You might be safer at the hotel as well…for a while."

"No."

"There are more of them. Safety in numbers."

"No." Audrey was adamant.

"Will you at least think about it?"

"Not unless you come too, and I know the odds of that. So I'm taking my chances with you and the mayor's heavyweights. Besides, I've just found you. I mean we've just gotten togeth—I'm not sure what's going on. I feel connected to you, and I'm not ready to let that go even for a while. Can you understand?"

Rae gathered Audrey in her arms and inhaled as if sucking in her spirit. The indescribable fragrance held the essence of Audrey—the combination of her hair, body, and breath in a concoction that would forever remind Rae of only her. "I understand perfectly. I wish I could be with you every minute. Promise me you'll be careful."

"Promise." Audrey kissed her and backed slowly away. "I think I'll go home and take a nap. This psychic business is exhausting."

Rae waved good-bye and reached for her ringing cell phone as Audrey left. "Butler."

"Detective Butler, I'm calling from the hospital lab," a pleasant female voice stated. "You asked for an analysis of Yasirah Mansour's blood. We have those results."

Rae flipped to a clean page in her notebook. "Go ahead, please."

"To put it in layman's terms, Ms. Mansour was administered an incapacitating quantity of chloroform. We can assume that the level was even higher than the test indicated because of breakdown in the system. A few more hours and it would've been completely untraceable. I'll send you a copy of the official report today."

Rae got the caller's name and thanked her for the information. Her skin tingled with the realization that she finally had a concrete clue. She dialed the records division and gave the clerk the particulars of the vehicle, licensing, and radius searches she needed. Audrey had provided several new threads to follow, and the lab report was another piece of the evolving puzzle.

A hazy picture of the suspect emerged: military trained, expert with a knife, injured in some way, knowledge of chloroform, access to the drug, dry-cleaning plastic, and an old white van. The military pool was also slowly shrinking. Not every combat-trained soldier received extensive medical training or language skills. And not every soldier who served returned with an injury. The suspect would have been discharged fairly recently to coincide with the timing of the attacks. At this point it was all speculation, but at least Rae had things to investigate; at least she was doing something productive.

CHAPTER SEVENTEEN

Audrey drove around the corner from the condo, pulled to the curb, and slumped forward against the steering wheel. Thank God, Rae wasn't telepathic or familiar enough with her tells to know how shattered she felt. She'd summoned most of her courage to share her conflict about using her psychic ability and the remainder to actually use it again.

The lifelong struggle and constant pull between two worlds was coming to a head. If she helped Rae with her case and word got out, the true test followed. Would "normal" people accept her and her abilities, or would they consider her a freak and discount her skills as a sham or merely a stroke of luck?

She had turned the question over in her mind repeatedly and had lost hope of a different outcome. Perhaps more people like Rae existed. Maybe she didn't have to choose *either* being true to herself *or* the outside world. For the first time she imagined being accepted for who and what she was. With the image came a sense of freedom she'd never experienced.

The pleasurable sensation was short-lived. What if using her skills unleashed the complete memory of her first assault? Was she ready to cope with the dreadful incident she'd hidden so carefully… and eventually face *him*? Could she unearth selected portions of her past while leaving others buried? Another either-or situation.

Merely reviewing the suspect's activities sucked energy from her like an eclipse swallows the sun. She couldn't help Rae if her body resisted each time. Sooner or later the darkness would consume her. She'd heard about psychics trapped by the dark side, sucked into an underworld of depravity and destruction. After touching the edge of this man's evil, she understood the possibility. But Rae needed her, and she owed it to Yasi and the other victims. She had to move past her fear.

Audrey jerked upright as someone tapped on the driver's side window. Her heart rate galloped as she momentarily thought he'd come for her again. When she saw the surly familiar face staring at her, she relaxed. One of the mayor's bodyguards who had been assigned to her stood with his hands raised as though ready to strike. She didn't feel completely comfortable around men who used their bodies as weapons, but she'd worked with them for a year and had learned to overlook their gruff exteriors.

"Ms. Everhart, are you all right?"

She forced a smile and rolled down the window. "Fine, Marc, a little weary. I'm going home. Why don't you take a break? I'll call you if I'm going out again."

His sharp gray eyes bored into her like pinpoints of magnified light. "I can't do that, Ms. Everhart. My orders are to protect you. Would you like me to drive you back to the apartment?"

"No, I can manage. Thank you." She motioned for him to step back and pulled away from the curb, feeling only slightly more capable than before. In the side mirror she saw his shoulders rise and fall in a frustrated sigh.

Everybody tried to protect her and she was grateful for the concern, but she really wanted to remember everything so she could help solve this mystery. Coaxing the ghosts from the corners of her mind and greeting them head-on wouldn't be easy. Where did she start to dig up the scraps of memory so long buried and denied? Perhaps working with Rae would provide the necessary catalyst.

When she opened the door to her apartment, Yasi was sitting on the sofa petting Cannonball. "Looks like you're feeling better. Did you sleep well?" She greeted her with a kiss on the cheek and sat down beside her.

"Better than you, apparently. How's Rae?"

She couldn't hide anything from Yasi. Sometimes Audrey thought she was psychic as well. "Frustrated. I'm hoping to change that."

Yasi wickedly waggled her eyebrows. "Are we speaking sexually or otherwise?"

"Both." Audrey stroked Yasi's long dark hair, unsure how to bring up what they needed to discuss. She mustered her courage again. "Yas, I'm sorry for—"

"Rae told you everything?"

Audrey nodded.

"I'm glad, but don't even think about apologizing for what happened to me. That's why we hid it from you. I knew you'd feel responsible."

"I didn't—"

"Do anything wrong. It wasn't your fault."

"But—"

"Let's help Rae find this guy—and I do mean *help*, not mount a two-woman vendetta or go after him alone like you did before. I mean help from a safe distance."

"Will you let me finish a sentence, ever?"

"Audrey, you could never hurt anyone intentionally. You were protecting yourself. If you'd known this man would hurt other people, you would've done anything to stop him. Am I right?"

"Yes."

"Then let go of the past and concentrate on what we can do now."

Audrey hugged Yasi and remembered why they'd been best friends all these years. They depended on each other, supported each other, and stood by one another no matter what. Maybe that was Yasi's gift to her at this moment. She wasn't alone, and courage doubled was a very good thing.

"I gave Rae my impressions of the case. I'm not sure I helped much though. It's been so long since I've actively tried to read anything or anyone. I'm not even sure I can do it properly any more."

"It doesn't go away, gets rusty maybe, but doesn't disappear. You know that."

Audrey rested her head against Yasi's shoulder and also stroked a purring Cannonball. She relaxed and enjoyed the serenity of the moment, absorbing it like the last rays of sunshine. As the emotions of the past few days surfaced, a knot formed in her throat. "I'm scared, Yas, scared and I'm not even sure why." The words tumbled out in a mixture of sobs and whispers.

Yasi hugged her closer. "What worries you most?"

"That I can't remember. Then I'm scared I will. I wonder if I've lost the gift and won't be able to help Rae. I'm afraid I still have it and will have to use it. I'm worried that people I care about are in danger because of me. And I'm terrified I can't do anything about it."

"But there is and you've already started. And you don't have to do it alone. We're all here, and we'll work it out together. Right now you need some rest. Why don't you take a nap? When you wake up, we'll start fresh."

"You're probably right." When Yasi nodded, Audrey started toward the bedroom. "If you need anything, call me. I'll drive you to the hotel later."

"Sounds good. Oh, I almost forgot. When I opened the paper this morning, I found an envelope inside with your name on it. It's on the counter."

Audrey recalled Marc tossing the paper from the front courtyard onto the steps as they left. "It was inside the paper?"

"Tucked in between the pages."

Audrey ripped the envelope open as she spoke. "The neighbors stuff announcements and invitations into everything. It's probably another—" The contents spilled onto the counter and Audrey stared in disbelief. "Oh, my God."

Glossy four-by-six photos of Audrey in various poses and stages of undress littered the worktop. Nausea churned in her stomach as she flipped through the pictures depicting scenes in every room of her apartment. Nothing was sacred—she was captured sleeping in her bed, showering in her bathroom, cooking in her kitchen, and even kissing Rae at the front door. Each shot was as clear and colorful as if the photographer had been standing in the room with her.

The room spun as she clutched a barstool for support. *He* had violated her private spaces. *He* had seen her naked—vulnerable in her exposure and in sleep. *He* had come and gone at will without her knowledge, without leaving a trace. She suddenly thought of Cannonball's irritable scratching and wondered if she'd tried to warn her. And *why* once again had her instincts failed her?

"Audrey…" Yasi stood at her side, arm around her waist. "We have to call Rae, and then we have to leave. No way are you staying here. You'll come to the hotel with me."

"I can't leave Rae."

"If my guess is right, she'll insist you do just that. Call her now." Audrey reached for her cell but her hands shook so badly she couldn't dial. "Let me." Yasi punched in the numbers and, when Rae answered, she handed the phone back to Audrey.

"Rae, pictures…in my paper." Her voice quivered in spite of her attempts to remain calm.

"Where's your bodyguard? Check and make sure he's at the front door."

Audrey made her way to the window and pulled back the curtain. Marc stood ramrod straight on her front stoop like the Queen's Guard at Buckingham Palace. "He's still there."

"Pack a bag. I'll be there in five minutes." Before Audrey could object, Rae hung up.

Time crawled as they waited for Rae to arrive. Audrey walked the length of the apartment stroking Cannonball and looking for ways an intruder might have gotten in. She shuddered to think of *him* creeping through her house while she slept, rifling through her belongings, and leering at her as she showered. She also became angry. A madman would not force her out of her home. She would fight back against the person who had damaged and disrupted her life.

Audrey heard voices at the front door and opened it to find Rae questioning Marc like he was a suspect. "What are you doing?"

"He's supposed to be protecting you." Rae turned to the bodyguard. "You didn't check the paper before you tossed it onto the steps?"

Marc gave her a look that would've easily intimidated a less-confident person. "I examined it for bulges that might indicate an explosive or incendiary device. It felt like a newspaper. What did you want me to do, read every line for a threat?" His tone indicated he thought Rae was the incompetent one.

Rae brushed past him and reached for Audrey the minute the door closed behind her. "Are you all right?"

"A bit rattled." Audrey clung to her, desperate for the safety she'd felt in her arms less than an hour ago. Everything seemed so right and normal when Rae was close. Had security and comfort always been missing from her life, or had the perilous situation simply made it more precious?

"Where are they?"

Audrey pointed to the kitchen counter and waited with Yasi as Rae examined the photographs. Rae carefully slid them aside one at a time with her pen. Her shoulders tensed, and Audrey could sense her anguish with each new image. The outrage seething in Audrey burned equally strong in Rae. Her body practically hummed with the suppression of it.

After she'd looked through all the photos, Rae placed them back in the envelope and walked from room to room. Audrey imagined she was visualizing the exact spot where this demon stood as he snapped each picture. Anger sparked from Rae's emerald eyes like daggers seeking a target, and Audrey loved her for it. Her detective would redirect her energy into the investigation until she found the suspect. And God help him when she did.

"Are you packed?"

Audrey knew the edge in Rae's tone was not directed at her, but she still recoiled slightly. She respected Rae's need to assume her professional persona and hoped Rae would understand her position as well.

"This is my home, and I want to stay." Rae and Yasi exchanged a look that said she was in for a fight from both of them. "I know you think I'll be safer somewhere else, but I can't keep running away."

Rae held her at arm's length and pinned her with a gaze so intense Audrey almost swooned. "I'm *not* playing Russian roulette with your life. You're much too important to me. *Please* go to the hotel with Yasi. You can look after each other much better than a couple of bodyguards. It's not safe here."

"I don't want to be away from you." Audrey knew she sounded desperate, but she had a strong sense Rae was also in danger. "I don't want to leave. I'm afraid for you."

"I'll be fine, and we'll see each other as much as possible. Besides, I still need your help. Please, Audrey, I'll be able to work faster and more efficiently if I know you're all right."

Yasi moved to her side. "And I'm not a hundred percent yet. I could use some assistance with these humongous bandages and a distraction from total boredom while I'm not working. It makes sense, Aud."

Audrey looked from one to the other and her heart ached with the concern scored across their faces. "All right, but you have to promise no more secrets."

They both nodded.

"I mean it."

"Promise."

They agreed in unison.

Loud voices bantering back and forth outside interrupted them. Rae motioned for her and Yasi to go into another room, and she approached the door with her hand cocked on her weapon. When Rae opened the door, Audrey recognized Trevor Collins, the department's crime-scene analyst. She understood the necessity for Trevor's expertise, and she trusted Rae to manage the situation as delicately as possible. But she felt like a bystander as virtual strangers stood guard over and rummaged through her life.

Rae stepped shoulder to shoulder with the hefty bodyguard, willing him to challenge her. She wanted to vent some of her frustration but was acutely aware of Yasi and Audrey's presence. Professionalism prevailed as she said, "Let him in, Marc. He's CSI." Marc stepped aside, obviously not happy with having to relinquish his stand twice in the same hour.

Trevor gave him a smug grin and rolled a heavy black equipment case into the apartment. He acknowledged Audrey and Yasi with a nod and addressed Rae. "You said this was a head-to-toe job so I brought my entire kit. What have you got?"

"Ms. Everhart's apartment has been broken into, no obvious signs of entry. Go over this place with a microscope if you have to. I want to know how he got in."

"How do you know he was inside?"

Rae flinched as she waved the envelope at Trevor. Two people too many had already seen Audrey's exposed body. She wouldn't allow even one more. "He took pictures from every room." She didn't allow him to touch the envelope. "I'll hang onto them."

"It would help if I saw the angle of the photos so I can determine where he stood."

"I've already done that. I'll walk you through it." Rae was deviating from the way business was done, and they both knew it. She didn't care. He'd process the scene her way or she'd find another CSI who would. Audrey had suffered enough.

"You're the boss." Trevor's frustration was evident.

"I'm sorry, Trev. I'm not trying to be difficult. Suffice to say the pictures are sensitive." She glanced at Audrey, held her gaze for several seconds, and lowered her voice. "I believe it's the Whisperer." When she returned her attention to Trevor, he nodded.

"I understand now. Tell me what you need."

Rae led him through the apartment, pointing out the intruder's vantage point for each photo. As they walked, she scoured the walls and ceilings for anything out of the ordinary. She stopped in the small common hallway between the living areas and examined scratch marks along the bottom of the woodwork.

"Cannonball." Audrey spoke from behind her. She had been so absorbed in her task she hadn't heard her approach. "She's been a bit skittish lately. Do you think she sensed someone had been in here?"

"It's possible. Cats are extremely intelligent."

Trevor would take three to four hours to complete his work in the apartment and get back to Rae with the results. She could relocate Audrey and Yasi in the meantime before dark. Rae made a quick call to have the incredible hulk removed from guard duty and another to ensure the necessary arrangements were in place at the hotel. As she loaded Yasi and Audrey's luggage in her car and secured CB in the backseat, she looked forward to dismissing the slightly overbearing yet highly efficient bodyguard.

"Marc, could you stay with Trevor until he finishes and secures the apartment? After that, you're free to go. I'm taking over Ms. Everhart's protection detail."

"My supervisor hasn't dismissed me." His dedication was admirable, but sometimes that very dedication made rent-a-cops almost comical. He stood his post even though he knew Rae had the authority to excuse him.

"For the purpose of this assignment, I am your supervisor. Consider yourself dismissed."

Marc's nostrils flared and his gray eyes drilled into Rae. "No disrespect, Detective, I'll have to check in." As he reached for his phone, it rang. He turned back to Rae a few seconds later. "Would you mind telling me where you're going—in case I'm needed later?"

"Sorry, Marc, need to know."

He gave her a mock salute. "I understand." As Yasi and Audrey passed on the way to the car, he said, "Take care, Ms. Everhart."

A few minutes later Audrey's cirque family surrounded their two friends like a protective shield and escorted them into the hotel. Rae conducted a security sweep of the accommodation, satisfied with the penthouse suite. The room was secluded if not a bit too isolated from the rest of the facility by a gym and restaurant level. She gave Sam and the others specific instructions and felt relatively comfortable that Audrey would be safe for the time being.

It took all her considerable logic to convince herself to leave Audrey in the care of a group of circus performers untrained in protection procedures. She still wondered if one of them might be responsible for the attacks. A fellow detective had conducted preliminary backgrounds on the male members of the group but had difficulty obtaining complete information from certain foreign countries. She didn't know if any of them had military training, but they all certainly had accents. Even a suspect as brazen as the Whisperer wouldn't risk an attack in front of so many other people. Rae prayed her logic was sound because she had to continue her investigation or the nightmare would never end.

As she drove back toward downtown, she called the records division to check on the business-license search she'd requested earlier. The clerk rattled off a partial list of dry-cleaning businesses no longer in operation around the dump sites. Even the incomplete list was daunting. Rae would have time to check only a few tonight. She told the clerk she'd pick up the results the following day, along with the motor-vehicle listings.

Rae pulled up to the first address and her heart sank. The building had been converted into a condo tower. Only the façade remained as evidence of the early architectural splendor of the structure. What a shame that progress often destroyed the beauty of the past to accommodate conveniences of the present. Marking the address off her list, she drove on.

A crumbling concrete wall and a patch of debris-laden ground welcomed her at the next location. The lot was bordered by dimly lit buildings and looked like a dingy snaggletooth smile. Rae parked and walked in the cool night air. She needed to think, to refocus her efforts. Running from place to demolished place felt too much like chasing her tail. The rubble of long-closed businesses and desolate lots couldn't possibly contain anything of value. As she started back to her vehicle, she heard a faint noise across the street and moved toward the sound.

A man sang slurred words with no hint of a tune. "Turned the water to blood…no, the water to wine. Water to blood, turned to a flood, moved out of the hood." The man laughed and repeated the chant over and over.

Rae followed his voice and found him lying on a soiled mattress behind a Dumpster. The elderly white male wore several layers of tattered clothing and a stocking cap. He was obviously one of the homeless people who populated the hideaways and underpasses of the city.

When she stepped out of the shadows, he sat up, wobbling from side to side. "Hey, what you doing in my house? Get out."

"I'm a police officer."

"Ain't done nothing wrong." His response, loud and angry, reflected years of living a drifter's life and countless confrontations with police.

"I'm sure you haven't. My name is Rae." Underneath the gruff exterior, she sensed a harmless and very lonely man. "Quite a song."

"I'm Larry." He looked her over, probably sizing her up with his streetwise instincts. "You've seen it then?" He struggled to stand, and she offered her hand to help. "The blood?"

She answered honestly. "I've seen enough of it."

"I had to move it was so bad."

"Where did you move from, Larry?" The conversation seemed pointless, but Rae felt compelled to spend a few minutes with him. Sometimes listening made all the difference in a person's life. She doubted anyone had listened to Larry in a very long time.

"Lived on Central Avenue for years, nice place in the back shed." He slapped his hand over his mouth as if he'd said too much. "The owners didn't mind."

"It's all right, Larry. Go on."

"Had a runoff for rainwater behind, like my own personal spring…till it turned to blood."

The man talked in nonsensical circles and each word carried the stench of stale booze. Rae started to leave but asked one final question. "What was in front of your shed?"

"A dry cleaners."

The twinge of excitement ran up Rae's spine like a rat up a drainpipe. "Do you remember the people who owned the place? What were their names?"

"Nice man, bitchy woman—Blake, that's not right. Blanketburg, Blimp-ton, no Blanken-ship, I think. That's it, Blankenship. When the water went bad, I had to leave."

"How long ago?"

"'Bout a year, I'd say? Sure hated to move. All this stuff gets heavy." He grabbed the side of the Dumpster and waved his arm as if proudly displaying all his worldly possessions.

"Where on Central?"

"Corner of Central and Second. You gonna move in my old place?"

"No, I might ride by." Rae calculated the timeframe and location with the other dump sites. Blankenship's was quite a distance from her search area. If the site proved to be relevant, the suspect had deviated from "normal" criminal behavior and used his home turf as a dumping ground. Maybe she was grasping at straws.

Larry looked at her like she was the drunk one. "Been closed for years."

"Perfect. Thanks, Larry, and be careful out here." As she rounded the corner en route to her vehicle, she saw Larry settle back on the mattress and take another pull from his booze bottle. She prayed the poison hadn't completely liquefied his brain.

Chapter Eighteen

Arya quietly opened the apartment door and slid inside. Butler had just left with his beloved and he had no idea where they were going. He'd been tempted to follow them, but he had more urgent business. A crime-scene analyst was going through her apartment looking for evidence of him. Arya needed to make sure he didn't uncover anything. Finding out where Butler had taken her would be easy later.

He had planned to wait until the analyst left to remove his equipment, but couldn't resist the opportunity to test his abilities. He had so few chances in the ordered environment of a *civilized* society. So far the police had proved a pitiful opponent. He'd eluded Whitt for a year, and Butler was no closer to his real identity though he hid in plain sight. Perhaps the crime tech would be a more worthy adversary.

The methodical analyst went through each room with skilled precision as the hours passed. Arya was impressed with his attention to detail. He was so focused he hadn't noticed Arya shadowing him through the small apartment like a predator. Perhaps he'd underestimated this man. He might actually locate Arya's carefully concealed devices and eventually his nest. The mechanisms he'd used could never be traced to him, but they might put his source on a law-enforcement short list.

As the analyst rifled through *her* belongings, Arya became more agitated. He had no right to handle her things, to invade her privacy.

He was not worthy. In the bedroom, he pulled her delicate lingerie from the drawer and held it up to the light, leering and imagining like all of his undeserving class. A bulge grew in the front of his pants as he raised the item to his nose and inhaled. Arya's blood surged and his contained fury exploded. He lunged, pummeling the offending agent with his fist and a lead-weighted slapstick.

Arya had no idea how long he pounded the analyst before he regained control. His lapses into rage were becoming more frequent and his ability to control them less predictable. Such disciplinary failures would result in mistakes and eventual capture. He couldn't afford such carelessness. His mission was coming to a close, and he needed to remain on target until he was finally and forever reunited with her.

He kicked the unconscious analyst, rolled him over, and bound and gagged him. He was not yet dead but very close. Why had he not finished the job? Arya hadn't hesitated to kill the redheaded man who touched her. Perhaps he would die yet. The knots were secured so the man would choke himself if he tried to break free. Gathering the analyst by the collar and belt, Arya shoved him into the bedroom closet and slammed the door. He picked up her panties from the floor and stuck them in his pocket.

Arya took his time retrieving the equipment, careful not to leave a trace in the apartment or his nest. As daybreak dawned he slipped out to find her and begin final preparations. Someone would discover the analyst, alive or dead. Even if he survived, he hadn't seen Arya and wouldn't be able to identify him. The analyst was irrelevant; soon he and his beloved would be on their way to a new life.

Audrey awakened in the morning to Yasi's urgent moaning next to her in bed, her face twisted with the kind of torment Audrey recognized from her own nightmares. A light sheen of perspiration covered her face and neck. "Yasi, wake up. You're all right. It's a bad dream."

"No!" Yasi screamed, and immediately six concerned faces appeared at their door.

Audrey purposely didn't touch Yasi, recalling her own terrifying images of being grabbed. "You're safe, darling. We're in a hotel. Remember?"

Yasi's deep-brown eyes scanned the room nervously before settling on her cirque friends huddled in the doorway and then on Audrey. "I remember." She took a few deep breaths and waved the others in. "Who announced the curtain call?"

"You did," Melvin and Tony answered together. They smiled at each other like Adonis bookends.

"Where else would we be? We're family." Audrey handed her a glass of water as their friends perched around the edges of the king-sized bed and fussed over her. She held Yasi, rocking and cooing reassurances until she relaxed in her arms.

While the others bolstered Yasi, Audrey thought about Rae and wished she were here as well. Then her family would be complete. Rae and her friends working together, united by the need to protect someone they loved. She couldn't picture the two coming together for any reason before all this happened. Maybe the division between her disparate worlds wasn't so great. Love and grief were great equalizers, but what would happen when the case ended?

She'd never felt such a desire to be with someone, to share every aspect of her life, and to plan a future. But she didn't have anything to offer Rae—not a loving family to dote on her, a large bank account, an impressive career, and certainly not the level of sexual experience she was used to. What would Rae see in a psychic circus brat with a penchant for attracting weirdoes? Her heart ached at the thought.

"Have you heard from Rae?" Yasi asked.

When Audrey returned her attention to Yasi, the others had left the room. As usual when she thought about Rae, her mind wandered and she lost track of time. She wasn't even able to read the woman beyond her surface moods. How frustrating. "No."

"Don't worry. I'm sure she worked all night and will call as soon as she can."

Audrey wasn't at all sure what Rae would and wouldn't do. She could only trust her heart and hope for the best.

"Would you mind helping with my bandage? It's a bit awkward to handle alone."

"Of course I don't mind." Yasi hadn't offered to let Audrey see her injuries before. She had hidden them, along with news of the Whisperer, until Rae told her the whole story. Suddenly the task seemed daunting. She was barely able to look at her own abdomen, sliced and scarred by the madman's blade. Seeing her best friend similarly disfigured would be almost unbearable. Audrey reminded herself of the earlier vow of courage and reached for the wrapping around Yasi's middle.

"Will you be all right?" Yasi placed her hand gently over Audrey's.

"I'll be fine. You're still you, and I still love you. This is one more thing we have in common, one more reason you'll never be able to get rid of me. Now lean forward."

She gave Yasi her bravest smile and unwound the bulky bandage down to the dressings. When she removed the final layer, the nerves in her gut twisted into an angry knot. Yasi's once-flawless skin was crisscrossed with slashes and patched with a combination of sutures, staples, and skin adhesives. Audrey mapped out in her mind the areas that would heal without leaving a trace and those that would forever haunt her friend. What type of person did this sort of damage?

"Hand me that small mirror on the side table," Yasi said. "I'd like to look when you've cleaned it up a bit. I want to know what someone else sees when they look at me now."

"Yasi, don't, not yet."

"I've got to get used to it…and I know it isn't easy." Her eyes held both question and apology.

"No, darling, it isn't." She gave Yasi the mirror and gently cleaned the wounds before reaching for another dressing. When she looked back, her mind flashed to another time, to a very similar injury.

A cold wind brushed across her face and added to the exuberance of the night. Even the throngs of people pushing in around her didn't curb her excitement. The show had been perfect, her performance outstanding. She was meeting her friends for a celebratory drink before heading home.

The crowd thinned as she veered off toward the neighborhood bar. Looking up at the quarter moon, she wished it were full. The night would be perfect. She skipped along the sidewalk like she'd done as a child and avoided the cracks. Whistling the theme song of her favorite TV show, she felt totally alive. Being in front of an audience exhilarated her.

She turned down the last side street before the bar and thought how dark it looked. Remnants of the shattered security light littered the path. A sweet smell wafted to her nostrils and she turned to search for the source. From behind, someone placed a piece of fabric over her nose and mouth. The smell grew stronger. Her eyes and nose watered, and the skin around her face burned. Drowsiness oozed down her spinal column and branched out into every nerve. She struggled momentarily before dropping to the pavement. The quarter moon disappeared, replaced by total darkness and recurring pain.

When she eventually tried to open her eyes she had no idea how much time had passed. She could make out only quick splashes of color and an occasional glint of metal in the muted light under the edge of her blindfold. A man's voice commanded her—to do what? She couldn't focus. The metal flashed again, burning and stinging. Everything was hard and cold. She felt like she was in a coffin, unable to move and certain of death. She screamed but the sound was muted too.

"Unspoiled," he whispered. "You are my unspoiled, Sanjana. Unspoiled." Over and over the same words and a horrible grunting noise.

"Please! No more!"

"Audrey?" Yasi's tone was urgent, edged with fear. Their friends had heard Audrey's cries and returned, standing around the bed, concern and uncertainty evident on their faces. "Audrey, can you hear me?"

The heady flash receded as quickly as it surfaced, but the memory remained. "Yes." Her voice was weak as she tried to recall every point before it vanished like a dream. But this particular vision wouldn't vanish. Each facet was as detailed as if etched in stone, crystal clear and terrifying. She excavated the facts but pushed the emotions back down, unable to deal with them yet. The feelings would return again, and the visions would be even more defined later. When they reappeared, she wanted to be with Rae. "I remember."

Sam lightly touched her shoulder. "What do you remember, Sanjana?"

She looked up at him and her heart pounded out of control. Suddenly she felt like a trapped animal. "That's what *he* called me. You're the only one who calls me that." What if Sam was the attacker? What if the others already knew and were protecting him? She felt hot and sick to her depths. She had trusted Sam with her life on many occasions.

Yasi took her hand. "Audrey, you don't believe Sam…you're obviously upset. Think about what you're saying."

Audrey forced herself to breathe and reflect rationally. Sam would never hurt her and Yasi or anyone else. He was the kindest, most nonthreatening individual she'd ever met in spite of his sizeable physique. Sam was not the Whisperer. The memory that had finally returned after a year had rattled her and she was struggling for understanding. "I remember my attack."

Her hands shook as she wiped at a tear trickling down her cheek. "I remember everything." Leaning back against the pillow, she flipped through the scenario again as if reading a book. She didn't want to lose one tidbit of information that might help Rae's investigation.

The emerging truth relieved, excited, and frightened her. She quickly read everyone in the room as if tuning into the news channel. Her intuition was razor-sharp and unobstructed. *He* would no longer be able to hide from her. She could read him as well…if she could locate him. Audrey felt a sense of freedom that had been missing for a year, but it came with a price—remembering every minute detail.

"I'll call your cop friend, Rae. She needs to hear this as soon as possible." Tony reached for the room phone, started to dial, then stopped. "I don't have her number."

Yasi pointed to her cell phone on the bedside table. "Use mine. Speed-dial number two."

As Tony made the call, Audrey and Yasi clung to each other, and neither spoke. Words could never explain or erase what they'd experienced. They valued the peace and consolation of simply holding each other.

After what seemed a very long time, Yasi nodded toward her still-exposed injuries. "When you're okay, would you finish my bandages? No rush. I'll commit each mark to memory." Holding the mirror in front of her for several minutes, Yasi stared at the reflection. "Oh, my."

"What's wrong?" Audrey tried to take the mirror. Seeing yourself carved like a side of meat wasn't easy.

"Wait. Look at this." She moved the mirror aside to give Audrey a better view. "When I see the cuts from this angle," she held her hands out and lowered her head, "it's upside down and backward. When you see them standing in front of me, you get the image the way he intended, the way he wrote it. That's what I see in the mirror."

Audrey tried to follow her logic. "What do you mean, *the way he wrote it*?"

Yasi's eyes were wide, as if she'd discovered something unique and profoundly interesting. "This is writing, Arabic—crude but definitely symbols representing words. Mine says *traitor*. That's what he kept whispering. Let me see yours."

"Yasi, we're not playing show-and-tell here. Relax." Audrey touched Yasi's forehead, certain she'd developed a fever and was overstating the significance of what she'd seen.

"Aud, I'm not kidding. I grew up in Morocco and learned Arabic along with a few dialects. This is definitely writing. Let me see your scars, please."

Audrey had never shown anyone except Rae the physical reminder of her assault. Now in the presence of these seven people seemed the right time and place. They were facing danger together, and she'd hidden her secret from them for too long. She raised her baggy sleep shirt and pointed to the area above her bikini panty line. One at a time, her friends stepped forward, looked at the scars, then hugged and kissed her. Each one was as wonderful as they would've been a year ago, if Audrey had trusted them. She turned to Yasi last. "What do you see?" She still wasn't making total sense.

"Yours says *unspoiled*, I think. Some of the bits are missing."

Audrey's gasp filled the air and hung like a layer of smog, echoing off the walls and reverberating in her ears. How could Yasi know that? She hadn't yet told her what she remembered. It was the exact word he'd whispered to her—*unspoiled.*

"I'm right, aren't I?"

"Yes…he kept calling me his unspoiled Sanjana. I'm not sure what it means—that he writes on people. That's sick—er. Maybe Rae has an idea. I'll call her again."

As Audrey reached for her mobile, she heard Rae's authoritative knock at the door. She jumped off the bed and ran to her. The protection of Rae's arms helped her make sense of what was happening. Everything seemed to be unraveling at the same time. If they were lucky some of the pieces would fit into Rae's case puzzle.

She clung to Rae, soaking in the warmth of her body and the steady pounding of her heart. "I'm so glad to see you." Regardless of what happened after the case was solved, Rae would not stop until Audrey was safe and her attacker behind bars forever. "I remember what happened a year ago—all of it."

"Are you okay? That couldn't have been easy."

"It was frightening, but I'm all right. At least I can actually fill in the missing pieces."

Rae whispered in her ear, "I'm sorry I wasn't here for you. We'll talk about it in private. I want you to come home with me." They stood, bound like an entwined ivy wreath, for several minutes until Rae stepped back. "I understand Yasi has some news as well."

Audrey tried to convey her uncertainty with a look so she wouldn't upset the others. "You need to ask her. Do you have the case file?"

Rae raised the manila folder and followed Audrey into the bedroom.

Yasi sat in bed, her nightshirt pulled up under her breasts, sheet over her lower abdomen, her injuries still exposed. "Look at this." She pointed to her abdomen. "I've come up with another clue. It's Arabic." Yasi explained what she saw, then asked, "Do you have pictures of the other victims' injuries? I'm willing to bet he did the same thing to them. He was sending some kind of deranged message."

Yasi studied the photographs as Rae spread them on the bed in front of her. "This one says *liar.*" She read the other scrawled markings: *unclean, destroyer, poison*. Audrey was first—*unspoiled,* and I was last—*traitor*. There's a pattern, isn't there, Rae?"

Rae slid the photos back into the folder and tried to suppress her anxiety. She didn't want to alarm Yasi or Audrey, but she owed them the truth. "Yes, it seems that Audrey was his chosen, the only clean or unspoiled one. After her, he's been sending messages about the unsuitability of everyone else. He may have targeted you because of your connection to Audrey, or he may see you as a traitor because you're Moroccan, more closely related to his *chosen* identity than the other victims. This is only a guess, a working hypothesis." Barry Hewitt, the weapons analyst, had originally raised the possibility of the attacker sending messages with the cutting patterns, but Rae hadn't given it much thought. Now it made more sense.

Yasi lowered her shirt and stared at Rae. "And it fits with my observation of an acquired, possibly a controlled, accent, doesn't it? And if I'm right, he knows that Audrey's International Cirque name, Sanjana, means *untouchable* in Sanskrit."

"Yes." Rae caught a questioning look from Audrey and knew she had a lot of explaining to do. "I'll tell you later. We need to go. I'd very much like to hear what you remember."

Rae started to leave, then turned back to Yasi and the others. "Will you be okay for a while?" Yasi nodded and Rae added, "Don't leave here unless it's absolutely necessary. If you have to, go as a group." She waited for everyone to agree. "I'm serious. This is important." Again they nodded. "And thanks for the help. I see why you're all such great friends."

During the drive back to her condo, Rae wondered if Audrey was second-guessing further involvement in the case and/or with her. Rae recognized distrust and insecurity rearing its ugly head. While she'd been tracking down leads, the distance between them seemed enormous, but when they touched again she felt immediately reconnected. She wanted reassurance her feelings for Audrey were real and reciprocated. But she most desperately needed to make sure Audrey was safe.

She reached across the seat and cupped Audrey's hand in hers. The warmth spread through her. Losing Audrey would suck the vitality out of her life and leave her in a hole so deep that hell would be a step up. She didn't want to imagine a future without Audrey beside her everyday and in her bed every night.

Audrey squeezed her hand. "I've missed you, Detective."

She missed me. That would have to be enough for the moment. Courting, wooing, and seducing took a backseat to tracking down a potential killer. "You have no idea how glad I am to hear that because I've sure missed you."

"You're focused on this case. Don't feel guilty about that. Let's figure it out…then get on with our lives."

"Sometimes this psychic stuff is pretty handy." Rae was relieved Audrey understood the urgency of their situation. She shuffled the latest bits of information about the case round and round in her head as she unlocked the door to her condo. None of it made much sense in the abstract, but perhaps Audrey could help put things into proper context. She still had only fragments of a suspect profile, with other pieces still coming in. If she was very lucky, Audrey would put the finishing touches on a slowly evolving silhouette.

Audrey brewed a pot of coffee while Rae set up the study for their work. When Audrey placed the tray on a side table, Rae wrapped her arms around her. "Could I have one kiss before we start?"

"You can have several, but no monkey business."

Rae skimmed her hands down Audrey's back and grazed her sides before capturing her mouth. Audrey's lips melted against Rae's as their tongues entwined, probing and searching for the depths of each other's soul. Rae wanted to forget the world and focus only on Audrey, her needs, her desires, and her pleasure.

Pain pulsed between Rae's legs, seeking relief. She tilted her pelvis back to alleviate the pressure, but Audrey grabbed her ass and reconnected them. It would be so easy to surrender to the desire clawing at her insides. She wanted this woman in every way imaginable, and she wanted to start right now.

Rae slid her leg between Audrey's and rubbed against her crotch, receiving an appreciative moan. "Monkey business," Audrey whispered.

"No, this is *our* business, and I can't wait." She backed Audrey toward the bedroom, careful not to break contact, purposely stroking her again with each step. Her body was on fire and she was beyond wet. When Rae reached up to ease Audrey down on the bed, her cell phone vibrated. "Shit. I'll turn it off." She reached toward her belt to silence the offending device, but Audrey stopped her.

"You can't. It could be important. I can wait."

"What if I can't?" But Audrey was right. This could be the call she needed most. "Butler."

"Rae, it's Tammy in the lab. Have you seen Trevor Collins lately?"

Rae kissed Audrey's cheek and adjusted her uncomfortably soaked underwear. "Not since yesterday afternoon. He was processing a scene for me."

"Well, nobody has seen him since."

Rae's attention crystallized on Tammy's words. "He's missing?"

"It seems so."

Chapter Nineteen

When Audrey and Rae arrived at her apartment complex, two patrol cars and an ambulance were parked out front, with a sizeable group of onlookers. Audrey opened her front door and the officers pushed by, eager to search for Trevor. Her psychic antenna pinged and not in a good way. She called after them, "Look in the spare-bedroom closet." Since she'd remembered the assault, her instincts were consistently on target.

In a few minutes, one of the uniformed officers rushed out, ducked behind a boxwood, and threw up. He waved for the ambulance attendants and motioned them inside but didn't reenter the apartment.

"How is he?" Audrey tried to alleviate the officer's embarrassment. She already knew Trevor was badly beaten and barely alive.

"He's in pretty bad shape. I don't see how he's still breathing."

When the paramedics rolled the stretcher by, Audrey looked away. The image in her head was vivid enough without seeing the real thing. She waited until everyone except Rae was outside before she went in. "Darling, where are you?"

"In the bedroom." Rae stood in the middle of the room staring into the bloody closet. "It was the Whisperer."

"I know. I can feel him everywhere, especially right here."

Rae looked at where she stood in the hallway between the rooms. "You mean you can read him now?"

"I haven't made contact with him directly, but I can certainly sense his dark energy." Audrey pointed to the scratches Cannonball had made along the baseboards. "That darn kitten *was* trying to tell me something. She was trying to get to him—up there." Audrey indicated the narrow attic door over her head. The space barely seemed large enough for a cat, much less an adult male.

"Do you have a step stool or small ladder?"

Audrey retrieved the stool, and within minutes Rae shimmied into the crawl space and disappeared. She felt uncomfortable waiting below and not knowing what Rae saw, but she certainly knew what she felt—more anger and disgust. She called up, offering the only support she could at the moment. "Focus on your job." Her best advice wouldn't help. She felt the same sense of violation and helplessness. Audrey heard Rae talking on her phone and shortly afterward she came down.

Rae dusted the sticky fiberglass insulation off her clothes, shaking her head. "That son of a bitch was *living* in your crawl space. He accessed it from the vacant apartment next door. And you never sensed anything." The comment wasn't an accusation but a mere statement of disbelief.

"All I ever got from him was noise. Whenever I was home I always had my stereo on to block outside interference. He had to have been on guard constantly to prevent me from sensing him. Imagine the control that takes."

"I've got the lab folks on the way to process everything. If he left one molecule of evidence, they'll find it."

Audrey nodded and walked into her bedroom, which she'd never sleep in again. The brightly patterned walls no longer felt cheerful and inviting. Her skin prickled and the air around her crackled with evil energy. "He put something in the wall, here." She ran her hand across the textured wallpaper and felt unusual bumps. "Here, here, and here." She walked through the rest of the apartment indicating various points, like a sniffer dog tracking drugs. "There are two in the bathroom, kitchen, and living room."

Rae's face morphed into an unreadable mask, her emotions sparking like fireworks. "Is this what I think it is?" She retrieved a knife from her boot and poked at a spot in the bath wall.

"Cam—cameras." Audrey could barely say the word around the disgust and anger rising in her throat. She tried to remember how many showers she'd taken recently, how many nights she and Rae had snuggled and kissed on her sofa, and how often she'd masturbated thinking about Rae since they'd met. "The cameras were everywhere. He removed them."

"That must be why he attacked Trevor. He was afraid he'd find them."

"Yes. He's been watching me for a long time, Rae. I think he killed someone else." Audrey couldn't say the name because she'd led him straight to the victim.

"Jeremy Sutton?"

Audrey dropped onto her sofa and sobbed. "It *was*…because…of me."

Rae tried to reassure her, but Audrey knew the truth. She didn't deserve consolation. She'd tried to play detective and instead got an innocent man killed. The Whisperer had followed her to Sutton's house, seen them shake hands, and killed Sutton because he touched her. He was a deranged man who considered her his property.

"Don't blame yourself, Audrey. Help me find him. Can you see who he is?"

She shook her head. "That's one of the few things I can't see right now." The pain in her chest lingered while the possibility of helping mitigated some of the sting. "I can give you more information from my assault." Audrey prayed it would be enough.

"Let's get to work. Time's running out, and he's becoming more violent. I'm surprised he left Trevor alive."

"He doesn't believe Trevor saw him…and he isn't afraid."

"Well, he should be. He's got both of us on his trail. He should be very afraid."

Audrey gave Rae an appreciative smile and waited as she instructed the patrol officers and a crime-scene analyst before they left. Right now Rae's confidence and her own stubbornness were the only things keeping her going. Once the case was over, she'd probably have the nervous breakdown she'd put off for the past year.

When they returned to Rae's condo, the mood had entirely changed from earlier. They had been close to making love again, but now they were more somber. Each had a job to do and couldn't avoid or delay any longer.

Rae pulled Audrey against her on the settee as though settling in to watch a movie. "When you're ready, I'd like to hear what you remembered today."

"I'm ready. When I start, don't interrupt. Let me finish completely…no matter what happens." The time had finally come to speak the whole truth…everything she recalled, felt, and believed about the first time she was assaulted. Rae would want it all. Audrey took a deep breath and let the memory surface. She didn't try to temper or hide the feelings this time, and she was unprepared for their intensity.

Waves of horror washed over her as fresh as the night it happened. She struggled against the bindings at her wrists and ankles until her skin chafed. The blade sliced through her like fire, and she flinched and thrashed from the sensory memory. His whispered words echoed in her head as if he'd screamed them, and she covered her ears to block the sound. When she tried to beg for her life, she gagged on the musty rag stuffed into her mouth. She cried aloud, prayed silently, and pleaded with her eyes.

He grunted and moaned like a man desperate for sexual gratification but unable to obtain it. The vehicle rocked with his rhythmic struggle and vibrated with the sounds of flesh angrily pounding flesh until he erupted in a frustrated wail. Audrey recoiled and waited for the next strike of the knife. She felt dizzy and near blackout.

When the darkness came, she saw everything in slow motion. She described it all in intricate detail. The pain stopped and she heard a soft voice calling in the distance. "Audrey, are you okay? Can you hear me?"

Rae. She was safe. "I'm all right now." Her voice cracked and her mouth felt parched. She was pressed against Rae's side and drenched in perspiration. "Water."

She took the bottle Rae offered and downed half before stopping. The cool liquid eased the dryness in her throat as her pulse calmed. "Do you want to ask questions or should I tell you what I remember about him?"

"Are you sure you're up for this? You look exhausted already." She stroked Audrey's arm reassuringly. "It can wait."

"No, it can't. I'll start and you can ask questions as I go." Rae nodded. "First, the smell was very sweet and on something that he placed over my nose and mouth."

"Chloroform, go on."

"I was inside a van, I'm certain because of the back-and-forth motion—and I saw it. The blindfold came partially off when he dumped me out. The van was old and white, as I said before. There had been an emblem on the side but was painted over, no license tag."

"Good." Rae jotted notes as Audrey spoke.

"I've already described the knife—definitely serrated and military issue. He's served in conflict, often. It's his preferred way of life." Audrey battled a resurgence of emotion as she recalled the atmosphere of turmoil inside the van. She hadn't been able to get into his head, but the turbulence surrounding him was thick enough to touch.

"He wore blue, medium-blue, like a uniform of some sort, not military. His hands, face, and feet were covered. He wore covers on his shoes…strange."

"Of course," Rae said. "The footprints at the community center and outside my window weren't real shoeprints, more like fabric. Some kind of cover would certainly explain that."

"And it would explain why I couldn't see his feet." Rae gave her a questioning look. "Don't ask. It's how my mind works—not always definite pictures, just flashes of seemingly unrelated pieces. I didn't actually see the blue uniform at the time, only the color and a sense of the uniform. You'll need to follow up on that."

Audrey was elated as more and more of the event emerged. She was beginning to understand Rae's attraction to the job of uncovering clues, chasing leads, and finding criminals—not that she'd ever want to be a cop. She loved the feeling that she and Rae were tackling something important together.

"What can you tell me about him? How he looked, felt, any sense of him at all?"

"Physically, he's lean and muscular, quite strong. I sensed extreme confidence and desperation—one professional, the other personal. Something is definitely torturing him, maybe physical damage or injury that challenges his self-concept."

Rae turned on the settee to face Audrey and stared at her as if something new had occurred to her. "Did he…I mean…"

Her voice was thick with emotion. The words seemed too painful for her to say, and Audrey knew immediately what she meant. The pressure of handling six unsolved cases had to be tremendous, especially when two of them involved acquaintances. She cupped Rae's face and stared directly into her eyes when she answered. "No, my darling. He didn't rape me or even touch me sexually, at least not in the conventional sense."

"What does *that* mean?"

"I'm not sure I can explain it. The air was definitely sexually charged. He thought I could give him something he desperately needed. I couldn't. It was almost as if he used the knife as a penile substitute without vaginal penetration."

"Jeez, he sounds like one sick bastard."

"It's a feeling and I'm no psychologist, so don't quote me." She gave Rae a quick peck on the cheek for reassurance.

"Did you detect an accent?"

"Yes, definitely not native. I couldn't place the area. Sorry. Yasi is much better with languages. It's an acquired skill. I read energy, she knows accents. He called me Sanjana, so he must have been to one of my cirque performances."

Each time Audrey revealed another tidbit about the Whisperer, Rae's face glowed with enthusiasm. She was pleased to be the source of Rae's renewed hope. She had seen her struggle for weeks, blaming herself for the lack of progress and taking personal responsibility for the victims.

"Anything else about his injury?"

"I'm afraid not, my darling. Remember, everything I've said comes with a big red disclaimer. These are only my perceptions, energy readings, and flashes of memory. It's now your job to find out if I'm right."

"Absolutely, and you've given me plenty to do. Thank you. I know it wasn't easy."

Audrey rested her head against Rae's shoulder and felt a rush of relief and satisfaction. Her psychic ability wasn't a fortunetelling novelty to hawk on the street or an embarrassment to hide. Her mother's prediction had come true—her skills served a useful purpose. Maybe times were changing and diversity of all types was becoming more acceptable. Or maybe it always had been and she was too afraid to try. Not any more, Audrey thought as she drifted to sleep.

Rae felt Audrey relax on her lap and realized she'd fallen asleep. She brushed a strand of blond hair from Audrey's forehead and stared at her completely tranquil face. She breathed the deep, even cadence of the unburdened. Keeping her secrets for the past year couldn't have been easy for a woman with Audrey's sensitivity. Rae had the feeling Audrey was finally free of the ghosts and nightmares, and she was honored to have witnessed the purging.

She eased Audrey down on the sofa, pulled a blanket over her, and crept into the kitchen. As much as she wanted to stay exactly where she was and hold Audrey while she slept, she wanted her safe more. She called records and held her breath as Loretta Granger located her search requests. While she waited, she asked, "Has anyone heard about Trevor?"

"His supervisor said he would be okay. He's got fractured ribs, a broken arm, internal bruising, and a serious concussion though." They shared a moment of there-but-for-the-grace-of-God silence that seemed universal anytime one of their own was injured. "Here are your results, Rae. I crosschecked all the variables you gave me—dry cleaners in the Central Avenue area against tax and utility bills. Then I ran those results against motor-vehicle registrations of old white vans. And—"

"And what?"

"Hold on, Sport. I have good news and bad news. Which do you want first?"

"Loretta, don't tease. Give it to me." Rae's skin tingled. Whatever Loretta told her would move her investigation in one direction or another, progress of a sort.

"Five dry cleaners in the area with white vans, three still in operation. That's the good news. The bad news is, of the two remaining, their former owners are both dead."

"What were the owners' names?"

"Blankenship and Albright. Blankenship was closer to Central and Second."

Rae did a quick mental calculation. "We're probably not looking for the owners anyway. I'd say a younger relative, maybe even a child. Can you check birth records for me?"

"Sure."

Maybe Larry the street urchin wasn't as pickled as Rae originally thought. He said he'd lived in a shed behind Blankenship's Dry Cleaners at the corner of Central and Second.

"Loretta, would you concentrate on Blankenship first? Also run a broad criminal-history check of Blankenships between the ages of twenty-five and thirty-five. Call my cell if you come up with anything, and thanks."

Rae hung up and dialed her local contact with the military. They had an understanding that, if they communicated, they wouldn't use names just in case. The information they needed from each other often required a violation of either military or public-sector disclosure laws. For that reason, they limited their exchanges to critical cases.

When he answered, Rae was clear and concise. She regurgitated the profile she'd developed, praying it would be enough, afraid it wouldn't be. "Former member, possibly covert ops, advanced medical training, language skills probably Arabic or similar region, between twenty-five and thirty-five, Caucasian male."

"That's too broad. Anything more specific?"

"He was probably discharged within the last eighteen to twenty-four months, maybe due to an injury. I know that doesn't help much. It's all I've got right now."

"Not enough defining parameters. Search results that large attract attention. Call me back when you have more." The line went dead.

Rae considered throwing her phone across the room, but feared she might wake Audrey. The request had been a long shot, and he was perfectly right to deny the search. She couldn't blame him for protecting himself. She'd jumped the gun. Rae was missing something and Audrey had the key—maybe not consciously, but she definitely had the answer.

After making herself a cup of coffee, Rae fired up her computer, anxious to see if Audrey's information meshed with known facts. Loretta had provided the names of two closed dry cleaners, and Rae pulled up the Web site of each one. Fortunately, many businesses left their Web sites online long after they closed, simply forgetting to delete them.

She checked the Albright Laundry first and scanned the pages for pictures. On the services page, she found two coverall-clad employees posed beside a white Albright van. The coveralls were dark. Rae enhanced the picture for a closer look—dark gray, not blue. She silently praised the Internet for once again saving her endless hours of legwork.

Her spirits lifted as she typed in the Blankenship search. On the home page, the man identified as the owner, Earl Blankenship, and his wife, Evelyn, stood with their entire staff, all dressed in medium-blue coveralls beside a white panel van. Bingo. The man and woman even seemed to fit Larry's description: *nice man, bitchy woman.* He had a kind face and genuine smile. Her nose was lifted slightly and the edges of her mouth curled into a sneer. She seemed to be unhappy with her outfit, the cameraman, or a smell in the air… maybe all three.

Rae was finally making headway. Though she hadn't identified the suspect yet, every ounce of her cop's intuition told her she was in his neighborhood, possibly even on his doorstep.

"What's new, darling?" Audrey hugged her from behind and nuzzled her back.

Rae closed her laptop and turned in Audrey's arms. "Say it again." She loved being called darling. No one had ever used such endearments with her. Perhaps her other lovers thought a tough cop wasn't the sweet-nothings type. The pet name sounded natural and sincere coming from Audrey.

"*What's new* or *darling*?" Audrey teased her, standing on tiptoes to kiss her earlobe. "Darling, my darling, sweet darling, strong-cop darling."

Rae cupped her ass and pulled them closely together. "Now you're definitely teasing me, so turnabout is fair play." She ground her hips into Audrey's and felt her surrender before she pulled away. "Sorry, no can do. I have leads to follow up." The disappointed look on Audrey's face mirrored the ache in her own body.

"I think *this* requires considerable follow-up."

Audrey kissed her with such passion Rae lost her balance, and they stumbled back against the counter. She languished in the softness and hunger of Audrey's mouth as their kiss deepened. The temptation to put everything on hold and concentrate on Audrey was seductive. They'd had so little time together recently, and Audrey deserved to be courted and cherished. But she couldn't be so selfish when other people's safety was at stake. If there was justice in the world, Audrey would still be interested once the case closed.

Rae reluctantly stepped out of Audrey's arms. The Whisperer's victims depended on her. One day she would deserve to call each one by name—the day she caught him. "I promise all the follow-up you need very soon."

Audrey looked at her with complete understanding and the closest thing to love she'd ever seen reflected in a pair of indigo eyes. "Back to the original question. What's new?"

Rae filled her in on the latest details between light kisses and ear nibbling. Her efforts to remain totally professional evaporated when Audrey was within reach. "Let's throw darts. I'm waiting for a couple of calls, and I need to concentrate. You're very distracting."

She took Audrey's hand and led her back into the study. "Do you remember your first lesson?" Audrey gave her a doe-eyed shake of the head so gorgeous Rae's insides quivered. She reviewed the basics of dart throwing and turned Audrey loose on one of the two boards tacked to the wall. Rae aimed at the other and was soon lost in the details of the case.

Position, aim, release, and retrieve. She landed three darts perfectly in the bull's-eye and went to pull them out. As she turned,

Audrey released a wobbly throw and the dart sailed toward her. She dodged, barely missing a head shot, but the dart spiraled into her left inner thigh. "Ouch." She stared at the dangling projectile, not quite able to believe what she saw.

Audrey rushed to her side. "Oh, my gosh. I'm so sorry. I guess I wasn't paying attention. I'm so awful at this game. You should never trust me with sharp objects. I cut my underarms when I shave. Rae, I'm sorry. Does it hurt? Let me—"

Rae placed her fingers over Audrey's lips. She was more upset than Rae. "It's all right. It didn't do any serious damage. My jeans took most of the impact."

"Take them off."

"Now you're talking." Rae reached for her belt and shucked her jeans to the floor before Audrey could clarify her intent. As her pants fell, so did the dart. A small streak of blood trickled down her thigh.

"You're bleeding. Sit down." Audrey grabbed a tissue from the end table, knelt in front of her, and dabbed the wound. "It doesn't look too bad. I'm so sorry."

Rae was amazed by the tenderness in Audrey's words and touch. She finger-combed her short hair and tried to reassure her. "Don't worry. I'm glad it wasn't a bit higher and to the right. I could've been out of commission for a while, if you get my drift."

Audrey suddenly sat back on her heels as if she'd been pushed. "That's it. Why didn't I see it sooner? It all makes sense now."

Audrey wore the same expression as earlier when she talked about her assault and the Whisperer. When she could, she'd explain. Rae couldn't picture a life constantly interrupted by the moods, thoughts, or feelings of others. Living daily under those circumstances required mental resilience and stamina Rae wasn't certain she possessed. Her admiration for Audrey increased exponentially as she waited for her next disclosure.

"He's injured in a horrible way. His manhood has been almost completely destroyed."

Rae wasn't sure what to say. War was responsible for atrocities of all kinds so it shouldn't surprise her. Was it poetic justice for a man capable of such heinous crimes or the cause of his pathology? "You literally mean his genitals, right?"

Audrey nodded. "How is that even possible without loss or disability of his legs?"

"I have no idea. Groin injuries have to be pretty common with lower-body trauma. Ballistic boxers are relatively new for soldiers."

Audrey looked like she didn't quite believe her comment about the boxers. "Will this help with your search?"

Rae reached for her phone in the heap with her discarded jeans. "Absolutely." She pulled her pants on as she dialed her military contact and added the additional detail. His answer sent a thrill up Rae's spine.

"I'll have a packet, complete with photos, delivered to your place before morning."

Rae hung up and turned to Audrey. "We're getting closer, thanks to you. Now I should probably get you back to the hotel."

Audrey's eyes sparked as she snuggled closer to Rae. "I don't suppose I could stay with you tonight?"

"I wish, but I have some things to run down. You'll be safer with the others." Audrey's expression changed. "I'm sorry. I'd love to spend the night with you, but—"

"I know, my darling. I know."

"I'll call you first thing in the morning and let you know how it's going."

"First thing? Promise?"

"Promise, so keep your cell handy. I know it has a tendency to run off on you." Rae reached for Audrey, but she darted out of her grasp.

"Then we should go, right now. If you touch me again, I won't be able to remain genteel and understanding."

CHAPTER TWENTY

Rae wiped the grime from a window at the rear of the Blankenship Dry Cleaners building and squinted to get a better look. The single streetlight in front cast shadows through the interior and hindered her efforts to identify the contents. She clicked on her Maglite and scanned as far inside as the beam allowed. Rolls of plastic on huge spools occupied half of one wall, and several racks of uniforms took up the other half. Forensic analysis would determine if this plastic was the same as that left at the dump sites with the victims.

She shifted and light bounced off a reflective surface, a hubcap. Rae focused the beam higher and her heart nearly stopped—an old white van was wedged between huge washing and pressing machines and partially covered by a blue tarp. The conveyor belt with abandoned pieces of clothing snaked around the top of the van, providing further camouflage. When she'd looked from the front, she missed the vehicle entirely.

Reaching into her right boot, she fished out her switchblade and flicked it open. She trained her light on the door lock and poised the knife to pry it open just before her professional monitor kicked in. *Damn it, damn it, damn it.* Just once she could bypass a precious search-and-seizure law. One lapse in a twelve-year career wasn't bad. She could slip inside, nose around, and *then* get a warrant. No one would be the wiser. If anyone asked about probable cause, she'd only have to tell one little white lie. The case was serious enough no one would blame her even if they did find out.

She positioned the knife blade perfectly to pop the lock and raised her elbow for leverage. *Shit.* She couldn't do it, not for the victims, not even for Audrey. If she bypassed procedure, she'd be a bad cop. If she covered it up, she'd be a lying bad cop. And if the Whisperer were convicted on evidence improperly obtained, she'd be a worthless, lying bad cop. She had to follow proper procedure. It was the only way to ensure he stayed in prison once she put him there and to maintain her self-respect and integrity. Morals and values were a pain in the ass.

Her gut told her the rest of what Audrey had experienced was inside the van. She'd have to go with the information she had and pray it was enough for a search warrant. She couldn't do anything else here for the moment. Waking a judge before dawn wouldn't help her case. She dropped the knife back into her boot and switched off the Maglite.

The blow landed in her gut, knocking the wind out of her. She doubled over, unable to breathe. As she gasped for a reviving breath, the sickly sweet smell scorched a path down her throat. Her nose and eyes burned and watered. She struggled against powerful arms but her limbs had turned heavy and sluggish. With a final surge, she kicked and heard a wail of agony before she collapsed.

Arya clutched his aching groin and drew heaving breaths to remain conscious. Butler had gotten in only one kick but it landed perfectly. If she hadn't been drugged, he would've been forced to kill her and his leverage would've vanished. He spat on her crumpled form at his feet. In ordinary times they would face off in a fair fight to the death, warrior to warrior. She would see his true superiority. But these were not ordinary times. Now she was his pawn, a means of securing Sanjana.

He'd offer to exchange the cop for her. In reality, he'd never release Butler. She had touched Sanjana, and she would die slowly and painfully as an offering to his beloved. The sacrifice would cleanse Sanjana and their life together could go on. A simple, perfect plan.

Arya considered his protective gear but it was time for full disclosure. Everyone would know the true identity of the Noble One before he and Sanjana were joined. He opened a black canvas bag and inventoried the contents. The assortment of restraints and devices of torture would work nicely. He loaded the bag and Butler in the trunk of her vehicle and drove to her condo. He had to get her inside and make final preparations before dawn. How appropriate for the ceremony to take place where she had defiled his beloved. Life was full of symbolism and his would live forever.

❖

Audrey paced the hotel suite and checked her cell phone for what seemed like the thousandth time since dawn. Rae had promised to call early this morning. Something was terribly wrong.

"Jeez, Audrey, how is anybody supposed to sleep with all this pacing?" Melvin asked. "Tony woke up in a pissy mood and demanded coffee without even a *please*."

"I'm sorry, Mel, but I have an awful feeling."

"Curtain call!" He yelled back toward the other bedrooms, and within seconds everyone scurried into the common area, pulling on whatever pieces of random clothing they'd found.

"What?" Tony didn't look happy but he could never resist a drama.

Hope, Grace, and Charity bounced in like teenagers ready for the next adventure, with Sam bringing up the rear, a supportive arm around Yasi's waist.

"Something is wrong, Sanjana?" Sam asked.

"It's Rae, isn't it, honey?" Yasi made her way to Audrey's side and encouraged her to sit with her on the sofa. "Tell us. What have you heard?"

Audrey felt awful for pulling her friends from sleep on nothing more than a feeling. She had been right too many times before, and they knew it. "That's the problem, I haven't heard *anything*. She promised to call first thing this morning."

Tony pivoted and started toward the bedroom. "False alarm. Insecure-girlfriend alert. I'm going back to bed."

Audrey continued. "And I have a strong sense that she's in real danger."

Tony spun on his heel and rejoined the group. "That's different. What can we do?"

"I'm not sure if *we* should do anything. I'm going to her place to make sure she's okay. Who knows, I could be wrong." Everybody stared at her like that was highly unlikely, and Melvin rolled his eyes.

Yasi, her constant source of grounding and stability, rubbed Audrey's back. "You can't go alone. Rae made us promise we'd protect each other."

"We stick together," Charity said. Grace and Hope nodded in agreement.

Tony concluded with his usual flair. "We're like rabid, caffeinated bats. If somebody messes with one of us, he messes with all of us."

Audrey didn't like the idea of her friends getting involved, but she loved them for wanting to help. "Yasi isn't well enough to be out. Why don't we split up? A couple of you come with me and the rest can stay here."

"I'm going." Yasi's tone left no room for discussion. "I don't care if I have to stay in the van, I'm going…we all are. Let's move."

Audrey was proud of how they all looked after each other. That's one of the things she'd missed most about her friends. How could she have doubted their loyalty? She was the one who had been disloyal, leaving without any explanation. One day she'd repay them.

As Melvin drove by Rae's condo and parked on a side street, Audrey looked around the area. Rae's car was in the driveway but not backed into her usual spot against the garage door. A large manila envelope leaned against the front door. Rae had been expecting more information, and it could be exactly what she needed.

Suddenly Audrey grew light-headed, and her vision blurred. The top of her head tingled with the warning of a psychic flash. She heard a summons in the distance, a dangerous siren call she didn't want to answer. She had no choice. He was finally allowing her in, insisting she connect, like a telepathic phone call.

"Sanjana, come to me. I am waiting. The cop is no longer a problem."

"He's in there…he has Rae. I think she's injured, not—" She couldn't say the word. "He's calling me. I have to go in."

"No." Sam spoke first, his booming voice echoing inside the vehicle. "You do not go in alone."

"I have to, Sam, or he'll kill her." She could feel the Whisperer's hatred of Rae. Audrey had to defuse his anger, redirect his erratic emotions.

"Is there a back door?" Tony asked.

"You can bet he's got it covered," Melvin answered.

Audrey grew impatient. "I can't sit here and wait."

Yasi, who had been listening and staring out the side window, spoke for the first time. "I have a plan. Girls, ring a couple of doorbells on either side of Rae's place. Pretend you've lost your cat. Then find a place on both sides of the house near the windows so you can listen."

Audrey had the feeling she was missing a vital piece of information she should have before confronting the Whisperer. "One of you bring me whatever's on the steps of Rae's condo. It could be important."

Melvin, always the pragmatist, played devil's advocate. "He won't answer the door."

"Exactly," Yasi said, "but it'll distract him for a few minutes so Tony can find a way in. Whatever it takes, get into that house."

Melvin looked shocked. "And then what, choke him with his feather boa?"

Tony came to his rescue. "Leave it to me. I'll create such a distraction he won't know which way to turn." He paused as if considering his statement. "How will I know when?"

"You'll know." Audrey warmed to Yasi's idea, risky and unrefined as it was. She still wasn't clear how they'd rescue Rae and incapacitate the Whisperer. She had to do something and these friends were all she had—or were they?

"We'll need more help." Audrey jotted down a phone number and a message and handed it to Yasi. Since you'll have to wait in the vehicle—sorry, love—call this number when Tony starts his distraction. The girls will give you the high sign. Say exactly what I've written."

"And what about me and Melvin?" Sam asked.

"Melvin at the front door, and you at the back." Audrey wanted her strongest friends at the points of exit if things went terribly wrong. "If he tries to get away, take him down."

"I should be with you, Sanjana," Sam said.

"You'll be there when I need you. You all will." Audrey looked at each one of them, trying to convey her deep appreciation. "Are you sure you want to do this? He's not a stable man, and Rae isn't one of us."

"She is if you love her." Yasi stared at Audrey, her brown eyes asking the question.

"I do."

"Then let's get on with it." Tony's statement conveyed more excitement than his expression, and she loved him for it. His enthusiasm was contagious and the others followed suit. "I can't wait to interrogate this cop and see if she deserves you…and us."

"Wait." Audrey didn't intend to give the Whisperer what he wanted too soon. She sensed his frenzy growing with each minute. When she arrived, she wanted his attention entirely on her. The more off-balance he was, the greater the chance their half-baked scheme would actually work. And Rae was undoubtedly planning her own way out. She would've given anything right now to be able to read Rae just once.

Audrey watched as the others took their places around the condo and marveled again at the depth of their devotion. She clung to Yasi's hand as if it were their last second together and prayed Rae would get to know and appreciate her very special friends. In a few minutes, Charity returned with the manila envelope from Rae's steps.

Audrey reached for it with a trembling hand and eased open the flap as if it might explode. She looked inside, then poured the contents onto her lap. Several pictures spilled out of the same man in different modes of military wear—dull-green training uniform, desert fatigues, and command blouse. The last photo depicted the man in civilian attire. A notation on the back indicated the shot was taken on the date of dismissal from service, twenty months earlier.

Audrey clutched the images and stared into the face of a man she'd seen every day for almost a year—Marc Pearson, one of the mayor's bodyguards. "Oh, my God. Not Marc. He's not capable of something like this. I would've known." She realized with a sudden wave of guilt that she *hadn't* known. She hadn't picked up anything from her attacker, and she'd never bothered to scan the mayor's protection detail because they'd been vetted for the job. Audrey simply assumed they were stable, reliable individuals. God, what had she done?

Yasi took the photos from Audrey and looked at them. "I've seen this man at our performances. He was there the night of your attack, waiting outside the arena when we left for the bar. You were running behind and we went ahead to get a table. As we walked away, he did too." Yasi stared at Audrey, her eyes full of regret. "We didn't wait for you. When we looked later, you'd already gone—It was like you vanished. We searched for months."

"Yasi, it wasn't your fault. Forget about that and let's stop him, now."

Audrey concentrated on the man inside Rae's condo, addressing him by name for the first time. "Marc, I know who you are."

As if reading her mind, Marc Pearson ranted. *"I am Arya, the Noble One. Come to me, Sanjana."* His intonation was no longer that of the Caucasian male she'd worked with the past twelve months.

Turning to Yasi, Audrey hugged her and kissed her cheeks. "I have to go in. I'll reason with him to let Rae go. Let's pray Tony can get inside. When you hear the commotion, call the number I gave you."

"Be careful, Aud. This isn't one of our crazy cirque acts. This is for keeps."

As Audrey walked toward the condo, she tried to imagine what she'd say to the man she'd worked beside for a year but had never really known—a man who had brutally attacked her twice and then taken his rage out on others. Words failed. She summoned her courage and knocked.

When Marc Pearson opened the door, Audrey stared into eyes so dark they appeared soulless. She'd never noticed the unemotional air surrounding him. He'd always seemed professionally detached. She tried to connect with her mind but he blocked her.

"We will speak aloud."

"Marc—"

"I am *Arya.*" His voice boomed and Audrey recoiled as the door slammed behind her. When he spoke again, he whispered in the lilted foreign accent she remembered. "Don't be afraid, but you *must* address me properly, Sanjana. I have waited so long for you. Many things have changed, but I will make everything right."

The fear and pain of that night returned and Audrey felt helpless. His whispered threats were like the knife's blade slicing through her flesh again. Her breathing quickened and her undergarments clung to the dampness of her skin. Audrey could hear the frustration in his voice and feel the rage of his energy as he moved closer. If all the sensations returned, she'd be incapacitated and unable to help Rae. She forced the images from her mind and pictured herself surrounded by a layer of protection. "Where is Rae?"

Arya turned on her and raised his hand as if to strike. "Your first concern is for *her*? *She* is the one who has defiled you, and *she* must pay."

Audrey was stunned by the vehement response. Her senses hummed with warning. She fought the urge to run, but Rae needed her. "I'm not worried for her. My concern is for your safety. If she's here, she could pose a danger." She forced herself to step closer to him and gaze into his flat, dark eyes. She needed to gain his confidence and see for herself that Rae was still alive. Sometimes feelings weren't enough, and this time she needed visual confirmation.

"She is harmless," Arya said. He led the way into the bedroom where Rae lay on her stomach, hog-tied on the floor with a gag over her mouth. When they entered, she struggled against the ropes that had already cut into her arms, her eyes pleading with Audrey to escape. Audrey wanted to go to her immediately but Arya watched for her reaction.

"You've done a wonderful job of restraining her. I want her out of here."

Her response was obviously not what either of them expected. Rae looked at her wide-eyed like she'd lost her mind, and Arya appeared confused. "Why?"

"This is our time, and I want us to be completely alone, undistracted."

Arya seemed to consider what she'd said but wasn't convinced. "You let her touch you. I saw you go into her bedroom, *this* bedroom, together. I watched from the window."

"You didn't see what happened, did you?" He shook his head. "I couldn't go through with it. I felt your presence and knew I had to save myself for you."

"You knew I was watching?"

"We're connected, surely you know that." Audrey tried to lie convincingly, though she rejected the bitter words with every ounce of her being.

"Prove you are loyal to me…only me."

"How?" Audrey shivered to think what he would require of her.

"Tell her and then I will cleanse you in her blood."

A scream rushed up Audrey's throat and almost choked her. Visions of the unimaginable flashed through her mind, and with each one her heart ached and her anger grew. She would have to give the performance of her life to save Rae. She forced one foot in front of the other until she stood beside Rae with her back to Arya. When she looked at Rae's bruised face, she wanted nothing more than to hold and comfort her. Audrey's energy drained as she made herself remain still. She prayed Rae would forgive her for the egregious lies she was about to tell. Audrey allowed her contrition to wash over her face and burn in her eyes as she began the distasteful delivery.

"I don't care about you. I never have. There is nothing between us." Tears pooled in Rae's eyes, and Audrey willed her to understand. "What you do with women is disgusting. I am not like you."

Arya smiled and moved closer to Rae as he pulled a serrated knife from his waistband. "And now you will pay for touching my Sanjana."

"No! Wait." She pulled Arya into the hallway between the rooms, desperate to put distance between Rae and the menacing knife he held. "I don't care what you do to her, but you know how sensitive I am. I don't like seeing people injured. Isn't there another way?"

Rae strained against the ropes biting into her arms and watched as Audrey lured Marc Pearson into the hallway away from her. The words she'd said burned into Rae like a brand even though Audrey hadn't meant any of them. Her words relayed one message while her eyes sent an entirely different one. Audrey's azure gaze infused Rae with the courage to fight.

When she'd woken up in the trunk of her own vehicle, she hadn't been sure if she'd ever see Audrey again. But this time Marc Pearson, aka the Whisperer, made mistakes. He was so certain of his plan and his ability to escape he hadn't taken precautions. He hadn't even searched her properly. Now she knew who he was *and* she was still alive. As long as she drew breath she'd fight.

While Pearson's back was turned, Rae twisted as much as possible for a better look behind her, then carefully positioned her hands under her feet at precisely the right angle. She would have only one chance to get this right. If she failed, she and Audrey would probably die slow, painful deaths. Rae flexed and extended her right foot until she felt her knife start to slip. Checking her position, she wiggled her foot again and the knife fell cleanly into her hand.

Rae caught Audrey's gaze and willed her to keep Marc occupied. An almost-imperceptible nod told Rae she understood. Rae turned the knife so it faced away from her body and flicked the blade open. Her skin stung and she felt the sticky blood in her palm. She eased the knife more to the midpoint and sawed at the ropes. The tight bindings limited her range of motion and progress was slow. After several strokes, the first layer gave way and her right hand slid free. It only took a few more passes to release her left.

Rae bent her legs closer to her body and cut them loose as well. She quietly lowered them and let the blood rush back into them. Gradually stinging replaced numbness and she could feel the lower half of her body again. She wanted to stand, but sitting would probably be as far as she got before Pearson detected movement and advanced toward her. She would have to rise and strike in one quick shift.

As Rae started to make her move, Pearson pulled Audrey's body against his and tried to kiss her. "No!" Rae yelled, and rolled over, trying to right herself. Pearson pushed Audrey aside and lunged toward her.

Audrey screamed, "Now, Tony! Now!"

The ceiling overhead opened up and Tony swung down from the crawl space like a kid on a monkey bar. He kicked Pearson in the back and sent him falling toward Rae. Audrey knocked the knife from his hand and it skidded across the floor. Rae raised her arms in self-defense and heard a crunching sound as he landed on top of her.

Rae's body ached and a hard object pushed into her chest. She smelled blood and felt its hot stickiness oozing over her. She labored to breathe, white spots of light floated in front of her eyes, and she heard voices close by.

"Rae, are you all right? Oh, God, please be all right." It was Audrey. Someone rolled Pearson off her. "She's hurt. There's blood everywhere. Get help."

"She looks…" Tony said.

"Don't even think that." A heavy pounding sounded in the distance. "Get some medical help, *now*. Oh, Rae."

Rae blinked and looked into Audrey's eyes. Tears fell and splashed onto Rae's face. "I think I'm all right."

They both turned and looked at Marc Pearson for the first time. Rae's switchblade protruded from his chest, and his dull eyes stared into nothingness.

Audrey hugged Rae and they rocked back and forth. "I'm so glad you're okay. I don't know what I would've done if you'd been killed. I love you. Do you hear me, Rae? I love you."

"And I love you…" Audrey's confession eclipsed Rae's relief at being alive. She couldn't imagine life going forward without her. The swell of love mingled with protectiveness. "What are you doing here? I told you to stay at the hotel with the others." Her words lacked conviction.

"Now that's gratitude for you." Tony stood with his hands on his hips. "As you can see, we're not at the hotel. We're here rescuing your ungrateful ass."

"Tony." Audrey gave him a reproachful stare.

"No, he's right. I'm sorry." As Rae spoke, the rest of Audrey's cirque family filed in. "I suppose you all had a part in this?" They nodded. "I don't know how to thank you. Audrey certainly has devoted friends."

"And you too, Copper," Melvin added.

"Yep, you're one of us now," Yasi said. "An adopted member of the family."

Rae finally stood and scanned the group. The Whisperer lay dead at her feet, she'd inherited a family, and the woman she loved also loved her. Everything considered it was a great day. "I can't imagine a better one."

As Rae reached for her cell phone, Sergeant Sharp and several patrol officers entered the condo. "How did you know—"

Not So looked around the room. "Somebody called and said we'd find a press release about the Whisperer at this address. Obviously they were mistaken."

"I don't think so." She inclined her head toward Marc Pearson's body. When Rae looked at Audrey, she rolled her eyes and tried her best to act innocent. Rae guided her toward the door where her friends were waiting. "Well done, all of you. Once you've given your statements to the officers, you're free to go."

"I want to stay with you," Audrey said. "These guys have to leave for another show."

"Could you wait at the hotel until I get there? I'll come as soon as I can."

"And you'll never leave me again." Audrey smiled. "Right?"

"Right."

CHAPTER TWENTY-ONE

Rae's hand shook as she knocked on the door of Audrey's hotel suite. Four hours had passed during which Rae tied up loose ends of the case, gave her statement about Pearson's death, and changed clothes. The adrenaline that had kept her upright and functional for the past few days had evaporated. Only her love for Audrey and the possibility of a life together kept her moving.

Had Audrey professed love in the heat of the moment, thinking Rae was dying, or was she sincere? She knocked tentatively. What awaited her on the other side?

When Audrey opened the door, Rae's breath caught in her throat. She was undoubtedly in love with Audrey, and she trusted that purely instinctual knowing.

Audrey grabbed Rae's T-shirt and pulled her inside the room, closing the door behind her. "Stop that."

"What?"

"Doubting my feelings for you."

"I thought you couldn't read my mind."

"I can't, darling, but a blind person could see what you're thinking." Audrey ran her hands up Rae's shirt, her fingers like fire against her skin, and kissed her. "Once you've told me the rest of the story, I'll show you how much I meant those three little words."

Audrey smelled of fresh soap and shampoo. Powder-blue short pajamas clung to wet patches of her curvaceous body. Audrey's damp hair spiked around her head in its customary disheveled style. Rae's apprehension evaporated.

"What story?" Her focus had plummeted to a spot well south of her brain. She sought Audrey's mouth again, hungry for the connection.

"The Whisperer. Who is Marc Pearson? What did you find out?"

"Oh, that." Rae reluctantly walked to the sofa facing the Kramer skyline and pulled Audrey down with her. She sat as close as possible with her hand on Audrey's thigh. She didn't want to talk about Marc Pearson. He'd taken too much of her time and too much of Audrey's life already. Rae wanted to replace the bad memories Audrey carried with newer, happier ones. However, closing this chapter would help Audrey heal.

"Your friend Loretta came through. She tracked the Blankenships' birth records and found the connection. Pearson's mother met Earl Blankenship when Marc was three years old. Apparently she wasn't fond of motherhood and wanted a fresh start. She abandoned him when Earl proposed. He never knew his wife had a child."

"How awful. So he grew up in the system, believing nobody cared about him and blaming his mother for abandoning him."

"Pretty much. At the first opportunity, he ran away and lived on the streets. He was a hard worker and made his way into the military eventually. The structured life provided the first meaningful order he'd ever had. War twisted his mind a bit further, and the groin injury was the last straw. He lost it."

"He was a tormented soul. Why did he fixate on me, and why did he hurt the others?" Audrey's voice broke.

"We may never know. He'd adopted a mixture of the Arabic, Muslim, Iraqi beliefs. When he saw you perform last year as Sanjana, maybe he began to envision himself as Arya, the Noble One. Or maybe he thought he could recover from his injury, so he kept trying. The doctors said he would never function sexually again. Imagine what that would do to a man's ego and self-esteem." Rae pulled Audrey closer. "I'm sorry I can't give you the answers you need."

"It's hard to believe I worked with him so long and had no idea of his true nature. And you're sure he was the Whisperer?"

"Absolutely. When I searched the Blankenship Dry Cleaners, I found all his paraphernalia—blue uniforms, plastic, rope, mask, gloves, and the chloroform. His knife was military-issue and exactly as you described. The lab is running trace analysis on everything, including the inside of the van. I wouldn't have solved this case without you, Audrey. I can't begin to thank you."

Lowering her head, Audrey swiped at a stray tear. "If I'd remembered sooner, four other women and my best friend wouldn't be going through the same hell I did."

Rae understood guilt and the toll it took. "We all make mistakes, wish we'd done things differently. You've put this right. I'll never be able to repay you, personally or professionally."

Audrey turned into her arms and threw her leg over Rae's. "Might I suggest a starting point? Of course, repayment could take a while, possibly years." As she nuzzled Rae's ear shivers shot down her side.

"I'm in your debt. Name your terms."

Audrey blushed and averted her gaze. Would she ever be comfortable initiating sex with the woman she loved? She wasn't even sure how to begin. She just wanted Rae—intimately, immediately, and eternally. "Anything?"

"Of course…what is it? I want us to share everything."

"Take me to bed. I'd like you to make love to me."

Rae smiled and mischief sparkled in her emerald-green eyes. "You mean *really* make love this time? I actually get to enjoy and appreciate every inch of you?"

Audrey play-slapped her arm. "Don't tease. Can I help it that you get me so excited? I've only waited my whole life for you." She outlined Rae's lips with the tip of her tongue and a spark coursed through her. Rae opened to her and their kiss deepened. Their energies merged as they claimed each other until she could no longer tell where Rae ended and she began.

Audrey barely broke their kiss as she rose from the sofa, pulling Rae toward the king-sized bed. "I will *try* to be patient…no promises." As Audrey walked, she shucked off her pajamas, leaving a trail.

"So much for patience." Rae said.

"Now you." Audrey sat in the middle of the bed and waited for Rae to undress. She loved to watch Rae's confident hands slowly unbutton her shirt and slide it from her arms. When Rae's firm breasts came into view, Audrey licked her lips in anticipation. The itch between her legs spread, tantalizing and warming her. When Rae unzipped her jeans and let them fall to the floor, Audrey rubbed her clammy palms together. The tuft of auburn hair between Rae's thighs beckoned to her.

"Come here." Audrey reached for Rae, her arms as empty as her heart had been for years. "I need to feel you—everywhere."

When Rae's body slid into place against hers, Audrey reveled in the sensations. Pebbled nipples pressed perfectly into her fuller breasts and seared her with heat. Rae's abdomen nestled like a glove over her scarred ridges, giving comfort and reassurance. And when Rae's pubic mound grazed hers, Audrey was instantly wet. She bucked against the firmness of Rae's pelvis. She wanted the friction, the slide and stroke that would relieve the mounting pressure.

"Pa-tience, remember." The hitch in Rae's voice suggested she was as affected by their closeness. The slick trail on Audrey's thigh confirmed it. "Roll over."

"I won't be able to—"

"If we stay like this, we'll both explode in seconds. Roll over, please."

Rae's face flushed, her lips rosy and plump from their kisses, her eyes brimming with desire. Audrey didn't need to be psychic to see Rae's love or the physical toll her restraint was taking. Audrey kissed a circle around Rae's gorgeous features and reluctantly rolled over. The bed covering bunched beneath her, exquisite against her swollen clit. She squirmed into the gathered ridge, seeking relief.

"No cheating." Rae smacked Audrey's butt with her hand then rubbed the spot.

She slowly lathered Audrey's ears, neck, and backside with teasing licks and kisses. Her hot mouth left a trail instantly cooled by soft breaths, sending shivers down Audrey's spine. Rae sculpted her body like an artist, admiring and appreciating. The skin-on-skin sensation was tender yet insistent, each touch an affirmation of love and desire. Audrey adored the sensitivity but her body demanded more physicality. "Rae, please."

Rae slid her hands up Audrey's sides before slipping underneath to cup her breasts. "Are you ready?"

"Oh…" Rae's body covered Audrey's back, hot and tight. The heat from Rae's crotch radiated against her ass and she ached to have Rae inside her. "Yes." Audrey raised her butt and rubbed against Rae's soft triangle of hair. At the same time, she touched herself and almost came with a single stroke. Her body had a mind of its own—twitching, aching, urging, and craving things she'd only dreamed.

"You're cheating again."

"I'm about to pop out of my skin. I want to come so badly. Please."

Rae gently rolled Audrey onto her back and palmed her breasts. "You have the most beautiful breasts."

She squeezed Audrey's aching flesh from base to tip, then flicked her tight nipples with her thumb. The touch tugged an invisible connection between her crotch and breasts and set the skin between ablaze. Rae buried her head between Audrey's breasts and rubbed them on either side of her face. "I think I could suck these to climax. Something about soft mounds and stiff nipples gets me off."

Rae closed her mouth over one of Audrey's breasts and lavished it with kisses and gentle sucking. The rhythmic oral stimulation milked her clit from the inside and almost sent her crashing into orgasm. "If you don't touch me soon, you won't have a chance."

Rae scrunched down between Audrey's legs. Folding her hands over Audrey's crotch, she rested her head on her hands. She stared into Audrey's eyes and pressed down gently. "So…how badly do you want me?"

Audrey's clit pulsed as if the teasing words had touched it. "So much it hurts."

Lowering her head, Rae gently blew on the point of ignition between Audrey's legs. Her body arched. She clutched the sheets on either side to keep from grabbing her clit. Rae tongued the valley between Audrey's thigh and torso, so close to the spot Audrey needed her. She squirmed sideways to force the connection but Rae skillfully darted away.

Rae cupped Audrey's hands and encouraged her to release the sheets. "Play with your breasts. I want to watch while I make you come."

Audrey's clit pounded painfully, as if Rae had physically captured and squeezed her sex in her palm. She reached down and forced Rae's mouth over her. "Take me now. I need you."

Audrey grabbed her own breasts and rolled the malleable flesh in her hands. She ached for Rae's mouth to satisfy her.

Rae flattened her tongue and licked in one luxurious stroke from Audrey's opening to the tip of her swollen sex. A burst of current shot through her. Audrey gasped as her body vibrated. Another stroke and she quivered. A third and she might lose control. Her clit hammered.

The powerful orgasm built inside her and she willed it to slow. Nothing had prepared her for these feelings. She wanted Rae to adore and pleasure her for days. She prayed for more as her body betrayed her.

Rae surrounded Audrey's clit with her lips and flicked with the tip of her tongue unrelentingly. The orgasm spiraled up Audrey's limbs and coalesced. She tensed, trying to slow the hurricane. "I'm close, Rae, so close."

Rae massaged Audrey's breasts and shifted onto her leg. "Come for me."

Audrey didn't have time to respond. Rae's tongue stroked and her lips sucked one final time. The dam inside burst and every ounce of arousal liquefied and poured from her. She entangled her fingers in Rae's hair and held her firmly against her, the warmth of her mouth cradling her quivering flesh. Each beat of Audrey's heart pounded between her legs and sent a shudder of release through her. Rae's lips closed around her again and milked several more tiny orgasms from her. When she could hardly draw another breath, Audrey released her grip.

"Jeez, that was…awesome seems so lame." Rae moaned, and Audrey realized she'd been so preoccupied with her own orgasm she'd lost track of Rae's. "What do you need, my darling?"

Rae whined urgently. "How about a couple of these?" She took Audrey's breasts in her hands. "And one of those." She nuzzled Audrey's sex. Rae slid up Audrey's body, legs still straddling her thigh, and rocked back and forth against her. She left a slick trail of arousal, and it ignited Audrey's passion again.

"They're all yours." Audrey placed her hands on either side of her breasts and offered them to Rae.

Rae kissed her with more passion than Audrey thought possible. "I love you, Audrey." She held Audrey's gaze as if she wanted to say more but then looked at her breasts like they were sacrificial offerings and sucked an erect nipple into her mouth.

Rae's stiff clit hardened even more against Audrey's leg as she established a slow, methodical suck-and-stroke rhythm. With each upward pull at Audrey's breast, Rae rubbed her sex along the length of Audrey's thigh. At the apex of each stroke, Rae's leg brushed against Audrey, urging her on.

"Can I touch you?"

Rae pumped faster. She took Audrey's hand and guided it between her legs. "Go inside—while I stroke." Rae's breath came in short gasps between breast sucks. "Won't take long."

Audrey squeezed her hand between her thigh and Rae's body. She flattened, palm up, and let Rae hump against her hand. She loved the delicate balance of power surging between them as Rae clung to the control Audrey threatened to wrest from her. Audrey slid her finger easily into Rae's opening, rewarded with a guttural moan and quicker pace.

With her free hand, Audrey pulled Rae tighter against her and raised her leg for firmer contact. Rae opened her mouth, releasing Audrey's breast, and clutched her shoulders. "Yes…oh, God, yes." She shivered against Audrey in a long, final stroke and collapsed.

Audrey left her finger inside Rae, the pulse of her orgasm like a heartbeat. It was the essence of life itself. "I love you, Rae. I will always love you." Audrey panicked. "Did you hear me, darling?"

"Didn't you feel what happened?"

Audrey nudged Rae's sex. Her clit bulged, rigid. "You're horny again…already?"

"You said you loved me. You've created a monster." She slid along Audrey's thigh and spilled into her hand once more. "God, I've never come so quickly."

"Maybe I'm not such a novice after all."

"You're perfect."

Audrey rolled Rae to her side and kissed her. "There is one thing I'm dying to try."

"Name it."

"I'm thinking of a number between sixty-eight and seventy."

Rae smiled. "One of my favorites."

THE END

About the Author

VK Powell is a thirty-year veteran of a midsized police department. She was a police officer by necessity (it paid the bills) and a writer by desire (it didn't). Her career spanned numerous positions including beat officer, homicide detective, field sergeant, vice/narcotics lieutenant, district captain, and assistant chief of police. Now retired, she lives in central North Carolina and divides her time between writing, traveling, and amateur interior decorating.

VK is a member of the Golden Crown Literary Society and Romance Writers of America. She is the author of three erotic short stories and one romantic short story published in Bold Strokes Books anthologies. Her novels are To Protect and Serve, Suspect Passions, Fever, and Justifiable Risk.

Books Available from Bold Strokes Books

Haunting Whispers by VK Powell. Detective Rae Butler faces two challenges: a serial attacker who targets attractive women, and Audrey Everhart, a compelling woman who knows too much about the case and offers too little—professionally and personally. (978-1-60282-593-2)

Wholehearted by Ronica Black. When therapist Madison Clark and attorney Grace Hollings are forced together to help Grace's troubled nephew at Madison's healing ranch, worlds and hearts collide. (978-1-60282-594-9)

Fugitives of Love by Lisa Girolami. Artist Sinclair Grady has an unspeakable secret, but the only chance she has for love with gallery owner Brenna Wright is to reveal the secret and face the potentially devastating consequences. (978-1-60282-595-6)

Derrick Steele: Private Dick The Case of the Hollywood Hustlers by Zavo. Derrick Steele, a hard-drinking, lusty private detective, is being framed for the murder of a hustler in downtown Los Angeles. When his best friend Daniel McAllister joins the investigation, their growing attraction might prove to be more explosive than the case. (978-1-60282-596-3)

Nice Butt: Gay Anal Eroticism by Shane Allison. From toys to teasing, spanking to sporting, some of the best gay erotic scribes celebrate the hottest and most creative in new erotica. (978-1-60282-635-9)

Worth the Risk by Karis Walsh. Investment analyst Jamie Callahan and Grand Prix show jumper Kaitlyn Brown are willing to risk it all in their careers—can they face a greater challenge and take a chance on love? (978-1-60282-587-1)

Bloody Claws by Winter Pennington. In the midst of aiding the police, Preternatural Private Investigator Kassandra Lyall finally finds herself at serious odds with Sheila Morris, the local werewolf pack's Alpha female, when Sheila abuses someone Kassandra has sworn to protect. (978-1-60282-588-8)

Awake Unto Me by Kathleen Knowles. In turn of the century San Francisco, two young women fight for love in a world where women are often invisible and passion is the privilege of the powerful. (978-1-60282-589-5)

Initiation by Desire by MJ Williamz. Jaded Sue and innocent Tulley find forbidden love and passion within the inhibiting confines of a sorority house filled with nosy sisters. (978-1-60282-590-1)

Toughskins by William Masswa. John and Bret are two twenty-something athletes who find that love can begin in the most unlikely of places, including a "mom and pop shop" wrestling league. (978-1-60282-591-8)

me@you.com by K.E. Payne. Is it possible to fall in love with someone you've never met? Imogen Summers thinks so because it's happened to her. (978-1-60282-592-5)

High Impact by Kim Baldwin. Thrill seeker Emery Lawson and Adventure Outfitter Pasha Dunn learn you can never truly appreciate what's important and what you're capable of until faced with a sudden and stark reminder of your own mortality. (978-1-60282-580-2)

Snowbound by Cari Hunter. "The policewoman got shot and she's bleeding everywhere. Get someone here in one hour or I'm going to put her out of her misery." It's an ultimatum that will forever change the lives of police officer Sam Lucas and Dr. Kate Myles. (978-1-60282-581-9)

Rescue Me by Julie Cannon. Tyler Logan reluctantly agrees to pose as the girlfriend of her in-the-closet gay BFF at his company's annual retreat, but she didn't count on falling for Kristin, the boss's wife. (978-1-60282-582-6)

Murder in the Irish Channel by Greg Herren. Chanse MacLeod investigates the disappearance of a female activist fighting the Archdiocese of New Orleans and a powerful real estate syndicate. (978-1-60282-584-0)

Franky Gets Real by Mel Bossa. A four day getaway. Five childhood friends. Five shattering confessions…and a forgotten love unearthed. (978-1-60282-585-7)

Riding the Rails: Locomotive Lust and Carnal Cabooses edited by Jerry Wheeler. Some of the hottest writers of gay erotica spin tales of Riding the Rails. (978-1-60282-586-4)

Sheltering Dunes by Radclyffe. The seventh in the award-winning Provincetown Tales. The pasts, presents, and futures of three women collide in a single moment that will alter all their lives forever. (978-1-60282-573-4)

Holy Rollers by Rob Byrnes. Partners in life and crime, Grant Lambert and Chase LaMarca assemble a team of gay and lesbian criminals to steal millions from a right-wing mega-church, but the gang's plans are complicated by an "ex-gay" conference, the FBI, and a corrupt reverend with his own plans for the cash. (978-1-60282-578-9)

History's Passion: Stories of Sex Before Stonewall edited by Richard Labonté. Four acclaimed erotic authors re-imagine the past…Welcome to the hidden queer history of men loving men not so very long—and centuries—ago. (978-1-60282-576-5)

Lucky Loser by Yolanda Wallace. Top tennis pros Sinjin Smythe and Laure Fortescue reach Wimbledon desperate to claim tennis's crown jewel, but will their feelings for each other get in the way? (978-1-60282-575-8)

Mystery of The Tempest: A Fisher Key Adventure by Sam Cameron. Twin brothers Denny and Steven Anderson love helping people and fighting crime alongside their sheriff dad on sun-drenched Fisher Key, Florida, but Denny doesn't dare tell anyone he's gay, and Steven has secrets of his own to keep. (978-1-60282-579-6)

Better Off Red: Vampire Sorority Sisters Book 1 by Rebekah Weatherspoon. Every sorority has its secrets, and college freshman Ginger Carmichael soon discovers that her pledge is more than a bond of sisterhood—it's a lifelong pact to serve six bloodthirsty demons with a lot more than nutritional needs. (978-1-60282-574-1)

Detours by Jeffrey Ricker. Joel Patterson is heading to Maine for his mother's funeral, and his high school friend Lincoln has invited himself along on the ride—and into Joel's bed—but when the ghost of Joel's mother joins the trip, the route is likely to be anything but straight. (978-1-60282-577-2)

Three Days by L.T. Marie. In a town like Vegas where anything can happen, Shawn and Dakota find that the stakes are love at all costs, and it's a gamble neither can afford to lose. (978-1-60282-569-7)

Swimming to Chicago by David-Matthew Barnes. As the lives of the adults around them unravel, high school students Alex and Robby form an unbreakable bond, vowing to do anything to stay together—even if it means leaving everything behind. (978-1-60282-572-7)

Hostage Moon by AJ Quinn. Hunter Roswell thought she had left her past behind, until a serial killer begins stalking her. Can FBI profiler Sara Wilder help her find her connection to the killer before he strikes on blood moon? (978-1-60282-568-0)

Erotica Exotica: Tales of Sex, Magic, and the Supernatural edited by Richard Labonté. Today's top gay erotica authors offer sexual thrills and perverse arousal, spooky chills, and magical orgasms in these stories exploring arcane mystery, supernatural seduction, and sex that haunts in a manner both weird and wondrous. (978-1-60282-570-3)

Blue by Russ Gregory. Matt and Thatcher find themselves in the crosshairs of a psychotic killer stalking gay men in the streets of Austin, and only a 103-year-old nursing home resident holds the key to solving the murders—but can she give up her secrets in time to save them? (978-1-60282-571-0)